GIVE UP THE DEAD

A Mediaeval Mystery

GIVE UP THE DEAD

A MEDIAEVAL MYSTERY

C.B. HANLEY

For A. G., who is even more
accident-prone than I am.

First published by The Mystery Press, 2018

The Mystery Press, an imprint of The History Press
The Mill, Brimscombe Port
Stroud, Gloucestershire, GL5 2QG
www.thehistorypress.co.uk

British Library Cataloguing in Publication Data.
A catalogue record for this book is available from the British Library.

ISBN 978 0 7509 8259 7

Typesetting and origination by The History Press
Printed in Great Britain

And the sea gave up the dead which were in it; and death and hell delivered up the dead which were in them; and they were judged every man according to their works.

Revelation, ch. 20, v. 13

Praise for C.B. Hanley's
Mediaeval Mystery Series

'*The Bloody City* is a great read, full of intrigue and murder.
Great for readers of Ellis Peters and Lindsey Davis. Hanley weaves a
convincing, rich tapestry of life and death in the early 13th century,
in all its grandeur and filth. I enjoyed this book immensely!'

Ben Kane, bestselling novelist of the *Forgotten Legion* trilogy

'Blatantly heroic and wonderfully readable.'

The Bloody City received a STARRED review in *Library Journal*

'The characters are real, the interactions and conversations natural,
the tension inbuilt, and it all builds to a genuinely satisfying
conclusion both fictionally and historically.'

Review for *The Bloody City* in www.crimereview.co.uk

'*Whited Sepulchres* … struck me as a wonderfully vivid
recreation of the early thirteenth century … The solid
historical basis lends authenticity to a lively, well-structured
story. I enjoyed the plight of amiable and peace-loving Edwin,
trapped by his creator in such a warlike time and place.'

Andrew Taylor, winner of the 2009 CWA Diamond Dagger
and three-times winner of the CWA Historical Dagger

'It's clever. It's well written. It's believable.
It's historically accurate. It's a first class medieval mystery.'

Review for *Whited Sepulchres* in www.crimereview.co.uk

'*Brother's Blood* [is] a gift for medievalists everywhere …
Hanley really knows her stuff. Her knowledge of life in a
Cistercian monastery is impeccable. More please.'

Cassandra Clark, author of the *Abbess of Meaux* medieval mystery series

'British author Hanley's enjoyable fourth medieval whodunit
will appeal to Ellis Peters fans.'

Review for *Brother's Blood* in *Publishers Weekly Online*

The Battle of Sandwich, 24 August 1217

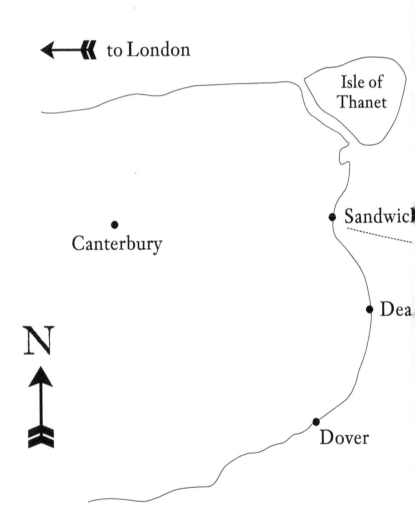

← ◀◀ to London

Isle of Thanet

Sandwich

Canterbury

Deal

N
↑
⏺

Dover

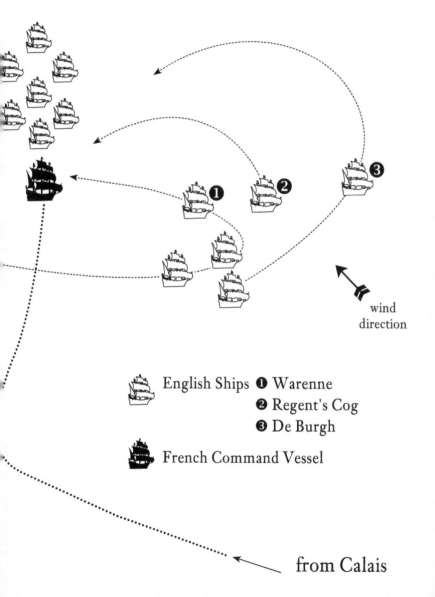

------------------- Route of English Ships

.... Route of French Ships

❶ Warenne

❷ Regent's Cog

❸ De Burgh

English Ships

French Command Vessel

wind direction

from Calais

Chapter One

The Thames Valley, August 1217

Edwin tried to hold his breath and avert his eyes, but it was no good; the devastation was all around them, the stench of burning was everywhere, and it had been going on for miles. Indeed, it seemed to be getting worse the further they rode. It was supposed to be the start of the harvest season, but he doubted very much if anything would be gleaned from these scorched fields or stored in the ruined barns.

They were even now passing through the remains of a village, the abandoned roofless houses accusing the interlopers with their charred and blackened beams. Towards the centre of the settlement there was some activity: repairs had been attempted to a number of cottages, a few vegetables straggled in gardens, and wary, sunken eyes peered out from windows. One or two children, bolder than their elders, approached the column of riders and held their hands out to beg. They were ragged and hollow-cheeked, and Edwin felt nothing but pity for them. This could have been his own village of Conisbrough: families settled in their homes around the church and the green, surrounded by fields of crops to feed them. The war had not reached far enough north to touch his home, for which he thanked God every day, but these people had suffered through no fault of their own. He began to reach for the purse at his belt.

A large hand fell on his wrist. 'Don't.'

Edwin looked across at Brother William, who rode beside him. 'But —'

The grip tightened as the monk spoke under his breath. 'Do it once and you'll be hounded, overwhelmed. You can't help all of them, and there's going to be plenty more like this, and worse, before we get to where we're going.'

Edwin knew he wouldn't be able to move his arm unless Brother William let go of it, so he nodded and, released, grabbed his reins again. Too hard and too suddenly, as it turned out: the horse didn't like it and he had to give all his attention to controlling the animal for a few moments. It had been the most docile mount they could find in the lord earl's stables at Conisbrough – the same one he'd ridden to Roche and back a couple of weeks previously – and he was certainly a better rider now than he'd been a few months ago, but being in the saddle all day every day was both tiring and difficult. By the time he'd regained control of the horse, they had left the children behind. He sighed and hoped that someone further down the long column might help them out.

It was unlikely, he knew, for they were not a light-hearted group out riding for pleasure but an army, heading to war, with compassion in short supply. They were stretched for some way along the road: the scouts and some lightly armoured mounted sergeants rode at the front, followed by the earl himself, together with his knights and lords and the higher-ranking members of his household; then those who were of lesser importance but still mounted, including Edwin and his companion Brother William, the earl's clerk. Behind them came the massed ranks of those who walked – foot soldiers, archers and servants of various types – and then the long skein of baggage and supply carts. Finally, a further group of armed riders ensured that the rumbling wagons didn't fall too far behind, and guarded them from any attack from the rear. The villagers hiding in the ruins of their houses would have to wait a good long time for their road to be clear again, for the column could only move at the pace of the slow and heavy carts. That was some consolation to

Edwin, at least. If he'd had to ride quickly as well as constantly he wasn't sure what shape he'd be in by now.

Their group would eventually get even larger, as they were on their way to meet with two other earls, friends and allies of Edwin's Lord William de Warenne, Earl of Surrey; they were also picking up more of the earl's own retainers as they went, from his estates that were seemingly scattered all over the kingdom. Then they would all head to the Kent coast. Edwin was a bit hazy on the details after that, but he did know that they were expecting to fight a great battle: Louis of France, son of the French king, who held most of the south and south-east of England, was having reinforcements sent across the sea. Once they landed, his host would be large enough to restart the war that had stalled after the engagement at Lincoln, and England would be devastated anew.

Thinking of Lincoln made Edwin shiver, despite the heat of the day. He had been there; he had seen the chaos and the blood and the death, and he never wanted to see it again. And yet here he was, riding helplessly towards more of the same, or possibly worse. He wasn't cut out for this.

Brother William broke into his gloomy silence.

'So, tell me again about your wedding. I would have liked to attend, to give you my best wishes and to see your pretty wife.'

He had hit on the one subject that could make Edwin happier. *His wife.* He had a wife. He was a married man. He could still hardly believe any of it – that he was wed at all, that Alys had come back to him when he thought she was lost, or that the most wonderful girl in all the world had somehow thought him worthy and had agreed to marry him. He felt the tension across his shoulders lessening, his heart lifting, the corners of his mouth turning upwards, as he recalled it all and the words tumbled out. Brother William had heard it before, but neither of them cared. The joy of his friends and family, the celebration in the village, the scent of the flowers in her hair …

He came to himself and realised he was still plodding ahead alongside Brother William, in the middle of a blissful daydream. How long was it since he'd stopped talking? How far had they ridden? He turned awkwardly in his saddle to see that they had left the village far behind. His companion seemed to be content with the silence, now he had heard the story of the wedding for perhaps the fifth or sixth time, so Edwin let himself sink back into his reverie as the surroundings washed past him. Were those a few green shoots appearing amid the blackened undergrowth?

It wasn't long before they came to another village – this fertile southern part of the country was more densely populated than the hilly north – which was in a similar state to the last one. No, worse: here the smell of burning was more recent, and the churchyard as they passed it held many fresh-dug graves as well as another half-dozen shrouded forms waiting their turn on the ground. Three of them were tiny, and Edwin found that the sight of them was enough to raise in him a feeling he hadn't yet experienced during the long journey: anger.

He turned to Brother William. 'If this is what Louis has been doing to England, perhaps it's better that we fight him. He needs to be driven out!' The unusual ferocity of his voice surprised him, and he wondered why the monk was shaking his head. 'What?'

'Ah, Edwin, you haven't seen much of war, have you? These lands belong – or used to belong, I'm not sure how it works when there's supposedly two kings in the country – to one of the earls who is supporting Louis, and this devastation was caused by the other side. King John burned it all last year, and before they'd had the chance to recover, the lord regent and his men swept through again a couple of months ago.'

Edwin could hardly believe what he was hearing. 'The king and the regent did this to their own people?' He would never understand these nobles, not if he lived to be sixty.

Brother William shrugged. 'They needed money and supplies, and where else could they get them from? They weren't going to raid the lands of the earls on their own side, were they?'

'But the people here – they have no say in which side their lord supports. Why should they have to suffer?' Edwin felt even more angry than he had been before, although he couldn't now work out against whom, or what he should do about it. He had no target, no outlet for his rage, and the frustration boiled inside him.

He looked again at the monk, his white robe dusty from the journey, and his eyes betraying all he'd seen before he took the cowl. 'You're going to tell me that it's war, aren't you, and that this is the way of it.' Brother William opened his mouth but Edwin cut him off before he could speak. 'Well, that doesn't make it *right*.'

He'd spoken more forcibly than he intended, but Brother William evidently didn't want to start an argument. He merely replied, peaceably, 'I didn't say it was. Pray for the Lord to help these people, because we can't and nobody else will. And pray for a swift end to the war.'

They rode on in silence.

———

Martin was enjoying the open space of the journey. The road ahead and the fields and woods laid out on either side were in marked contrast to the constricting, suffocating walls of the abbey where he'd spent the week before they set out. In fact, they'd been there less than a week, hadn't they? It felt like much longer, time seeming to stretch out and stand still while they were there. Dear Lord, but how could anyone *want* to spend their lives like that? It was incomprehensible.

He was riding just behind the earl, alert in case he should be needed for anything, but at the same time daydreaming about how he was going to prove himself in battle, earn fame and renown, take another step towards his knighthood, be awarded money or lands … and the first thing he would do would be to buy himself a horse that was actually big enough. He was riding the roan courser that was the tallest the Conisbrough stable afforded, and which had gradually been recognised as his personal mount for that very reason, but his legs still dangled. Nonetheless, they were used to each other and he was comfortable in the saddle as the day wore on.

He wasn't quite sure where they were now, although it was somewhere south of the Thames. They had originally been travelling on the main road that they always used when the earl rode to his southern lands – the one that ran from York to London – but London and its environs were in Louis's hands, so they'd turned off at St Albans and were now making a wide circle around the capital. There had been a day's delay while the host, bit by bit, crossed the Thames at Wallingford, but they had made steady progress since then. Martin still thought it was a bit slow, personally – he reckoned they'd only made about ten miles so far today – but Humphrey, the earl's new marshal who was in charge of the travel arrangements, seemed satisfied. Fortunately, the distance they covered each day, or the planning for the next, wasn't Martin's problem to worry about. He actually felt rather carefree as they went along, looking forward to a great gathering of armed men and the chance to prove himself, enjoying the fact that Adam, the junior squire, didn't seem to feel the need to talk endlessly as they rode, and safe in the knowledge that he wasn't in charge of anything except keeping the earl comfortable and supplied with everything he wanted – and he'd been doing that most of his life.

As the sun grew lower behind them Martin's mind started to turn to where and when they might halt and make camp. They'd passed through a few villages during the afternoon, but they were poor places where the people didn't look like they took much care of their surroundings – had they no pride? – and none of them had afforded anything even approaching a decent inn. Probably they would camp in open ground, which would be preferable anyway as far as Martin was concerned.

Eventually a process of to-ing and fro-ing between Humphrey, the lord earl and some of his knights who travelled this road more often resulted in the halt being called. It was still light, and a smaller group might have pressed on for another hour or so, but they'd have to wait for the baggage carts to catch up, and then allow time to erect the tents before it was dark. Martin stretched, aware that he'd been dozing in his saddle for a while, and looked about him. It was a good spot: a flattish area – always better for putting up tents and particularly for struggling with the earl's pavilion, which was large and unwieldy – but with a slight rise off to the east which would allow for guards to be posted with a good view around them, and a gentle slope down to a stream that would afford fresh water.

He whistled as he dismounted, handed his reins to Adam and went straight over to his lord to see if he had any immediate instructions. Later he'd stretch his muscles hauling on ropes to help the men set up the earl's camp, check that the horses had been properly picketed, and there might even be time for a bit of sparring practice before it got completely dark. All was right with the world.

———◦———

Edwin heaved a sigh of relief as word reached them and the column ground to a halt. With aching slowness he eased himself down from the back of his mount, holding on to the saddle and stamping his feet a few times to get the feeling back into his legs. Brother William had likewise dismounted and was stroking his horse's nose. He took his pack down from the animal's back and swung it over his shoulder, the stout cudgel he carried everywhere narrowly missing Edwin's head.

Brother William patted the horse again. 'I shouldn't really be riding such a fine mount, of course – we monks are only supposed to make use of mules. But if I find the man who decided that that would make me too slow, and let me ride a courser once more, I will bless him all his days.'

Edwin managed a tired smile. Brother William looked as fresh as he had done when they set out this morning, while he felt like his limbs were all made of lead.

The monk was sympathetic to his weakness. 'Here, pass me your reins, and I'll go and picket them both. You sit down.'

Edwin shook his head at the proffered hand. 'Sitting down is the last thing I want to do, believe me. Come, I'll take them both, seeing as I'm going. And you'll be much more use than me at …' he gestured vaguely, 'helping to set things up.'

'Very well.'

Both sets of reins in hand, trying not to tangle them up, Edwin set off behind all the other men who were leading horses. He stumbled around the piles of fresh manure as he went – he might be tired but he didn't want the tent to stink all night – and followed the crowd. There would be a picket somewhere. Yes, there it was. Men more experienced than he, old campaigners, knew how to organise such matters, and if there was one thing Edwin knew about the nobility, it was that they took great care of their horses. It was no surprise that their area was the first part of the camp to be sorted out each night.

He waited his turn as various squires dealt with some very fine-looking animals indeed, nodding at Adam when he saw him. His and Brother William's horse stood patiently after another long day's trek – did horses get bored? – and Edwin told them that the wait would not be long now. He risked patting his own mount on the nose.

When he reached the picket he concentrated with extreme care as he tied the reins around the fence exactly as he had been taught.

If anyone was going to be humiliated by his horse getting loose overnight, it was not going to be Edwin.

Similar attentiveness was being displayed by the small figure in the place next along from him, and Edwin recognised him as he turned. 'Peter?'

The boy jumped at being addressed by name. But then he saw who it was, relaxed a little and nodded. 'Edwin.' He scooped up an armful of hay from the stack someone had placed nearby and put it in front of the animal he was tending. Then he reached into the bag he was carrying, rummaged around and dug out a brush. 'Sir Roger trusts me to see to his horse every night now. On my *own*.'

His pride was so evident that Edwin felt himself smiling despite his exhaustion. 'You serve him very well.' He looked more closely and saw that, in the few weeks since he had last seen the boy at midsummer, his cheeks had filled out and the tunic no longer looked quite so oversized. And he hadn't fled when Edwin had spoken to him. He was a different child from the starving, terrified waif he'd known in Conisbrough.

Once they had completed their tasks, they turned to walk back to the main camp, now with tents mushrooming everywhere and the smoke from cooking fires drifting into the evening sky. They threaded their way through groups of men, piles of baggage and webs of tent ropes until their ways parted.

Peter squinted up at him. 'Are you coming to see Sir Roger?'

He certainly wouldn't mind the calming presence of the young knight, so it was with some regret that Edwin shook his head. 'I need to go and see if my lord the earl needs me for anything. But please, do give Sir Roger my greetings and say I will be glad to speak with him later if he has leisure.'

Peter stared straight ahead of him for a moment, his brow furrowing, and Edwin knew that his message would be passed on word for word. He gave the boy an affectionate pat and turned away.

The earl's pavilion was easily recognisable among the smaller, plainer tents of the camp. Fortunately, Edwin had been at the picket long enough for it to have been set up in his absence, so nobody had asked him to help and then sworn at him for getting in the way. The earl was currently sitting just outside it on a folding chair, sipping wine while his servants hurried in and out with mats, hangings, wooden kists, furs, blankets and the pieces of the bed ready to assemble. They were being directed by Humphrey, and Edwin was struck once more by the quiet and efficient way in which he went about his business – so different from the shrill self-importance of his predecessor. *May he rest in peace*, he added to himself.

Martin was attending the earl, as was Brother William, who was breaking the seal on a letter as he spoke. 'From the Earl of Salisbury, my lord.' Edwin took up an unobtrusive place nearby, hovering in case he was needed.

The earl waved for his clerk to continue as he finished the wine and held the cup out to Martin for a refill.

'The lord earl sends his greetings, et cetera,' said Brother William, as he scanned down the parchment. 'He has sent his messenger on ahead … prays you may give him credence … he expects to be with you here at or just after nightfall.'

The earl grunted. 'Good. That will give us some time to catch up tonight before we get any further around London.'

Edwin tried to dredge up the correct earl from his memory, recalling his recent lessons with Sir Geoffrey; the Conisbrough castellan had been drilling him over the summer in the names, devices and relationships of the higher nobility. He was determined that Edwin should not make a fool of himself now that he was in the earl's service, for if it became known that Edwin was from Conisbrough then any signs of stupidity or ignorance would reflect badly on him. No, that wasn't quite fair, thought Edwin. It was part of it, to be sure, but Sir Geoffrey had been a lifelong friend of Father's, and Edwin was sure that part of the old knight wanted Edwin to do well for his own sake too.

Anyway, Salisbury. That was one of the easier ones: he was the young king's uncle, an illegitimate brother of old King John. Edwin had never seen him but he knew him to be around fifty years of age, an experienced military campaigner and a long-time ally of the earl. Oh, and he was called William, of course; no surprise there, as half of the realm's earls and lords shared the same name. And his device was … ah. Edwin tried to picture the colourful rolls Sir Geoffrey had shown him. Something to do with lions?

Belatedly he became aware that the earl was summoning him. 'Yes, my lord?'

'Was Sir Hugh expected today?'

'No, my lord – tomorrow.'

The earl sighed. 'Shame. Still …' he drummed his fingers on the arm of the folding chair. 'Roger is here, I know. Go and find him and bring him here.'

'At once, my lord.'

Edwin was halfway through his bow when Humphrey appeared at the earl's side to tell him that all was ready within. The earl nodded, stood, and disappeared inside the brightly coloured walls of the pavilion as Edwin straightened.

The smell of many cooking fires assailed Edwin's nostrils as he made his way through the camp. He reached the point where he had left Peter and then followed in the direction he thought the boy had taken. Somewhere around here, surely? Yes, there he was. That halo of bright blond hair was unmissable, even at dusk.

Sir Roger was sitting on a low stool outside a plain tent that had been patched more than once. His men – just ten archers, no sergeants – lounged around in a circle, while Peter sat cross-legged, polishing a sword that was already so bright he could see his face in it.

'Edwin!' The knight stood, a welcoming hand outstretched. 'Peter said you might stop by.' He smiled down at the boy. 'And as you see, I am "at leisure". Please, sit.' He indicated the one stool.

Edwin took his hand with genuine pleasure. 'Sir Roger. Thank you. But I'm afraid I haven't come to talk – the lord earl wishes to see you.'

'Very well. Will you show me the way?'

Peter, alert to his lord's every move, had already stowed the sword back in the tent and was now hovering a little uncertainly.

Sir Roger looked down at him. 'I think I can manage without you. There are plenty of other boys around the place – why don't you go and play for a while?'

Peter's face lit up and he scampered off. Sir Roger caught the eye of one of his men and gestured with his head at the small departing back.

'I'll keep an eye out for him, my lord, never fear.'

Sir Roger nodded as he turned back to Edwin. 'He gets nervous around too many people, and especially the lord earl.'

As they made their way back through the maze of the camp, Edwin reflected that Peter wasn't the only one.

———•———

Martin sighed as he finally pushed the bowl away from him and then stretched his arms out until his shoulders cracked. 'Ah, that's better.'

Adam, who had finished his meal long since, gave him a brief smile before returning his attention to the chessboard. His hand hesitated and hovered over several pieces before he prodded his queen forward a couple of spaces.

Edwin, who was his opponent, looked up. 'I've never seen anyone eat as much as you.' He flicked a knight sideways and took one of Adam's bishops almost absent-mindedly.

'Well, there's a lot of me to fill.' Martin stood and then cursed as he knocked his head on one of the horizontal tent poles. He rubbed the sore spot and ducked as he moved over to them. 'Who's winning?'

'Who do you think?' replied Adam, as near to being irritable as he ever was.

Martin clapped him on the back. 'Never mind.' He'd been taught the basics of chess once, but he was so hopeless at it that nobody had minded when he gave it up. But the earl was very keen, as was Sir Geoffrey, and it annoyed him when he couldn't find a decent opponent away from Conisbrough. At his order Adam had been learning for several months, and he was now considered reasonably competent although nowhere near the earl's standard. Edwin had taken up the game a week ago, on the first evening of their march. He'd lost to Adam the first two nights, drawn a stalemate the third, and won every game since, taking less and less time about it each evening. Martin chuckled at Adam's frustration and turned away to the task he'd been looking forward to all day.

The bag was exactly where he'd left it; he hadn't trusted anyone else to unpack it from the baggage cart. He untied the string and then reached inside to remove the contents, pulling it out and then unwrapping the protective linen with reverence. And there it was, in all its glory. His new great helm, a reward from the earl for his recent services and a surprise gift presented to him just as they had left Conisbrough. The very latest in style, with a round flat top and plate all round, not just a face mask at the front like Sir Geoffrey's. Breathing holes, eye-slits, rivets … he knew every tiny facet and piece of it, and it was hardly less fine than the earl's own. He took up the polishing cloth but sat with it idle in his hand as he gazed in wonderment at his prized possession.

'You'll stand out, you know.'

Martin gathered his wits. 'What?'

'If you polish it any more. When the sun shines on it, every eye will be on you. Check, by the way.'

There was a sound of annoyance from Adam, but Martin wasn't going to let anything spoil his mood. 'Well, maybe it'll blind them all so they're easy pickings.' He hummed to himself as he started work.

When he was happy that the helm couldn't be in any better state than it was, he wrapped it carefully and stowed it back in the bag. Then he moved aside the hanging that separated their service area from the main part of the pavilion and the earl's curtained-off private area at the far end, to see if he was needed.

The earl and Sir Roger had been deep in conversation since their evening meal, continuing while the squires had been dismissed to eat theirs, and they were still going now. But the earl saw him and gave him a brief nod, so Martin took his usual position a few paces behind his lord and began to listen. They had now thankfully moved on from politics to possible battle tactics, and he wanted to learn all he could. But he'd barely heard the word 'archers' when there was a commotion outside.

With a brief look at the earl for permission, he strode to the pavilion entrance, pushed aside the flap that functioned as a door, and addressed the duty guard. 'What is it?'

The guard nodded at several riders who were dismounting by the light of flaming torches and braziers. 'Newcomers, sir.'

Martin caught the flash of blue and gold on the surcoat and turned back. 'The Earl of Salisbury has arrived, my lord.'

The earl waved. 'Good, good, bring him in.'

Martin bowed to the leader of those outside. 'My lord, if you would come this way?'

Salisbury grunted. 'Warenne in here, is he?' He took off his gloves and thrust them at his waiting squire before pushing past Martin into the pavilion.

Inside, the earls were greeting each other. Sir Roger was bowing and taking his leave. Humphrey had appeared and was already directing servants to lay food. Salisbury sat down with the earl, but there would be little immediate rest for his attendants – two squires and a page were hovering around him, still covered in dust from the dry summer road. The youngest boy looked exhausted, drooping as he placed a table by his lord's elbow. As he turned to fetch a cup he tripped over his feet, regained his balance without damaging anything, and was rewarded by a sharp cuff on the ear from the eldest.

Martin looked more closely. It had been a while since he'd seen them, but yes, that was definitely Philip. Martin's heart sank, but he tried to remind himself that he was older and stronger now. The middle one, currently with his back to Martin as he filled a plate from the dishes on offer, might or might not have been a bigger version of the boy Martin vaguely remembered … yes, now that he turned to offer the plate to Salisbury, Martin could see that it was. What was his name again? Guy? No, Gregory, that was it. He had a fading bruise on the side of his face.

The small boy spilled some wine as he lifted the jug. Martin stepped forward before Philip could hit him again, but Adam was quicker. 'Here, let me help you with that.' Martin couldn't help noticing that the page's initial reaction to being addressed was to flinch and duck. They themselves were going to get a new page as soon as the Earl of Arundel joined the host, and Martin promised himself he wouldn't be too free with his fists.

Once Salisbury was supplied with his meal, and candles had been placed to enable the two earls to see each other while they spoke, he flicked his fingers at the squires and page, and they took plates of their own and filled them. Martin pointed to the service end of the pavilion and they all made their way through. He was mildly amused to see that Edwin was still staring at the chessboard and did not even look up as they entered.

Philip sat on the stool opposite him and banged his plate down. 'There you are. I didn't see you out ...' He stopped as Edwin looked up and he realised his mistake. Martin stepped forward to forestall anything Edwin might say. He didn't know Philip.

'I don't think my lord will need you for the rest of the evening. Why don't you ...' He rolled his eyes in what he hoped was an obvious manner and Edwin stood up.

Now that Philip could see Edwin properly, in his nondescript clothes, he gaped in exaggerated surprise. 'You let a servant sit with you?'

Edwin opened his mouth, but Martin gave him a shove before he could say anything. 'He isn't a servant.' Martin put his face close to Edwin's ear. 'Just go. I'll tell you tomorrow.' Edwin looked puzzled, but he did as he was told.

Philip was still looking about him. 'Changes in the household, eh? I wonder why that could be?'

Martin had no idea whether the question was genuine or whether Philip knew the truth and was trying to make trouble. The chessboard caught his eye and he thought of something Edwin had said earlier; perhaps attack would be the best way to defend. 'That's none of your business, and I suggest you start eating that before your lord needs you again.'

Philip's eyes narrowed. 'My, we have grown up, haven't we?' He looked down at his plate and smiled. 'I haven't got enough here. Matthew, give me some of yours.'

The page, whose head had been drooping over his own meal, looked up. His eyes were huge in the shadowy candle-light, but he said nothing as he held out his plate for Philip to scrape most of the food off it. Martin caught Adam's gaze over the boy's head and saw his mouth set in a straight line. He sighed. There was going to be trouble, and he was going to have to be the one to deal with it. So much for a simple campaign and a good fight.

It was not long before all of them were summoned back to the main central part of the pavilion. Salisbury had finished eating, so Gregory stacked the plates back on the side table ready for the servants to deal with in the morning. Salisbury told them all to be off to check that his own pavilion was now ready and said he would be along in a while. They all dutifully trooped out, little Matthew holding the tent flap open for his elders. As he was about to follow them into the night, Adam stopped him and pressed something into his hand – a piece of bread, if Martin was not mistaken.

'You two can get to bed, too,' said the earl. Martin gestured for Adam to head off to the curtained sleeping area. He himself checked that the jug of wine between the two earls was full and replaced a couple of candles that were burning low. He grimaced in irritation as hot wax splattered on to his hand, but it was nothing he hadn't experienced a hundred times before. He waited until it was cool and then scraped it off before bowing and moving to the sleeping area.

Adam had already unrolled both straw palliasses out on the ground next to the wooden bed and was stretched out on one of them. He couldn't have been there more than a few moments but he was already fast asleep. Martin took off his belt and boots and lay on the other. He dozed.

He was woken – had he even been asleep? – by the sound of voices.

'I told you it was dangerous to come back to the lord regent's side so soon.'

'We had to! After Lincoln, and when it became clear that de Burgh was going to hold Dover ...'

'But now look where we are, cousin. Louis in London, and a huge fleet of reinforcements on the way. If they get through —'

'They won't.'

'But what if they do? We were in a good position with Louis, could have been in line for rewards once he was crowned.

But we wavered and went back. If he wins now then we'll lose everything. It might be time to reconsider.'

'No. That would be the worst thing we could do. To keep changing allegiance smacks of weakness, and that won't do us any good either way.'

'What does Arundel say?'

'It doesn't matter what Arundel says. He has lands but no blood. We're the ones who are the young king's relatives.'

'It matters not who is related to whom. What matters, cousin, is who is going to be wearing the crown next year – or next week.'

'We cannot go back, I tell you!'

'Do you have a better idea?'

'Let me think.'

There was silence for a few moments.

'We stay with the regent. If he wins, we're his loyal men. If Louis wins, then we submit to him but say we were bound by honour to support our blood kin.'

'Hmm.'

'Know your enemy, man. Louis is absolutely wedded to his notions of "honour", more fool him. He'll fall for that.'

'It's too risky. He's likely to win, so I say we go back to him now.'

'I say not. I say we put all our efforts into making sure the young king keeps his throne, for that puts us in the best position.'

'I'm not convinced.'

'We're in this together, remember? And all men know we're allies. If you go down then you'll drag me – and Arundel – down with you.'

'I'll have to think on it.'

'You do that!'

'I will!'

Martin heard the sound of one them, presumably Salisbury, leaving. In his half-awake state, odd thoughts ran through his head.

They did sound alike, didn't they? You could hardly tell which was which when you couldn't see them. But then they were cousins, weren't they? He yawned.

The earl, for it must be he who was still in the pavilion, paced up and down. Martin could hear 'But what to do?' repeated a couple of times, and then the sound of a chair being kicked as he swore under his breath. Then he came through to the sleeping area.

Martin roused himself, and he was careful to say nothing, to give no indication that he had heard anything, as he helped his lord prepare for the night. Then the earl settled himself in the bed, the ropes creaking under the feather mattress, and fell asleep.

Martin returned to his pallet.

It was still dark when he awoke again, confused. He was normally a heavy sleeper – why was it not dawn yet? Was anyone still arguing? No. Then what had roused him? A thought of candles came into his head, and he scratched at his hand where the wax had stuck. No, it was gone. What was he thinking of? He should go back to sleep, get some rest before tomorrow's ride. Why was he still thinking of wax and flames?

Ah, it was because he could smell smoke.

Too much smoke.

And a crackling noise.

Jolted thoroughly awake, he sat up and reached out a hand to the heavy curtain. As soon as he pulled it back he choked, scrambled to his feet and began shouting, all at once. The pavilion was on fire.

Chapter Two

Something was amiss. Martin quite clearly had some kind of history with that other squire, and a history that wasn't pleasant. Edwin spent the short journey back to his tent worrying about his friend: Martin could, of course, take care of himself on a physical level, but he wasn't quite as tough as his size made him out to be. And there was a considerate side to him that not many others knew about. After the wedding, Edwin, Alys and most of the villagers had packed into his – their – cottage and shared out whatever they could bring at short notice: simple fare at the hungry midsummer time of year. They had barely settled down to it when a commotion was heard outside and, to everyone's surprise and delight, several of the men from the castle kitchen entered, laden with bread, cheese, ale and meat pies thick with mouth-watering gravy. It wasn't until afterwards that Edwin found out that Martin had promised Richard, the earl's cook, almost everything he owned if he would only divert a portion of the hall's evening meal down to the village celebration.

Brother William was already asleep and did not stir as Edwin entered the tent and rolled himself in his blanket. He didn't really need it, as the night was warm, but he felt better for having it wrapped about him. Safer, if such a thing was possible under the circumstances. He thought he would probably lie awake for most of the night, but the day's ride had tired him and his self-made cocoon was comfortable.

The shouts woke them both up in the middle of the night, and they scrambled out into a smoke-filled darkness alive with cries and shadows. Edwin stared in horror at the blaze, but Brother William was already pulling him. 'Quickly!'

They ran towards the flames. Surely it couldn't be – but it was. Dear Lord. The earl's own pavilion. Where was he? And Martin and Adam? Edwin cast about frantically, feeling panic rise, until he saw with a wrench of relief a huge figure silhouetted against the orange glow. That could only be Martin. And there was the lord earl and Adam, both bent double and coughing. Thank God.

Edwin rushed over. 'My lord! Are you all right?'

The earl straightened and nodded, still gasping. 'Yes.' He pointed. 'But … my treasure.'

It took Edwin a moment, but then he realised. Several of the kists that were brought into the pavilion each night were stuffed with bags of pennies and other precious items, ready to use for paying his knights and men. How would this be done if the silver drained away in a molten stream? And there were letters, pieces of parchment, all in wooden boxes – they would be destroyed.

Brother William had already hurried off to join the line of men passing buckets of water up from the stream. Adam was still struggling to breathe. Edwin was the only one with no immediate task. 'I'll go, my lord.'

He felt the heat starting to singe him as he approached the pavilion, hands held up to shield his eyes. Thick smoke poured up into the night sky, and flame belched out from the open doorway. Edwin searched for the giant shadow, found Martin and grabbed his arm. 'Come with me.'

The flames were loud, and so were the shouts of men. 'What?'

Edwin stood on his toes to get nearer to Martin's ear and bellowed. 'We have to save my lord's treasure!'

Martin heard him this time. 'But how? We can't get through that!'
Edwin pulled harder at his arm. 'Round the back!'

He succeeded in dragging Martin away and round to the rear of
the pavilion, where more water was being thrown on to the wet
canvas and all the nearby tents were being hastily struck and moved.

Edwin realised he hadn't put on his belt and dagger, and cursed.
He pointed to the wall of the pavilion, at the sleeping end. 'Cut
it open!'

'What?'

'I said cut it open! It doesn't matter if you ruin it – it's going to
burn anyway!' He pulled Martin's knife from his belt and plunged
it into the taut canvas, dragging it down with both hands to open
a vertical rip. He jumped back as a burst of heat boiled out, but no
flames yet. He stabbed the knife again, trying to enlarge the hole.

Martin belatedly realised what he was doing, grabbed the edge
of the cut and heaved. This tore a hole large enough for Edwin to
squeeze through, and he made his way in. The smoke was thick,
choking, but the heavy hangings separating the area from the rest
of the pavilion would keep the worst of the flames out for a few
moments more. Edwin tried as best he could to cover his nose
and mouth as he groped his way around. There. Wood. A corner of
something. He started to drag the kist.

It was heavy. How long would it take him to get it back to the
rip in the canvas? And for how long could he hold his breath?
Suddenly Martin was beside him, and the kist moved as they heaved
it together. A third man joined them, and then others were there
outside as they reached the hole. Edwin took a huge gulp of air and
then pushed his way back in. How many kists were there? And had
they all been together?

By the time he'd made it out with another box he could hardly
breathe at all and he collapsed in a heap on the ground. Someone
bent over him and he recognised Sir Roger's voice. 'Edwin! Edwin,

are you all right?' Edwin couldn't speak but he managed a nod. Sir Roger straightened and turned back towards the pavilion, but the flames had now reached the sleeping area. 'I don't think we'll —'

A small figure darted past him and dived through the hole. Sir Roger shouted after it. 'Peter! Come back!'

And then Edwin watched as the flames burst through the pointed top of the pavilion, creating a funnel, a natural chimney for the fire. It roared up into the night and the remaining canvas ignited with a whoosh, a huge flaming torch lighting up the night sky before it caved in on itself and disintegrated into a scorching whirl of flying cinders.

———

It was dawn.

Edwin stood among a circle of men staring at the sodden and steaming heap of ashes. It could have been worse, he supposed. The pavilion was entirely destroyed, as was much of its furniture, but no man had lost his life, and the earl's treasure and correspondence had been saved.

No boy had lost his life, either, but Peter was soon going to wish he had, judging by the way Sir Roger was berating him. As Edwin had found himself yelling hoarsely at the flaming pavilion he had seen a shape, head down, running towards them: a tall figure carrying something that kicked. Both he and Sir Roger had thanked God, and the knight had said nothing at the time, overwhelmed by his relief. But it appeared he had merely been saving up his efforts.

Leaving the others to continue damping down the ashes, Edwin cleared his throat to dislodge some of the grit and made his way over to see if he could intervene.

Sir Roger was in full flow, arms waving. 'What were you thinking? I told you to stay near my tent! You could have been …'

Little Peter had tears streaming down his face, making tracks through the soot. He kept his head down and his hands behind his back as he endured the tirade, saying nothing. Edwin saw the tears drip to the ground. He stepped over to the boy and put a hand on one heaving shoulder. 'Please, Sir Roger.'

The knight stopped in mid-sentence. For a moment Edwin thought the outburst was going to be redirected towards him, but Sir Roger merely expelled a long breath and glared at them both. 'You tell him, then.'

Edwin looked from one to the other, the boy miserable and the knight as animated as Edwin had ever seen him. He knew why. 'Peter. You disobeyed an order, didn't you?' The boy sniffed and continued to stare at the earth under his feet. 'But you did it because you thought Sir Roger might be in danger?'

Peter looked up and gave half a nod.

Sir Roger opened his mouth, shut it again and folded his arms. 'Go on.'

'My lord, I couldn't see you, and I thought – I thought …'

Edwin saw realisation dawning in the knight's face. 'You thought I was in the pavilion?'

'Yes, my lord.'

'So you ran in to find me?'

'Yes, my lord.'

Sir Roger sighed. 'That still doesn't excuse disobeying my orders.' But the anger had gone from his voice, and Edwin and Peter both knew it.

Peter risked meeting his gaze, his eyes red-rimmed. 'Sorry, my lord. Please – please don't send me away.' His voice trembled and the ground engaged his attention again.

The knight crouched and laid his hand on Peter's shoulder. 'Look at me.' The boy obeyed. 'I'm not going to send you away. But you *must* do as you're told. You could have been killed, and then where would I be?'

Edwin saw Peter's first flicker of hope as Sir Roger continued. 'I was worried about you, do you understand? You're a good boy, and … I'd miss you if you weren't around.'

Peter's eyes grew wider. Slowly, slowly, his face changed, and it was like the sun had risen.

Sir Roger rolled his eyes. 'Oh, all right. Off you go, then. Go and clean yourself up and see if the men have left anything for us in the pot.' He called after the departing back. 'But do as you're told next time!'

Peter spared a glance for Edwin on his way past. 'I'll always protect him.' His tone was so adult that Edwin almost laughed, but he managed to swallow it just in time.

Sir Roger turned to him and Edwin braced himself, but it wasn't necessary. 'You see things very clearly,' was all the knight said to him, followed by, 'I should give him a beating, really, to remind him to obey orders next time. Sir Geoffrey would have done it to me when I was younger.'

There wasn't really an answer to that except to agree.

'But I haven't the heart. I'm sure he's had plenty of beatings in his life for less.'

Edwin's throat was sore and he wasn't sure how much longer his voice was going to hold out. 'He has. But … he's a different boy since you took him on.'

The clear blue eyes looked into Edwin's own. 'I felt the Lord telling me to do it, and I'm glad I did. But now I must get back to my men, and the lord earl will no doubt have work for you to do. And we'll still have to march today, even if we don't start until later.' He headed off.

Edwin went to find the earl. He was in conversation with Salisbury, as men around them packed what was left of his belongings on to the baggage carts, so Edwin didn't venture too near.

He spotted Martin, dipping his hands into a bucket and splashing water on his head in what was an unsuccessful attempt to remove the soot. Martin raised a streaky face. 'Are you all right? No burns?'

'No. Just a few holes in my tunic from flying sparks. You?'

Martin held out his left hand, which had a raw-looking red mark on the back. 'Just this. Could have been much worse.' He gestured to where the two earls were speaking. 'My lord is pleased with you.'

Edwin brightened, despite the pain in his throat. 'Is he? Good. I'm glad we managed to get it all out. The money, I mean – I know you lost the chairs and things.' A sudden thought struck him. 'What about the chess set?'

Martin burst out laughing, continuing until it turned into a cough. 'Trust you to think of that. No, sorry, it's gone. But my lord hates to travel without one, so I'm sure he'll pick up another from somewhere when he gets the chance.' He stood, wiping his wet face with the sleeve of his tunic and smearing it even more.

Edwin was struck by another horrible thought. 'Your new helm!'

'It's all right. I'd put it in one of the kists so as not to leave it lying out in the service area. So we saved it along with the treasure and parchments.'

'Thank the Lord. I know I joked about it, but I wouldn't want you to lose it.'

'Me neither. Now, let's see if we can find something to eat before we set off.'

They made their way past the now deserted remains of the pavilion to where Humphrey had set up the service area of the earl's camp: a stores tent, cooking fires, and a neat array of kitchen equipment. Humphrey was trying to talk to several men at once but he saw them and signalled for one of the servants to bring them food and drink. They sat on a couple of upturned buckets, and Edwin took a long and grateful draught of the weak morning ale before he started appreciatively on a bowl of warm pottage and bread.

He paused after a few moments. 'How did it start?'

Martin wasn't listening. Edwin waited until he'd cleared half the bowl and then repeated himself.

'The fire, you mean?'

'Yes.'

Martin was dipping a piece of bread into his pottage, and he hesitated. 'Well, that's the strange thing.'

'What is?'

'There were candles in the tent, of course, but we always make sure to put them well away from the walls and from any of the hangings. The only ones left out when I went to bed were the ones on the central table.'

Edwin paused with bread halfway to his own mouth. 'You went to bed and left candles lit?' His pottage dripped and he hastily shovelled it in.

'No, I mean – of course I wouldn't normally, but my lord was still up and talking to the Earl of Salisbury. He told us to go to bed.'

That sounded odd to Edwin. He hadn't been serving the lord earl for very long, it was true, but from what he'd learned and seen so far, he was almost never unattended. 'And Salisbury's squires?'

Martin spoke with his mouth full. 'Also gone. He told them to go and check everything was ready for him in his part of the camp.'

This was curious indeed. 'I wonder what they wanted to talk about?'

Martin shrugged. 'None of my business. I dozed straight off. Although, come to think of it, they did have a bit of an argument just before Salisbury left.'

'What about?'

Martin looked about him and lowered his voice. 'I was half asleep, but it sounded serious. Something about supporting the young king, about de Burgh holding Dover and stopping the fleet before they could get to Louis.'

'Nothing else?'

'Something about all being in this together, and all men knowing they were allies.'

Edwin pushed his bread round and round his bowl.

'Stop doing that.'

'Doing what?'

'That. Staring into the distance like that, like you're looking right through everything. *Thinking.*'

Edwin laughed. 'You want me to stop thinking?'

'What I mean is, stop making it complicated. I'm sure a candle just got knocked over by accident.'

'Hmm.' Edwin continued to push the bread, sopping up the last trace of pottage. 'And Salisbury's squires definitely didn't come back?'

'No.'

The answer was curt, even for Martin. Edwin looked at him more closely. 'There's something you're not telling me, isn't there? About that squire. The oldest one.'

Martin stood up abruptly. 'I have to get back to my lord. I'll see you later.' He shoved his bowl at the nearest serving man and loped away.

———•◦•———

They were late setting off. Edwin didn't feel as though he'd been in the saddle very long, but it was already noon. The stink of smoke still lingered, but whether it was from his own clothing or from the burned-out village they had passed through, he didn't know. This one had been completely deserted, no sign of life except for a couple of rats slinking through an overgrown garden. One or two of the men had strayed off the road to see if there was anything to be scavenged from the roofless, sightless buildings, but they came back with little more than a handful of scorched dried peas and some apples that were too green to eat. Edwin wondered about the people who had once lived there, and then wished he hadn't, as it weighed on his mind. This time Brother William made no effort to cheer him, his mouth set as he stared ahead. Then he crossed himself and Edwin realised he had been praying in silence as he rode.

Just after noon they reached a crossroads, where a group awaited them. Edwin recognised Sir Hugh Fitzjohn as their leader and brightened a little. The grizzled knight was a great friend of Sir Geoffrey's, and he had briefly been Edwin's companion when he'd first found himself part of an armed host a few months ago. He looked as though he'd been addressing his assembled men, but he stopped and bowed as he saw the earl approaching.

The column itself did not halt, but the earl nosed his horse to the side of the road to accept Sir Hugh's greeting and to acknowledge the men who knelt before him. Edwin cast his eye over the group. Sir Hugh's squire was behind him, and there were six other mounted sergeants, a dozen foot soldiers with varying degrees of armour, and – he scanned along the line – nineteen archers. Behind them were servants and baggage carts, neat and well packed. Sir Hugh had been on campaign many times before.

The mounted sergeants fell in with the rest of the column; the foot soldiers and archers picked up their equipment and waited for the horses to pass; those driving the baggage carts prepared their animals and looked back to see if the end of the column was in sight. Edwin spotted a man and a boy in the back of one of the carts, which was unusual, but he couldn't blame them for hitching a ride – this road was endless. The captain of the archers began pushing his fellows into a straight line, although he seemed to be having quite an altercation with one of them. Edwin heard an aggressive 'Say that again!' but he'd ridden too far past to catch the unfortunate man's reply.

Sir Hugh himself was invited to ride with the nobles, and his squire joined the others. The squire looked out of place: unlike his fellows, who were all boys of various sizes, he was a grown man in his forties. Alan, if Edwin recalled correctly: he'd been Sir

Hugh's squire since he was a boy but had never been able to afford knighthood so had remained in his master's service as the years and decades went by.

The road continued; the horse in front kept walking; Edwin allowed himself to fall into something of a stupor as the afternoon wore on. He was tired after being awake much of the night, and for once he was grateful for the horse and its steady rhythm.

It was later in the afternoon by the time he next paid attention to his surroundings, and he could sense a change in atmosphere. What was it?

He heard Brother William mutter something under his breath and followed the other's gaze. They had entered another village, this one inhabited and with repaired houses. The streets were deserted but Edwin heard a shriek and saw a soldier come out of one of the buildings brandishing a smoked ham. Two or three others were pushing their way into other homes, one even kicking down a door. They were being directed by Philip, the Earl of Salisbury's eldest squire.

Edwin knew with a sinking heart that he was about to get into a great deal of trouble, for he couldn't stand by. He prepared himself to get down from the horse, even as he heard another cry, a real scream this time.

He was not as quick as Brother William, who had already dismounted and was pulling the wooden cudgel out from his pack. He thrust his reins at Edwin.

'But Brother, you said…'

'I know what I said, but I'm not having this.'

Edwin watched in consternation as the monk marched over to the houses. Martin appeared beside him, with Adam just behind. 'What's going on?'

Edwin gestured to where Brother William was shoving a surprised man out of the way and taking up a position in the doorway of a house; a woman and several children were just visible inside. The altercation had attracted Philip's attention and he was making his way over, the others now at his back.

Martin swore, pushing past. 'Stay here. Stay out of it.'

He was loosening his sword in its scabbard as he strode, and Edwin had to hurry to catch up. 'No, Martin, stop —'

'Stop?' Martin gestured. 'They will kill him, monk or no.'

Edwin tried to grab his arm but he was shaken off. He looked back. A number of those riding or walking past as part of the column were looking over with interest, but, seeing the senior squires of the two earls, they sensibly decided it was none of their business and moved on.

The men were now in a loose half circle about the doorway – four of them, with Philip behind. He was urging them on. 'What are you waiting for?'

One of the soldiers replied, a little uncertainly, 'But my lord, it's a monk ...'

'Which should make it all the easier, you halfwit. One monk? An untrained cleric against four armed men? Go on, get it over with.' He gestured at the small heap of stuff they had piled up: nothing to him, thought Edwin, but a huge loss to these people, who have suffered enough. 'Get rid of him, kill him for all I care, see what's in there – you can see if she's got a daughter hidden away if you're quick, and we'll be on our way.'

Brother William did not move, except to loosen his stance and tap the end of the club into his left hand. Edwin realised he was the only one who knew what was about to happen, so he ran and pulled at Martin again. 'You don't understand.'

Martin turned and Edwin was taken aback by the fury in his eyes. 'I am not going to let him do this, do you hear me?'

'But it won't. You haven't seen —'

Their altercation had drawn Philip's attention. 'Oh, and look, the boy and the servant have come to even up the numbers. How sweet.' He put one hand on his sword, still in its scabbard. 'You want to try me again, Maaartin?'

The drawling emphasis on his name seemed to ignite something within Martin. If Edwin didn't get through to him soon, the Lord only knew what he was going to do. And there was no need. He threw himself in front of his friend, pushing his hands flat against his chest, knowing that he had no chance if Martin decided to throw him to one side. 'For God's sake, will you *listen* to me!'

'*What?*' Martin's expression remained one of fury, but he was still in there, somewhere.

Edwin lowered his voice. 'You don't need to intervene. Really. It is not Brother William who will end up dead.'

The eyes focused on him properly. 'Are you mad?'

'No. But I know something you don't know. And neither do they.' He still had his hands on Martin's chest and he could sense the hesitation. He was getting through. '*Trust me.*'

Chapter Three

Martin was looking down at him. 'What do you – no, never mind. Are you sure? Swear to it?' Their eyes locked and Edwin nodded. Martin turned to Philip. 'Go ahead.'

Philip was taken aback. 'What?'

Martin gestured. 'I say let them get on with it. Your men look like they're out of condition – I'll give you sixpence on the monk.' He looked sideways at Edwin and muttered under his breath. 'I hope you're right.'

Lord, Edwin hoped he was too, or the consequences were going to be too terrible to contemplate. But he knew what he had seen, that day on the road at midsummer.

Philip, uncertain now in the face of their strange confidence, waved his men forward. Two had swords, one an axe and the other a dagger. Brother William held his cudgel with a casual air that Edwin recognised, and he allowed himself a discreet smirk.

'What in the name of God's blood is going on here?'

Edwin jumped as the bellow came from behind him. A burly man on a horse was making his way over from the column. At the sight of him, the four assailants, as one, dropped their weapons.

The horse was going to go through him rather than round him, so Edwin hastily removed himself from its path. The man had a voice that would carry across a battlefield. 'Pick those up! Get back in line! And by God's blood, if I see you attacking a man of the Church again I'll have you all whipped and dragged behind the carts.' He glared as they did as they were told and then scurried off, heads down.

Philip drew himself up and opened his mouth, but he was no match for that booming voice. 'The lord earl requires your presence, sir.' Even Edwin winced. 'Now.'

Edwin watched as Philip struggled with himself and then decided to make the best of a bad situation. 'As my lord wishes, of course. Thank you for alerting me.' In a final, petty gesture he kicked at the pile of booty, sending the ham and a couple of loaves of bread flying, and bursting open a bag of peas. As he passed Edwin and Martin he gave them both a look of loathing. 'Unfinished business, Martin. And –' he looked at Edwin as though he were something to be scraped off the sole of his boot – 'new business with you, it would seem.'

Edwin heaved a sigh of relief as he left. He felt the tension draining out of him and moved forward.

'Stay back, if you please.' It was Brother William.

Martin's face was a jumble of conflicting emotions. 'But —'

'I don't mean to offend, Martin, Edwin, but to these people armed men are armed men. Please, wait there.'

Edwin watched as Brother William spoke to those inside the house, invisible now, and made the sign of the cross over them. As he left the village, several other women and children came out of their houses. Some called out for him to bless them, but most remained in silence until the three men were all well away. As he reached the main road and mounted his horse, Edwin looked back to see the children scrabbling in the dust for the scattered peas.

It was evening. Martin knew that the earl's temper was becoming short, and it was no wonder. The Earl of Salisbury had offered to share his own pavilion until such time as a replacement could be procured – and Martin hoped to heaven that the man Humphrey had sent on to the lord earl's castle at Reigate would ride quickly – so they were all crammed in there. They'd managed to rig up a bit of privacy for the earl when he slept by moving the hangings around to create more and smaller compartments, but that didn't help here in the service area, which was now both tiny and holding more people than it was supposed to.

A bag of correspondence had just caught up with them – a single man on a horse could move much faster than the unwieldy host, so news was received every couple of days – and Martin handed it to Brother William, who tipped it out on to the corner of the table.

No sooner had he done so than a splatter of red liquid splashed all over the parchments, and the monk jumped back with an exclamation to avoid his white robe catching most of it. He turned and started to shout before realising that the person before him was the page Matthew, holding a jug and quaking with terror. Philip was several paces away, but Martin wasn't fooled.

Brother William shut his mouth and concentrated on mopping up the spill with a cloth which Adam passed him. Martin jerked his head at the page, who, clearly unable to believe his luck, fled through to the main section of the pavilion.

Martin watched the monk closely. He'd been in the household since midsummer, and to be honest Martin hadn't really paid him that much attention. He was merely a figure in a robe drifting around, talking to the earl about letters and boring administrative matters, thus giving Martin the time to let his attention wander. He seemed to be quite friendly with Edwin, but that was natural, he supposed, as they shared some of the same responsibilities and were together at the times when everyone else was out training or hunting.

However, Martin had in the intervening time spent a week in a Cistercian abbey, during which he had (if he was honest with himself) totally misjudged at least two of the men there, so he'd better not make the same mistake again. Brother William's right hand, now he looked at it properly, was strong, and the forearm that emerged from his robe as he wiped up the spilled wine was thick and muscled. This was not a man who had spent his youth sitting down with a pen.

The earls' meal was arriving, so Martin and Adam went through to the main space, leaving Brother William patting the remaining letters dry and starting to sort them.

Later, after everyone had eaten and the servants had been dismissed, the earl decided to walk about the camp to speak with his knights and show himself to the men. He elected to take Adam with him, so Martin, disappointed, occupied himself in checking that everything was as it should be in the cramped space set apart as their sleeping area. There wasn't much to do, so he took the opportunity to sit down, take his boots off – too small, as they always were, and pinching his feet – and stare into space for a while.

He closed his eyes and allowed himself the luxury of thinking of Joanna, conjuring an image of her face. It was all so hopeless. As companion to the Lady Isabelle, the earl's sister, she had spent many years at Conisbrough during which he could admire her from afar, and during the last year he had come to know her better and (he really was being honest with himself tonight – why was that?) to love her. How cruel, then, that she should be torn away from him just as he recognised his feelings: the Lady Isabelle had gone to her new home following her marriage to Sir Gilbert, and Joanna had no choice but to go with her.

Martin sighed. He kept trying to create scenarios where they could or would meet again, but they grew ever more fanciful. She would remain at Pevensey with her mistress; he would follow the earl around the country, but as his lord's preferred residence was Conisbrough, almost the entire length of the realm would separate them. The only tiny chink of light he could see was the possibility that she would remain unmarried until he could become a knight and have a manor of his own. That might happen within the next few years, and then he might be able to get his father to talk to her family, and then her cousin might consider the offer … there were far too many *mights* in there, but it was his only hope, so he could imagine it if he wanted to.

Far away in his daydreams, it was some moments before Martin realised that voices were coming from the other side of the hanging. It was Philip – no mistaking that tone – and the Earl of Salisbury. He was trapped. They evidently had no idea he was there, and, although he hadn't been deliberately hiding, if he were to be discovered now it would look like he had been eavesdropping. The only thing to do was to stay as still as possible, hope that they would not come in here (and they would have no reason to, surely?), and wait, either until they went away, or possibly until others came back to the pavilion and he could attempt to mingle with a group.

Of course, it wasn't polite – wasn't knightly – to eavesdrop, but now he was here he couldn't help it.

'… not pleased to hear that Tom Godsblood had to come over and find you.'

'I'm sorry, my lord.'

'It's fair enough to plunder an enemy's lands, but it was unnecessary to do it yourself, and you kept me waiting.' There was a slight pause, and Martin stiffened, trying not to breathe too loudly, until he heard the clink of jug on goblet and the sound of liquid being poured. Salisbury continued. 'But, worse than that, you could have insulted the Church, which I can't afford, and you almost made yourself look very stupid, which would reflect badly on me.' There was the creak of a chair, and Salisbury's voice was filled with menace. 'I will not tolerate those who embarrass me, is that clear?'

Even Philip wouldn't dare talk back to that, and indeed, he sounded more subdued than Martin had ever heard him.

'I understand, my lord. It won't happen again, I swear it.'

Salisbury grunted. 'The way I heard it, Warenne's men were certain that monk was going to win the fight. Which means they knew something you didn't, which means you were about to go into battle without all the information you needed.'

'Yes, my lord. I'll learn from this.'

'Know what you're getting into, boy, before you make any kind of move.' Salisbury took a gulp of whatever he was drinking. On the other side of the hanging, Martin was so close he could hear him swallow before he continued. 'Remember: you need to know your enemy.'

———•———

Edwin inhaled. The cool evening air was filled with the smoke of cooking fires, but it was a friendly, homely smell and much nicer than the stale, cramped pavilion. He had not been needed by the earl, thank the Lord, so he could get away for a while. He had initially returned to his tent, where Brother William was already snoring away – his time in the abbey, with its constant broken nights, had given him the ability to fall asleep at will whenever he had the opportunity – but he was not tired enough to sleep. Instead he wandered through the camp in search of Sir Roger and company. He found him, but he was in conversation with Sir Hugh Fitzjohn; Edwin hesitated.

Sir Roger saw him hovering and beckoned him over. Edwin was greeted by both knights and invited to sit. He was pleased that Sir Hugh remembered him and was able to give him news of Sir Geoffrey, who had been his friend and companion for many decades.

The conversation turned to the afternoon's altercation, which both knights had heard about but not seen in person. Edwin was able to give them a full account, watching as they first puffed out their cheeks in disbelief and then became outraged.

'No discipline!' Sir Hugh thumped his hand down on his knee.

Sir Roger was shaking his head. 'And to steal from women and children.'

'Stealing anything from anyone shows a lack of control and authority, unless it's foraging for supplies on specific orders. By God, I wouldn't stand for such a thing from my men, and indeed I was telling them so when we all met up on the road. Discipline must be maintained in a host, else there is chaos. And you say it was a *squire* who was leading them? Joining in, encouraging them, rather than trying to stop it all?'

Edwin nodded. 'Yes. Philip, who is the Earl of Salisbury's senior squire.' There was more he could say, but that was Martin's business, not his, so he kept his counsel.

Sir Hugh called over to Alan, who was, as Edwin now noticed for the first time, unobtrusively unpacking, sorting and making everything neat in Sir Hugh's tent. 'Do you hear that?'

Alan inclined his head. 'Yes, my lord. If I'd done anything like that when I was a boy, you'd have had me out of your service before sunset the same day, and I would have deserved it.' He returned to his task.

The three of them continued to chat as the light faded, turning to the more general subject of the present campaign, and before long Edwin became aware that food was being passed around. Sir Hugh, who enjoyed greater resource than Sir Roger, had a dedicated cook in his contingent of men, and the bowls smelled appetising.

Little Peter lifted his nose and sniffed appreciatively, making Sir Hugh laugh. 'You're welcome to join us. In fact, it's just you and the ten archers, is it?' he asked Sir Roger, who nodded. 'Alf!'

A man sitting by the cooking fire turned, and Edwin recognised the man he'd seen in the baggage cart earlier. He kept stirring a pot as he replied. 'Yes, my lord?'

'If Sir Roger here pools his supplies, can you manage cooking for another twelve men? Well …' he looked at Peter with a straight face, 'eleven men and a boy who looks like he could do with some more of your good food?'

The man still didn't move, but Edwin saw his nod in the shadows of the firelight. 'Of course, my lord. But perhaps he'd better taste the goods before he decides?' He ladled something into a bowl and passed it to the boy who crouched next to him. The lad brought it over to Sir Roger, who took out his spoon and dipped it into what looked to be a thick broth. Edwin watched, his mouth beginning to water, as the knight tasted, savoured, and finally expelled a long breath.

'No offence to my men, who do the best they can, but I'll happily take service with you as a foot soldier, Sir Hugh, if this is the food on offer.' He scooped up another mouthful.

'Done, then,' said Sir Hugh, cheerfully. 'Bring some of that over for the rest of us, Alf, and make sure everyone gets his share.'

The man by the fire heaved himself up to a standing position with some difficulty and took up two bowls. As he came towards them he was in silhouette, the fire behind him, and Edwin could make out only a figure with a pronounced limp. Then, as he drew nearer, Edwin gaped, for the man had only one leg. Where his left shin and foot should have been, there was a wooden pole.

Alf had handed one bowl to Sir Hugh and he was standing patiently with the other held out towards Edwin. Edwin realised he was staring and shut his mouth. 'Sorry, I didn't mean to … what I mean is …'

'Not to worry, my lord. It takes most men like that when they first see it.'

Edwin took his meal without thinking. 'Oh, I'm not a … but how? I mean, what happened …?'

There were immediate groans of protest from around the fire, where the cook's boy was distributing the pottage to the rest of the men.

One of them, the captain of archers Edwin had seen by the side of the road, spoke up. 'Oh Lord, never ask him that – not unless you've got the rest of the night to hear his tales of crusades to the east, anyway. Bigger hero than old King Richard, he was, if you believe it all.'

Alf opened his mouth to retort but Sir Hugh cut him off. 'Now then, John, Alf, settle down and eat your supper while it's hot. Plenty of time for tales later on.'

Edwin tucked into his meal, trying to identify the combination of flavours – how had the man produced something so delicious with only campaign rations? – as he looked about him. They were in a large but tight-knit circle, facing inwards as they ate, situated in a central part of the main camp; others were passing by constantly behind them, just out of the light of the fire, insubstantial shadows flickering past rather than real men.

Once all were served, Alf and his boy sat down to eat too, the cook gratified as he looked at the wolfing going on around him. The boy finished quickly and then went to hover in front of the captain of the archers. 'Is it finished yet?'

John, as Sir Hugh had called him, folded a last piece of bread into his mouth and spoke through it. 'Get away with you. You think I haven't got more important things to do?' He passed his empty bowl to the child and watched him turn away, disappointed, but as soon as his back was turned John reached behind him and pulled something out of a bag. Edwin handed over his own dish and watched with interest as John took out his knife and started whittling. It was too dark to see clearly, but whatever he was doing, he was paying great attention to it, holding it to catch the best of the light from the fire.

By the time the bowls were all collected, John had finished whatever he was doing to his satisfaction. He put the knife behind him, sticking it into the back of the log on which he was sitting as he admired his handiwork. 'Dickon!'

The boy looked up from behind the towering collection of dishes he was now carrying. He stacked them by the cooking fire, where a butt of water stood ready, and made his way over. His face lit up as John held out the prize, and as the light flared Edwin could see that it was a carved wooden figure of a knight on horseback. Dickon took it and held it up. 'Oh, John, it's wonderful. Look, Father, look!' He scampered over to Alf, and John tried unsuccessfully to keep his face stern.

Alf took the knight and turned it over in his hands before passing it back. 'Very fine, John, very fine. You spoil the lad.' He turned to the boy and pointed at the bowls. 'Pots first – play afterwards.' He took up a stick and used it to raise the handle of the metal cooking pot and remove it from the fire. 'Leave that one until it's cool, but get the rest done now.'

With extreme care, Dickon placed the knight down on the blanket on which he had been sitting, before sighing, putting on a canvas smock which was far too big for him, and rolling up his sleeves. Peter, who had in the shadows been putting away more food than ought to be possible for a child his size, joined him and passed a first bowl, though whether he was looking more at the water butt or at the carved knight was a moot point. John laughed. 'Maybe I'd better start on another one.' He moved to the nearby stack of firewood and started to root through it, looking for a suitable piece.

Edwin stretched his legs out comfortably as he listened to the two knights talking. Then his eye fell once more on John, who had re-seated himself and was feeling around behind him. 'Has someone taken my knife?' He made his way round to the back of the log, crouching and groping his way along it. 'Come, now, which one of you has it?'

The other men made various negative noises, one or two shifting to see if they could see it. John's voice became more irritated. 'You know I use that knife all the time. It's not as good as my tools at home, but it serves well and I want it back. If any of you has taken it in jest, let him return it now and I'll say no more.'

By now several of his comrades were looking round, but Edwin thought they had little chance. John had been sitting at the outer edge of the circle, with strangers passing behind him constantly. Who was to say one of them hadn't seen a handy-looking knife and decided to help himself to it? He was about to say something when his eye was caught by a new figure at the edge of the firelight, and he jumped to his feet as he recognised the earl.

'My lord.' Sir Hugh had seen him too and was also standing, gesturing to all to do the same. The earl moved towards them, Adam a pace behind. 'Stay, stay, all of you. Sir Hugh, let us walk.'

The two of them made their way through the men and strolled off, speaking of the campaign. Seen from behind they were almost anonymous: two figures much of a height, wearing nondescript cloaks over the fine tunics that would mark them out from other men.

Some time passed, John still unable to find his knife and he and various companions spreading further out to look for it, inside and around the tents. Edwin had settled back and was just starting to wonder whether Sir Roger ever played chess. His eye fell on Alf, who was laboriously dragging a large object with a dome-shaped top nearer to the fire. What …? Oh yes, he could see it now – a small bread oven on a wheeled board. Of course, men needed bread every day and they couldn't carry it all with them.

Alf called to Dickon, who was just wiping the last bowl. 'Fetch the brushwood and then you can play, as long as you don't stray too far.' The boy brought him some ready-tied bundles of twigs, lit each one by dipping it in the cooking fire, and pushed them in the oven. The he picked up his precious knight, and with a look at Peter they were both off out of sight.

Edwin watched as Alf sealed the door of the oven and turned to pour flour and water into a shallow trough, along with a handful of leftover dough from the last batch. Just like his mother did at home: that was what you did to make bread that rose properly, although Edwin didn't know why. Soon Alf had a dough and was kneading it with a rhythmic motion that made Edwin feel dozy as he watched. The cook left it to warm near the fire and shuffled in a sitting position over to the pot he'd left earlier, poking the remaining contents with a long spoon. 'Good. Dickon? Oh, never mind …'

He began to haul himself to his feet – foot – and Edwin roused himself. 'Can I help you with something?'

'My thanks, sir. The later in the day, the more trouble I have with my leg.' He tapped the wood. 'Would you kindly fetch me the crock of butter out of that cart?' He pointed.

Edwin groped around in the back of the cart until his hand fell on cool pottery. The crock was bigger than the one his mother had at home, but similar: keeping it in shade or in a bucket of water kept the butter reasonably solid even on a warm day. He passed it to Alf. 'Here. And it's just Edwin, please.'

'Edwin. Good old name. I'm Alfred myself, but I've always been Alf to my friends.' He held out a floury hand and Edwin shook it. Then he dolloped some butter into the trough and poured more flour on it.

Edwin was curious. 'Is that to make a different kind of bread?'

Alf shook his head without stopping his work. 'No – pastry this time. Lard is better, but butter will do when there's no lard to be had. First bake of the oven is the hottest, so that's for the bread; but once you've taken that out it's still warm and good for a few pies.'

'Pies? With what?'

Alf nodded at the cooking pot. 'Leftover pottage. Can't waste it, but the pot has to get clean and go back in the cart for tomorrow's march. If you leave the cold pottage in it all day and then heat it up again it can make men sick. And men get sick all too easily on campaign without adding to the danger.' He picked up the ball of stuff he'd made and began to pull it into fist-sized pieces. 'If you cook it in a pie now and then eat it in the morning, it doesn't spoil.'

Edwin watched as he deftly made cup shapes and then started to ladle the thick and congealing pottage into them. Something struck him. 'Doesn't that mean you're awake most of the night?'

'Aye. But the men need their bread, and the lad and I get to sleep in the cart during the morning. It's not so bad. And I'm lucky Sir Hugh will have me at all, being how I am.'

Edwin took the opportunity to ask, tentatively, about his leg, wondering if the subject might be a painful one. He needn't have worried, though, for Alf was happy to tell what sounded like a well-worn tale about a battle in the East, and how he'd been lucky to survive, 'what with having been treated by one of them heathen Saracens rather than a proper Frankish surgeon.'

They were interrupted by a commotion breaking out in a nearby part of the camp. Edwin and several others stood, trying to make out what was happening, taking a few steps in the direction of the hubbub, but it was by now fully dark and looking at their own fire had spoiled their night vision.

Edwin heard his name being called, and Adam panted into the circle of light. 'Edwin. Sir Roger. Come quick.'

Edwin felt his heart thump, and Sir Roger, issuing from his tent, reached for his sword. 'Adam, what is it? Are you hurt?'

Adam shook his head and held out something that glinted in the firelight. John pushed past the men crowding round and grabbed at Adam's arm. 'Where did you get that?'

'Is it yours?' Edwin could see that Adam was holding up a knife.

'Yes, it is, where did you get it?'

Adam looked from him to Edwin and back again. 'You'd better come too, then. Because someone has just thrown it at the lord earl's back.'

Chapter Four

Martin heard them before he saw them. Salisbury apparently did too, for both he and Philip went outside. Martin took his chance: when the group of shouting, gesticulating men burst into the pavilion from the darkness outside he stepped into the flurry, confident that nobody would know he'd been inside all the time.

Everyone was talking at once. He spotted Edwin and grabbed him. 'What's going on?'

Edwin looked grim. 'Someone threw a knife at the earl.'

Martin gaped in horror. 'What? Who? Is he …?' But a quick glance assured him that his lord was fine.

'It hit Sir Hugh, though it only grazed his arm and tore a hole in his sleeve.' Edwin gestured to where the grizzled figure, sword drawn, was standing in the doorway and blocking anyone else's entrance.

'Then how do you know he was aiming at my lord earl?'

Edwin drew him to one side. 'I saw them walking together. From the back you couldn't tell which was which, especially in the dark. And I was worried about the fire, anyway. Surely this is someone realising his first attempt failed, and trying something more direct?'

Martin nodded. 'I should have listened to you.' He looked at Sir Roger, who had joined them. 'We need to protect him while Edwin finds out what's going on.'

'Agreed. And he may need protecting in more ways than one.' Sir Roger looked over to the centre of the group, where the earl was by now engaged in a shouting match with the Earl of Salisbury, jabbing a finger at him. 'In a moment he is going to say something he will regret.'

Sir Roger went over to them and Martin heard his smooth, calm tones. Behind the milling men Martin caught sight of Philip's smirking face as he stood by and watched the altercation. The old rage, like a nagging sore, came back. He looked down at Edwin. 'Funny, isn't it, that we should have had a journey free of incident all the way from Conisbrough, and all this only happens when they join us?'

He could see Edwin's mind beginning to work, so, satisfied that he'd made his point, Martin elbowed his way through the press. The earl saw him. 'Martin. Get all these people out of here.' In his agitation he'd forgotten that the pavilion wasn't his – Martin could hardly push the Earl of Salisbury and his household out. But he couldn't disobey, either, so he contented himself with finding a few men who looked like they'd just tagged along for the excitement and bundling them out past Sir Hugh.

Eventually he, the earl, Adam, Edwin, Sir Roger and Sir Hugh were left with Salisbury and his household, and things calmed down a bit, although the pavilion's reduced central space still felt crowded. The rushing around of bodies had made all the lamps and candles flicker, and they had not yet steadied themselves, so everything was jumping. Sir Hugh's squire, Alan, belatedly arrived and started to look at his master's arm, but even in the terrible light Martin could see that the scratch was just that, and it wasn't bothering the old knight in the slightest.

Both earls had calmed themselves, but there was still something in the air, and it wasn't just the sweat from too many bodies. Salisbury took charge, pointing at Adam. 'You, boy. I heard you say that a man had claimed the knife as his?'

Adam looked uncomfortable. 'Yes, my lord, but —'

Salisbury waved him into silence. 'Bring him in, we'll hear what he has to say for himself and then hang him.'

Both Edwin and Sir Roger bit back protests as Sir Hugh gestured to Alan. The squire spoke to someone outside the pavilion, and soon a man was escorted in, his arms pinioned by two guards. He had a bruise on his face – unless it was just dirt, Martin wasn't close enough to see – but was otherwise unharmed.

Salisbury addressed Adam again. 'This is him?'

Adam looked around for help, but none was forthcoming. 'Yes, my lord, but —'

He was cut off once more, this time by Salisbury cuffing him around the ear. 'Don't talk back to me, boy – just answer my question.'

'How dare you!'

The retort had, thankfully, come from the lord earl, the one person in the pavilion who could address Salisbury in such a tone. 'How dare you discipline one of my squires in my presence?'

'I'll dare what I like, cousin, in my own tent.' They stood eye to eye, Salisbury marginally taller but the earl with his heavier muscles tensed. Lord, thought Martin, I'm sizing them up as though they're going to fight. What will I do if they do?

Salisbury looked away first. 'Never mind the squire. This man here threw his knife at your back – what are you going to do about it?'

In normal circumstances, Martin thought, the lord earl would not hesitate to have the man punished. But now he seemed to be more concerned with continuing to argue with his fellow nobleman. 'Did he now?' The earl ran his hand over his beard, considering. 'Roger, Weaver.' He turned and Martin saw them tense. 'You both had something to say a moment ago. Say it now.'

They exchanged a glance and Martin saw Edwin indicate that the knight should speak. 'By your leave, my lord. This man here was using the knife, which was stolen from him some time before it came near you. Edwin and I, and Sir Hugh, all heard him asking who had taken it and then looking for it.' He glanced at Edwin, who spoke with some reluctance. Martin knew how much he hated being asked to speak in front of his betters.

'I agree, my lord. And also ...' he tailed off, but nobody stopped him so he continued, falling over his words in his haste to get them out. 'When Adam came with the knife, John clearly said it was his, in public, before he knew what had been done with it. My lord, if he had thrown it at you he would never have done such a thing, surely?'

Over at the edge of the tent, Philip made a derisive noise that was just loud enough to be heard but subtle enough to be mistaken for clearing his throat. Salisbury snorted more openly. 'You think so, do you? And what's your word worth?'

Edwin had no reply to make, thankfully for his own safety, but the earl had had enough. 'He's my man, as are the *knights* Sir Roger and Sir Hugh, so if they all swear to the truth of this –' he looked about to see them nodding – 'then I will accept the man's innocence. Let him go.'

The prisoner, looking hugely relieved, as well he might, left the pavilion as fast as he could, followed by the other soldiers. The two earls stared at each other for a long moment before – divine intervention, surely – a lantern spat and spluttered out next to them, causing them both to look round in surprise. The moment was broken and each retired, saying no more, to his sleeping place.

Martin jerked his head at Adam to tell him to accompany the earl, and then he joined Sir Hugh, Sir Roger, Edwin and Alan near the pavilion entrance.

Sir Hugh was the most senior, so Martin left it to him to say what they were all thinking. 'We must stand guard.'

Sir Roger nodded. 'Agreed. But where? Outside?'

Nobody wanted to raise out loud the idea that the danger might be inside the tent. Edwin looked like he wanted to say something, so Martin nudged him. 'What?'

'Sirs … maybe – I mean, you'll know better than me – but —'

'Spit it out, Edwin, we all know you.' Sir Hugh wasn't a man to waste words.

'Perhaps, if you mounted a guard both outside the door here, and around the back of the pavilion? Don't forget, there's only a wall of canvas separating him from anyone wanting to get in. And perhaps Martin could sleep with his feet across the entrance to the sleeping area, so anyone trying to approach that way will trip and wake him up?'

Martin found himself nodding in agreement. 'It's so small in there that I'd probably have to do that anyway, but yes, good idea.'

The knights exchanged a glance. 'I and my men will take turns at the back, Sir Hugh, if you and yours would do the same here. And that leaves Edwin free to … pursue any enquiries he might want to make.'

Sir Hugh nodded and scratched absent-mindedly at the wound on his arm, now scabbing over and making his torn tunic stick to the skin. He spoke to Alan. 'See to it.' The squire bowed and left, and Sir Hugh clapped Edwin on the shoulder. 'Good. Off you go, then. If you need anything, ask Alan.'

Martin watched as Edwin slipped out into the night. He and the others looked at each other before Sir Hugh spoke once more. 'To work, gentlemen, and let us pray we all survive the night.'

⸺•⸺

It was late the following afternoon, and Edwin was dozing in his saddle. He had been awake most of the night but had discovered nothing at all beside what he already knew. John had finished the carving, stuck the knife in the back of the log on which he had been sitting, and had spoken with the boy and the cook. He had moved to the firewood stack and then back again. It had been dark, and many men from the camp had been passing by. Nobody had seen the knife being taken, but equally, nobody could account for it later being thrown at the earl. There was no other explanation.

On the positive side, there had been no further attack on the earl during the day so far. He had told all to Brother William – who had enjoyed a good night's sleep – so he was confident that the monk would keep his eyes open for trouble even if Edwin didn't.

They had heard Mass that morning before setting off, as it was Sunday, and then continued on their way. The circular detour was now almost complete and they were around to the south of London; even at this distance Edwin could see the smoke rising from the hundreds – no, thousands – of hearths in the great city, and he wondered what it was like there. Perhaps it was similar to Lincoln, the only other city he had ever visited. Remembering that naturally led to thinking of Alys, and his mind was pleasantly engaged until it was time to stop for the evening once more. The light in her summer-blue eyes as they held hands at the wedding feast …

Good news awaited the earl as the camp was erected: Humphrey's man had done his work and two carts containing the pieces of a second pavilion and various items of furniture had arrived from his castle at Reigate. There would be no more need to share with the Earl of Salisbury, thank the Lord. Once it was erected and the earl installed inside, lord of his own domain once more, they had a new visitor: the Earl of Arundel.

Edwin was pleased to note to himself – *thank you, Sir Geoffrey* – that he would have recognised the newcomer by his device. He wasn't armoured or wearing his surcoat, but both of his squires and a few other household members who accompanied him wore a patch on their tunics that was red with a gold lion. Arundel – another William, of course – was about the same age as the earl and was greeting him like an old friend. Which he was, of course: the earl's wife, who had died when Edwin was a child but whom he vaguely remembered seeing at Conisbrough, had been Arundel's sister.

'And so to business,' Arundel was continuing. 'I bring you your new page.'

Edwin looked on expectantly: a new member of the earl's close household was always of interest, and he surely had to be better than the last page, who had been sent away in disgrace.

'Where is he?' Arundel was looking around him in irritation, his dramatic flourish spoiled. 'Step forward, Hugh, and greet your new lord.' He located his son, pulled him out from the group of retainers behind him, and shoved him into the centre of the space.

There was a long pause.

The silence was in danger of stretching to an embarrassing length, but eventually the earl broke it by saying what Edwin, and surely everyone else, was thinking. 'And he's seven, is he?'

The boy was *tiny*. If he'd been asked, Edwin would have put him at around five years of age, if that. Surely he wasn't old enough or strong enough to be sent away from his home? These nobles did things differently from normal people, but still …

Arundel tried to laugh it off. 'He's a bit of a runt, I grant you, and so is my elder son. But when a man has seven daughters he'll take whatever he can get.' He poked the child in the back. 'Make your obedience, then! As you've been taught.'

The boy – Hugh, had his father said? – managed to bow before the lord earl, who still looked nonplussed. He turned to Martin, who was as ever standing behind him in silence. 'Can you do anything with him?'

Martin was still staring, but he collected himself. 'Of course, my lord. My lords,' he added, hastily, with a look at Arundel. 'I'm sure he'll be a fine addition to your household.' He tried to give the boy an encouraging smile, but Hugh took one look at the looming figure and immediately bit his lip as though trying not to cry. Edwin felt sorry for him, but there was nothing he could do now. He would try to be reassuring if he saw him later.

The earl sighed. 'Very well then. Martin – no, Adam – go with him to collect his things, bring him back here and show him what's what.'

'Yes, my lord.' Adam bowed and beckoned to the boy, who, thought Edwin, still looked near to tears but with at least the relief of having been publicly accepted into service and then sent out with the less intimidating of the two squires.

The earl was also standing, intending to take a walk through the camp with the Earl of Arundel. Edwin exchanged a glance with Martin, who put one hand on the dagger at his belt, nodded silently and followed them out, so close to his lord that he almost trod on his heels.

Edwin wasn't sure what he should do while the earl was away, but he hadn't been invited to follow, so he would have to wait here until he was needed. He busied himself tidying up a few cups, replacing them on the side table, and straightening the chairs.

After some while a man entered, sent through by the guard outside. It was Turold, one of the Conisbrough garrison who was often employed by the earl as a messenger. He was carrying a leather bag of correspondence, which he held out to Edwin.

Edwin took it from him. 'Have you come all the way from home? I thought I'd seen you with us.'

Turold shook a dusty head. 'No, you're right, I was here – got sent out a few miles to meet with two others and collect it all together so they could get back. Anyway, it's all there and I'm off to see if I can find a drink.'

Edwin thanked him, watched him go, looked at the bag, and then almost jumped out of his skin as Brother William appeared suddenly before him.

'No need to raise your eyebrows at me like that, Edwin. I'm not possessed of supernatural knowledge – I saw him arriving and knew what must be in the satchel. Come.' He led the way through to the service area and hummed under his breath as he tipped up the bag and emptied the letters on to the table.

Recovering himself, Edwin smiled. 'Such cheerfulness, Brother – what would the lord abbot say if he heard you? And on a Sunday, too?'

Brother William pursed his lips. 'Something about precept fifty-four, probably. Or have I just made it worse in saying that?' He shuffled through the pile. 'These have come in from different places, I think. Yes, look, this one is from Sir Gilbert down in Pevensey, but this is Sir Geoffrey's seal. Some of these have come all the way from Conisbrough.'

Edwin moved closer to the table.

The monk held up two letters with the same seal. 'Two from Sir Geoffrey, in fact. Why would he …?' He turned them over. 'Ah, that explains it. One is for the lord earl, and the other' – he held it out – 'is for you.'

Edwin had never received a letter before. Why would Sir Geoffrey be writing to him? Was something wrong? Something must be wrong. He felt panic rising, panic that was made worse when, astonishingly, Brother William pushed a second folded parchment at him. 'And another one for you. Plain wax seal, but also in Father Ignatius's hand. My, you are popular today.'

Edwin took it without speaking, suddenly finding it difficult to breathe. What if …?

Brother William paused and spoke less flippantly. 'Edwin. Don't look so worried. No doubt this one is a message from your lovely wife telling you how much she misses you. And the other – well, if Sir Geoffrey knew that someone had to ride all the way here to bring his letter to the lord earl, maybe he thought it would be no extra trouble to dictate one to you too.' He patted Edwin's arm before turning back to the rest of the correspondence. 'I'm sure everything is fine.'

His fingers trembling, Edwin moved to break the seal on Sir Geoffrey's message, but just at that moment the earl entered the pavilion, and the chance was lost. He tucked both letters into his belt. They returned to the central space, where Martin gave him a quick shrug to indicate that nothing untoward had happened. Edwin stood straight while the earl settled himself. He could feel the letters burning a hole in his tunic, but he must wait. He must. However long it took.

The earl held out a cup for Martin to pour wine into, and flicked his fingers at Brother William to begin.

'Sorry, my lord, these have only just arrived this moment, so I have not yet had time to open and read them. Some may not be worthy of your personal attention.'

The earl sighed. 'Well, I'm here now and we're not going anywhere for a few hours, so we may as well get on with it. You can skip any that aren't important as we go along.'

Brother William nodded and broke the first seal. 'From Sir Gilbert, my lord.'

The earl sat forward with more interest. 'Let's hear that one, then. Is my sister with child yet? No, too early to know, I suppose. But anyway, continue.'

The monk scanned his way down the parchment. 'He greets you well and offers his respect … he will not be joining the host as he has been asked to remain at Pevensey in case any of the French fleet sails that way –'

'Shame,' interrupted the earl. 'But yes, makes sense. Go on.'

'Ah, let me see … your sister is in good health, my lord, she is grateful and thanks you for arranging the match … all is well, though she has had to find a new companion as the girl Joanna has been recalled by her cousin and married off …'

He continued, blithely unaware of the life that had just been shattered. At the mention of Joanna's name Edwin looked across at Martin, standing behind the earl as usual, and now he watched in sympathy as his friend's face registered first fleeting pleasure, then shock and dismay, and finally collapsed into ragged, total despair.

Martin didn't move or make a sound, but Edwin knew what was going on in his mind as he stared straight ahead. His heart wrenched for him. And for Joanna.

Brother William started on another missive, but Edwin wasn't listening and he didn't think Martin was either. He longed for the audience to be over so that Martin could escape, knowing he'd want some time and space to himself, but there was still a pile of unopened letters and the earl looked settled in his seat.

Edwin tried as hard as he could to concentrate, despite feeling Martin's turmoil. He was helped by Brother William's next words: 'From Sir Geoffrey, my lord.' He became acutely aware once more of the letters in his belt. Maybe the message for the earl would give him some clue.

'The usual greetings, my lord … all is well at Conisbrough … harvest … new bailiff has arrived … he craves your attention in a personal matter, asks your permission to —'

He stopped dead.

The earl looked up impatiently. 'Well, get on with it – he asks my permission to what?'

Brother William cleared his throat. 'He asks your permission to get married, my lord.'

There was a collective intake of breath.

Rather unexpectedly, the earl burst out laughing. 'Does he indeed?' He slapped the arm of his chair. 'Well, the old dog. What is he, sixty if he's a day? Sixty-five? There I was thinking that manor would come back to me, and now someone's caught his eye and he might get himself an heir.'

Edwin could hardly believe what he'd heard. Sir Geoffrey? Married? Good Lord. He'd been a bachelor all his life, utterly dedicated to the earl's service. He did have a manor of his own, but he only visited it for two weeks a year to check it was still functioning. Married? Edwin shook his head.

The earl was continuing. 'Let's hear it, then. Who? A widow of sensible age? Or the pretty young daughter of a neighbour?' He seemed in good humour as he sipped his wine. 'Do tell.'

Brother William bent his head back to the letter and found his place. He ran his finger along the text. 'Craving your attention … married … he wishes to wed …' he tailed off again, but this time it was with a choke and an expression of absolute horror. He looked at the earl, then at Edwin, then back to the earl again. Edwin went cold. Surely …

The earl's good mood was fading. 'Well? Come on, man!'

Brother William managed a sort of strangled noise. 'My lord … Sir Geoffrey asks your permission to marry Anne, the widow of Godric Weaver and the mother of Edwin.'

For one moment, everything was still.

Edwin wondered how close he was to the doorway, but his feet seemed pinned to the ground. He couldn't move. He watched as the earl put down the cup he was holding, very slowly and very precisely. Edwin would never forget the noise it made as it touched the table. Such an everyday sound for such a life-changing moment.

The earl stood and turned towards him, still moving with that slow deliberation. Oh Lord. Waiting for the eruption was almost worse than enduring it.

'You.' It was a low growl of a word, but there was venom behind it. Edwin took a step back. Behind the earl, Martin was shaking his head, desperately trying to communicate something to him, but he had no idea what.

'*You*. I take you into my household. I raise you up. And this is how you repay me?' The finger was pointing in his face, accusingly, sharply. Too close. Edwin gulped and tried to step back again, but he was already against the canvas wall.

The earl was working his way up. 'You've been planning this all along, haven't you? Standing in at my councils, working out how you can get more, how you can get rich, how you can rise above your station?'

Edwin shook his head and tried to gabble out a denial, but there was no point.

'But this? Getting your mother into Geoffrey's bed? A manor to inherit? A woman only just widowed, for God's sake, and a peasant to boot. Why, she —'

'*Don't say anything about my mother!*' Dear Lord, had those words really just burst forth from his lips? In his terror, had he dared talk back to the lord earl, one of the most powerful men in the kingdom? Martin was really shaking his head now. Edwin wasn't sure his legs would even hold him up any longer, never mind allow him to escape.

In any case, it was too late. Hell was unleashed. Edwin wasn't conscious of most of what was going on, but it involved shouts, curses, strikes, kicks, things being thrown … he staggered, took the blows, covered his head as best he could and tried simultaneously to curl up and to run away. The earl's family was said to descend from the devil, and at this moment Edwin could well believe it. The noise, the shock was too much for him. It was overwhelming. He could feel panic rising, hear his voice gabbling and begging and denying. What was he saying? He didn't know.

Something hit him in the face as he cowered, something with a hard metal edge which stung and left him with blood trickling from the corner of his mouth. He had to get away. But where? How?

Brother William was also in the earl's service, but he was a monk and therefore in slightly less physical danger than anyone else. Edwin felt, rather than saw, the muscular body pushing its way in between him and the furious earl. The blows stopped, although the cursing continued. He stumbled towards the pavilion entrance and reached it to the accompaniment of the words 'Out! And never come back! Ungrateful – disloyal – treacherous

– get out! And think yourself lucky!' Something hit him between the shoulder blades and he stumbled through the flap. Martin was there, shielding him, pushing him, whispering as best he could. 'Get away but stay in the camp. He might cool. I'll try to find you. Go now – quick as you can. Go!'

And then Edwin felt a final, powerful shove which landed him on his hands and knees outside the door. The cursing was still going on inside. Tears were streaming down his face, mixing with the blood. Somehow, he managed to get to his feet and then he ran, blindly, into the dark.

———•———

Martin couldn't think straight. He had no idea what he was doing. What was he supposed to be doing? He stared right through an overturned stool as he restored it to its place and picked up the scattered cups. The metal goblet that had hit Edwin in the face had blood on it, so he wiped it with his sleeve.

Brother William was there. He was speaking soothing words to the earl – a Godsend, for Martin didn't think he could get a word out of his own mouth if he tried. Edwin's mother. And Sir Geoffrey? And had Edwin …? Surely not. But if not, then that meant that the lord earl was wrong and had just accused a good man unjustly. That couldn't be right, either. And Joanna …

He felt himself swaying and reached out to steady himself against one of the tent poles. *Pull yourself together, man.* If some talk makes you collapse, how will you manage in battle? But Martin knew he would much, much rather be facing a fight than standing here feeling the way he did right now.

Adam came in, the tiny new page in tow and a cheerful expression on his face. Well, thank God they'd been out of the way while all this happened.

The space was a bit tidier and the earl had stopped shouting, but he was still fuming, and Adam sensed something. His smile faded and he looked enquiringly at Martin. Martin had to do something. Say something. 'It's fine, don't worry. I'll tell you later.'

He took a step towards them, saw Hugh flinch, and stopped. Then he went closer again. He was tall – the boy was just going to have to get used to it. But good God, the child's head was barely higher than Martin's knee. How on earth was he going to manage his duties?

Martin rubbed a hand over his face and crouched down. He took a deep breath and held out his hand. 'I'm Martin. I'm the earl's senior squire.'

To his credit, the lad squared his shoulders and replied without faltering, though it looked like it took some effort. 'I'm Hugh. I'm proud to serve the lord earl, sir.' He shook hands.

Well, that was something at least. 'I'm sure you are. And you don't need to call me sir – just Martin will do. And you know Adam already. And that's Brother William, my lord's clerk.' The boy nodded. Martin could see Adam looking around, presumably wondering where Edwin was, but he couldn't let that conversation start now. He stood once more, before Adam could say anything. 'Good. Now, take your things round into the sleeping place and stow them – Adam will show you the box where we keep our gear. Then come back here and we'll start getting ready for my lord's evening meal. Clear?'

Hugh nodded, and Martin thanked heaven he seemed willing at least. And he wouldn't always be so small. The boy could be pushed to the back of Martin's list of worries. He turned to immediate practical tasks, the very regular, repetitive work of every evening helping to prove to him that a small part of the world was still the right way up. Sir Hugh was to dine with the lord earl this evening, so they would need more dishes, but of course Humphrey would know that, and in fact there he was already, directing various servants.

Adam and Hugh reappeared so Martin set them to work, instructing Adam to get Hugh to practise pouring water from a jug into a goblet. He wouldn't let him loose on the wine until he could do it three times in a row without spilling a drop. He pointed out the newcomer to Humphrey, who replied with a completely straight face that he'd probably be able to recognise him again among all those in the earl's household.

Martin risked casting a glance over at his lord. Brother William had succeeded in calming him, and they were continuing to go through correspondence. From what Martin could pick up of their conversation, the monk had managed to choose the dullest letters from among the pile, and they were currently engaged in something to do with the fitting out of a ship.

All was ready by the time Sir Hugh arrived, and Martin greeted him at the entrance. As the knight entered, Humphrey was on his way out and the two of them came face to face.

From the way they were standing, Martin realised that they knew each other, although he couldn't work out how that might be. They stared at each other for a long and awkward moment before Humphrey remembered his place and stepped aside with a bow.

Martin expected Sir Hugh to clap him on the back, because that was what Sir Hugh did to everyone he knew, but instead he just nodded the barest acknowledgement as he brushed past into the pavilion's main space.

Humphrey made to leave but turned back as he did so, and he had a strange look on his face that Martin couldn't quite interpret. Sadness? Anger? Bitterness? Or a mixture of all three?

But then he was gone, and Martin had more important things to worry about. Later on, he'd tell Edwin —

It all came crashing back on top of him and he stumbled. Edwin. Joanna. Dear Lord, he had the whole meal and the rest of the evening to get through, in front of all these people, until there was even the slightest possibility that he could slip away and get a few quiet moments to himself.

Somehow, he didn't know how, he managed to stay upright and not spill anything as the earl and Sir Hugh ate their meal and drank their wine. Humphrey had managed to conjure up several dishes of meat and sauce as well as the more usual campaign pottage, and they both put away copious quantities as they talked of the current campaign and the likely forthcoming engagements. Normally Martin would have been interested in this last, listening attentively and learning as much as he could. But tonight he just wished they would stop talking. Was the evening never to end?

Eventually the squires were dismissed, and they took the remaining dishes through to the service area. Adam started tucking in, but for once Martin wasn't hungry. Neither, it seemed, was Hugh, who just stared at the bowl in his hand as though he were looking straight through it.

Martin observed him more closely. The boy looked dead on his feet, as well he might. There was also a certain redness of eye and biting of trembling lip. Martin remembered his own first day as a page, young and in a strange place, and sighed. He took up a piece of the white manchet loaf – the saints alone knew how Humphrey managed to produce anything so fresh and light while they were constantly on the move, but it was his job to do so, Martin supposed – and held it out. 'Hugh, take this and go to bed. We can manage without you for the evening.'

The boy could hardly move, so Martin took his arm. 'Come on.' He hustled him quietly through the main space, where the earl and Sir Hugh barely looked up from their conversation, and into the sleeping area. There were now three mats on the floor around the bed, rather than two, so Martin pushed him down on to the nearest and crouched to wrap a blanket around his shoulders. 'Eat if you feel like it, or sleep first and keep it in case you wake later.' He made as if to stand but then stopped and patted the tiny shoulder. 'Everything will be all right.' He left so that Hugh could cry in peace, knowing from experience that it would make him feel less bad if he thought nobody knew. In truth, Martin was aching to do the same himself, but not yet. Not yet.

He returned to the service area and shovelled in half a bowl of something without really noticing what it was. Then there was everything to stack, ready for the servants to remove. Then there was … he couldn't do it any more.

Adam was standing in front of him. 'I can manage by myself if you want.'

Martin could barely take in what he was saying. 'You can?'

'You're not yourself. Is it something to do with Edwin? Brother William said something earlier that I didn't quite catch, and he's gone to look for him. If you want to go, go. I can cover for you.'

Martin looked at him gratefully. 'Yes. I'll just … get a bit of air for a while. Thank you.' He went outside and took in a deep breath of the night air, so much fresher than inside the pavilion. He needed to find Edwin, but more than that, he really needed some time to himself. The camp was full of men – many of them would be asleep by now, but he still couldn't count on any privacy. Where …? Ah, yes, of course. He headed for the horse picket.

When he found his own mount he stroked its nose for a while and then sat down, heavily, in a pile of hay. He wanted to weep, but instead he just stared into nothing as he hovered on the edge of the abyss his life had just become.

He had no idea how long he had been there when he felt the first griping in his belly. Lord, he would have to be more of a man than this. He might feel like everything was collapsing around him, but he had the earl to serve, he was on a campaign, he was going to be a *knight*. They didn't let themselves feel weakness like this.

He stood and was seized by a wave of cramping and pain. He was dizzy. Surely his thoughts couldn't have done this to him? Was he actually ill? He should get back to the pavilion, and get to bed – that would be the best thing.

He managed to get about ten yards from the picket before he vomited spectacularly, fortunately facing away from the horses. Heaving and retching, hawking and spitting, he picked himself up. Bed ... no. The cramps – he needed to get to the latrines, and quickly.

By the time he'd left half his insides in one of the camp's stinking latrine pits and vomited again on his way back to the pavilion he was almost crawling. How he was going to sit on his horse in the morning, he didn't know. Perhaps he could just get to his mat and curl up without anyone else noticing and sleep it off.

There were strange noises coming from the part of the camp behind the pavilion – groaning and whimpering. And there were still lights on inside, despite the lateness of the hour. He staggered in, grabbing at a pole for support, to find a hellish scene. The earl was slumped forward in his chair, clutching at his stomach, a bowl of God knew what next to him and vomit down the front of his tunic. Adam was in a heap on the ground, pale as death, and little Hugh, although apparently not afflicted, was rushing from one to the other in a panic and with tears streaming down his face. He looked up as Martin appeared, first with hope and then with increasing dismay.

Martin thumped to his knees between Adam and the earl. 'Hugh,' he managed, swallowing hard. 'Go and fetch Ed– Humphrey, or Brother William, or any of my lord's men you can find. Go.' He pointed vaguely in the direction of the part of the camp occupied by the earl's household, and the boy disappeared. Martin tried to stay focused. 'My lord?' The earl only groaned. 'Adam?'

Adam's eyelids flickered as he recognised the voice. 'Martin? Are you –?'

Martin reached out to grip his arm. 'I'm here. What – what happened?'

Adam tried his best. 'Ill – sick – the earl first, then me. After you went out. And Sir Hugh left. Think … maybe something … in the food.' His voice trailed away as he passed out, and Martin lowered his dead weight to the floor.

Martin was just conscious enough to take in the full meaning of what Adam had said. Beside him, the earl spewed uncontrollably once more. Dear God. Had he been poisoned?

Chapter Five

Edwin stumbled blindly through the camp. What was he to do? Where was he to go? Could he even go back to his tent? It belonged to the earl's household so maybe he shouldn't. And anyway, he didn't want to go back there, not yet. He didn't want to lie down, because then it would all overwhelm him. He must keep going. But where?

Someone had put out an arm to stop him; someone was talking to him. He made an effort to see straight and recognised John the archer. 'Sorry, what did you say?'

'Are you here to see Sir Hugh? He's gone off to have his meal with the lord earl, I think.'

Mention of the earl made Edwin's knees buckle, and he struggled to stay upright. But wait. Sir Hugh. Maybe Sir Hugh would speak to him, would advise him, would have *some* idea of what was going on and what he should do about it. 'Can I wait here until he gets back?'

'Surely. Come and sit by the fire.'

Edwin followed him through the twilight to where Sir Hugh's men had set up their camp for the night. He nodded to Alf and found himself welcomed by the others, even the men he hadn't spoken to before.

John sat next to him and cleared his throat. 'I'm not a great talker, but I wanted to thank you.'

'Thank me?'

'For speaking up for me last night. I reckon I'd be strung up from a tree now if you hadn't spoke up and saved me.'

He held out his hand and Edwin took it. 'To be honest I think you were saved more by the fact that my lord was irritated by the Earl of Salisbury, but for what it's worth, you're welcome.'

'You may be right, for these great men will hang us on a whim if it suits them.' John sounded bitter, as well he might, given his narrow escape. 'But not everyone would have done what you did in front of them all, and I owe you.' There was a murmur of assent from the others round the fire, and John nodded to Edwin before returning to his fellows.

Edwin gazed into the fire as both the light and the world around him began to fade. Had that all really happened? Or had he just imagined it all? Was it a nightmare from which he would wake?

It wasn't a nightmare and it had really happened. Brother William had opened the letter and read it out to the earl …

Letters. He had letters of his own. Perhaps they would shed some light on this whole sorry situation. He reached to his belt and pulled them out. He turned them both over in his hand, desperate to know what was inside but somehow loath to begin. He tucked Sir Geoffrey's away again and broke the plain seal on the other. Father Ignatius's writing, but Alys's words.

Most worshipful husband,

Hot tears sprang into his eyes. He wiped them away with the back of his hand and started again.

Most worshipful husband,

I send you my greetings and my deepest affection. Know that I and your mother are in good health and await your return to us. Your mother begs to inform you that she wishes to marry again, to the honourable knight Sir Geoffrey who has asked her to be his wife. She asks you to understand that she does this with love for him, with honour to you and with respect to your departed father. She hopes you will find pleasure in this news in your absence. If it please you and you have the opportunity, send us word of you and your health. I pray that you are well and in God's grace, and that you will return to me soon so that we may enjoy to the full the good things from God. From your most beloved wife, farewell.

Edwin sat in silence for a few moments. Then he opened the second letter.

Sir Geoffrey, knight of Rochford and castellan of Conisbrough, to Edwin son of Godric, of the lord earl's household, greeting. I send this by the hand of Father Ignatius to tell you that I have asked the lady your mother to be my wife. Your father was my friend and I am pleased to protect his widow and driven by a deep love for her. I send also this news to the most noble lord earl by the same messenger and I pray that he may accept it. I pray you will speak with him on the matter and that I may greet you as a son when next we meet. Given on the feast of the Assumption at Conisbrough.

Well, there was no doubting the news, at least. It was no dream. He looked again. What was there to learn behind the words? Both of them wanted this marriage. Both spoke of love – and what it must have cost Sir Geoffrey's pride to say that out loud to the priest while he was dictating, Edwin didn't like to imagine – and of respect for his father. Poor Father. But he was cold in his grave and had spoken to Mother before his death about her marrying again. She was much younger than him so an early widowhood had always been a real possibility. Edwin earned enough that she need not marry again if she did not want to, but clearly she did. Which meant that this would make her happy. Which meant that, despite his shock, despite his own situation, this marriage was something he had to support, even though Sir Geoffrey could have little idea of what it had already cost him. But how to go about it? It seemed impossible, though perhaps if he put his mind to it, some idea would occur to him.

Edwin was so lost in his thoughts that he had not noticed Sir Hugh returning to the camp. Indeed, the knight had to touch him on the shoulder to get his attention. Edwin leaped to his feet.

Sir Hugh's face showed that he knew everything. 'Foolish old man. What's he thinking, in God's name? And you? Come in the tent and we'll talk.'

Thank heaven, he had not cast Edwin out in loyalty to the earl. Edwin followed him into the tent; it was nowhere near as luxurious as the earl's pavilion but had room for a small table and a couple of folding stools as well as a wooden cot and a straw mattress next to it. Alan lit a rush and placed it carefully on the table before leaving them alone.

Sir Hugh's face and his bushy beard loomed in the poor light. 'So. What did you know of this?'

Edwin shrugged. Lord, he was tired now. He could feel the strength draining out of him each moment. 'As I told my lord, nothing. That is – I knew Sir Geoffrey would always protect my mother, for my father's sake if nothing else, but this? No.' He rubbed his hand over his face.

Sir Hugh nodded. 'Very well. The lord earl is very angry about it – with you, with Geoffrey – at the moment, but perhaps in time he may calm. In the meantime, I offer you a place in my own household.'

That made Edwin sit up straight again. 'Sir Hugh – I can't – I thank you – but – what if my lord gets angry with you too?'

'No doubt he will. But when he thinks all this through and remembers your service to him – and Geoffrey's – he will be grateful to any man who stopped you leaving and getting yourself killed by yourself on the road.' He paused. 'I'm afraid I don't have need of a man of your … usual talents, but I'm sure you can fight or shoot, so just stay with the men, keep your head down and keep away from the lord earl for now. At least we'll see you fed and sheltered.'

Edwin said nothing, overwhelmed in more ways than one.

Sir Hugh put out his hand. 'Do we have a bargain?'

Edwin took it and, to his surprise, found that Sir Hugh's hand, thick and calloused as it was, had a slight tremor. He looked quickly into the other's face and saw what he hadn't noticed before – the grimace of a man trying to hide pain. 'Sir Hugh! Is it your arm?'

The knight shook his head. 'No. Just a griping in my belly. Something I ate, perhaps.' He winced as a loud noise came from the direction of his stomach. 'At my age, you know … anyway, perhaps you'd better go.' He stood and hustled Edwin towards the tent entrance. 'And call Alan.'

Even in the poor light Edwin could see that Sir Hugh's face was ashen, and he now clutched at his stomach with both hands. Edwin hurried out and found Alan only a few yards away. On hearing the news, he did not exclaim or panic but merely nodded and looked over Edwin's shoulder. 'Alf. Find me bowls, if you please. Dickon, fetch cloths out the cart.' He turned back to Edwin. 'Just some bad camp food, I expect. I'll look after him.'

Edwin was glad that Sir Hugh was in such capable hands, so he wandered back to the fire. Nobody else seemed to be suffering, so hopefully the situation wasn't serious.

It hit him like a dash of cold water. Of course nobody else was ill, for they had not eaten the same food. Sir Hugh had eaten with the earl. And if he was sick, then …

To bemused looks from his new companions, Edwin hurried off into the dark.

Martin opened his eyes. Where was he? Wooden poles above him – not the chamber in the castle keep – no, they had left – campaign – yes, he was in the pavilion. He was lying on his back and there was a candle somewhere behind his head. Someone was sitting next to him on the ground.

It was Humphrey. 'Martin? Can you hear me?'

Martin licked his lips. 'Drink?'

An arm slipped under his neck and raised his head; a goblet was put to his lips. Watered wine. He slurped some and lay back. 'My lord?'

'He lives, thanks be to God. He's in his bed and Brother William is watching over him.'

Martin stared at what he could see of the pavilion roof. When he had mustered the energy to speak again, he managed, 'Adam?'

'He's here next to you, but he hasn't woken yet. He was in a very bad way – I think he must have eaten more than you.'

Martin managed to turn his head and saw a recumbent form a few yards away. Little Hugh, his own face tear-streaked, was wiping Adam's face with a cloth. Martin made an indeterminate questioning noise, which Humphrey fortunately seemed to understand. 'He's fine. He says he didn't eat anything.'

The food. Yes, thought the part of Martin that could still think through the wool in his head. But there was something else. Someone else … 'Sir Hugh?'

'He is also ill.' It was a different voice this time, and Martin felt Edwin kneeling next to him.

That wasn't right, was it? Something – there was something … 'You shouldn't be here. My lord … angry.'

He felt Edwin pressing him back down. 'Don't worry. I'll go again before he knows I've been. I was with Sir Hugh when he fell ill, so I came to see if you were all right.'

Martin made a vague gesture with his hand but couldn't get any more words out. He lay still and listened to Edwin and Humphrey continuing the conversation.

'Sir Hugh said it must have been something he ate, and I knew he'd taken his meal with the lord earl.'

'It must have been something in the food, God forgive me. My lord, Martin, Adam and … Sir Hugh all had the same meal and are sick. Hugh here and Brother William did not and they're both fine.'

'Anyone else?'

'Three of my men are also ill.' Even in his stupor Martin caught the grim tone of Humphrey's voice. 'So at least I know who's been sampling dishes when they shouldn't.'

'Just the three?'

'Yes. The rest of the men had pottage and bread. It must have been something specifically in the dishes for my lord. But I'm sure only fresh meat was used …'

Edwin's voice was also serious. 'I don't think you need to worry about the quality of the food. But I would like to know exactly who prepared it, and who might have gone near it while it was cooking.'

Humphrey's voice was incredulous. 'Surely you don't think –'

'I do. And I'm going to find out who did it. In the meantime, I'll pray for them all to recover swiftly.' Edwin leaned over Martin and touched his shoulder. 'Try not to fret. Just take care of yourself.'

Martin mumbled something, but he wasn't sure he made sense even to himself. Another wave of pain …

Edwin made as if to rise, but Humphrey stopped him. 'And … how is Sir Hugh?'

Martin was concentrating on his belly and heard only murmuring as the conversation went on, except for a sharp 'How did you know?' from Humphrey and a low chuckle from Edwin. Then a few more words and Martin heard him going out of the tent.

Humphrey sighed and then turned back to Martin. 'Could you manage another drink?'

Martin nodded as the wave receded, and felt himself being lifted once more. He sipped.

'Good. How do you feel?'

Martin thought about that for a few moments. 'Pain – I have pain in my guts. On fire. And weak – don't think I could stand if I tried. But I don't think I'm going to be sick again.'

'Good. Sleep now, and I'll see if I can do anything for my lord and Adam.'

Martin let the darkness engulf him.

———•———

There was little time the next morning for recriminations. They had to keep moving, lest they arrive at the coast too late. From the position he had taken up at a discreet distance from the earl's pavilion, Edwin had seen the earls of Salisbury and Arundel make separate visits and emerge looking sombre.

The earl, Sir Hugh and both squires had survived the night. None of them was well enough to ride, and Edwin watched as a litter was fashioned and slung between two horses to carry the earl. The others were loaded into the back of carts, swathed in blankets; Martin had managed a half-sitting position but Sir Hugh was still flat and poor Adam had barely stirred. Edwin muttered a prayer under his breath. Two of Humphrey's three men had looked a little better when he'd slipped round there first thing, but the third was groaning and thrashing in pain.

He had tried to speak with the earl's cook as dawn broke; the man seemed genuinely horrified at the thought he might be suspected of wrongdoing, and Edwin believed his earnest protestations of inno-cence. What could he possibly hope to gain from poisoning his own lord in such an obvious way? He was no murderer, although he might be justly accused of laxity in his duties. From what Edwin could gather, he'd cooked the meal, keeping it separate from the common fare as usual, but had left it unattended several times: once to visit the latrine and twice to get some more supplies out of a baggage cart, where he'd stayed chatting for some moments. In the meantime, the food had been left cooking and many men were passing by. Edwin could picture the scene and, with a sinking heart, he realised that it would have been relatively easy for someone to drop something noxious into the earl's meal and walk off. He wouldn't need to hang around to see the results of his deed: it was quite clear from the fine ingredients which meal was for the earl and which was for the common men.

Edwin sighed as the remains of the camp were packed up around him. Time to go. He should find his horse and … oh. Still, he'd always hated them, hadn't he? And he was used to walking. He'd manage.

He'd already retrieved his scrip from the tent that Brother William would have to himself for the foreseeable future, so he slung it over one shoulder and made his way back to Sir Hugh's men.

To start with, the walking was fine. But he'd got unused to it in the months since he'd been in the earl's service, and by noon he was beginning to forgive all the horses he'd ever ridden. Plus, the clouds of dust being kicked up by the feet of hundreds of men were choking; he hadn't realised how far above it all he'd been on horseback. He coughed and tried to wave some of it away from his face. But he had to keep on, and besides, Peter was in the group just ahead of him, trudging along with Sir Roger's archers, and Edwin certainly wasn't going to admit to being footsore ahead of a boy of nine.

To take his mind off his feet, he turned to John, who was whistling as he strode. 'Have you been in Sir Hugh's service long?'

'Oh, yes, more years now than I care to remember. Up and down the land, and even over in France two or three years ago.'

'France?'

John gave him a quizzical look. 'Aye, France. Big place, over the sea. Led by that whoreson Louis and his father. Old King John invaded, trying to get back the lands he'd lost, but he was useless and it was a disaster. We got beaten at a place called Bouvines and we didn't all come back. The nobles did, of course – Salisbury up there was captured and ransomed, which didn't happen to many of us poor so-and-sos, I can tell you.'

His expression was sombre. Edwin thought that he'd perhaps not chosen the best topic of conversation. How to bring it round? 'So, you're away from home and family? Do you have a wife and children?'

This time John gave a mocking laugh. 'Me? Oh yes. Big family man. Three daughters, all trouble, all grown, wed and out of my sight. Three wives, all dead in childbed, and three sons all dead likewise.'

Edwin was sincerely wishing he'd never opened his mouth.

'Not to worry, lad. You weren't to know. Anyway, now I'm free as a bird, so I just find me a woman whenever I want, and no worries or troubles about keeping a house over her head.'

Edwin looked around at the mass of men. 'Not many women round here.'

He got a disbelieving snort this time. 'You're not looking in the right place. Find me tonight and I'll show you.'

Edwin made no reply.

John continued, waving dust and flies away from his face. 'Anyway, now you know me, some questions for you. How did you learn to read? I saw you last night with letters. You're a clerk?'

'Oh, no – but my father was the bailiff on my lord earl's estate at Conisbrough so he had our priest teach me to read. You need to, if you're going to be a bailiff. Manor courts and records, that sort of thing.'

'Oh, a bailiff, are we? Well, I should be glad you're even talking to me.' He touched his hat in mock salute. Edwin couldn't help noticing that it was filthy and didn't look like it had been taken off his head in several years.

'I'm not the bailiff. After Father died I was – well, it's complicated – the earl wanted me to …' he tailed off. 'I don't know who I am now.'

John gave him a friendly clout on the shoulder that sent him staggering and reminded him of how sore his feet were. Damn.

'Never mind that, then. Here's a more important question: can you shoot?'

'Not very well, I'm afraid. I practised a bit when I was younger but there were plenty in our village who were better than me. But if I'm going to be one of Sir Hugh's men, I'd better learn, hadn't I? I think I'd rather be an archer than a foot soldier with a spear.'

'Oh, aye, archers have a better time of it. More skill, you see.' John tapped the strap across his chest which held the long bag in place on his back. Most of the others had stowed their bows in the carts when they set off that morning, but John evidently preferred to keep his close at hand. 'And you've no armour, so you don't want to go wading in hand-to-hand if you can help it. If there's light tonight when we camp, I'll set up and we'll see what you can do. The lads haven't practised for a day or two, so they'll need to loosen up themselves.'

'Thank you. I'd like that.' Edwin sighed. 'Sir Hugh has been kind, so I don't want to let him down.'

'Good. It's settled, then.'

They marched on, the dust getting into their throats and the heat reflecting back off the road like a shimmering furnace.

It was the middle of the afternoon when the column gradually ground to a halt. Edwin couldn't see what was going on, but eventually the order reached them that all men were to prepare themselves for entering hostile territory. Thankfully someone passed an aleskin up the line at the same time, and Edwin took a grateful swig, wiping the liquid away as it dripped down his chin. He could feel a headache developing and he hoped he could stave it off for a while longer.

John began to bark orders at his archers and soon they were all collecting and stringing their bows, and hanging quivers of arrows from their belts. Sir Hugh's foot soldiers donned such helmets as they had and held an assortment of weapons at the ready. Edwin loosened his dagger in its scabbard but didn't know what else to do. John spotted him and pushed a bow into his arms. 'Here. We have some spares. Take this for now – we'll see about finding one that best suits you later on.' He grinned, wolfishly. 'If we're all still here.'

Edwin gulped, but there was nothing for it. He tied the quiver to his belt with care and hefted the bow. Dear Lord, whose was this? He could barely pull the string back halfway. If it came to combat he'd just have to hope that nobody noticed his arrows weren't going as far as anyone else's. *Please God let nobody else's life depend on me this day*.

Sir Roger pushed his horse through the throng, there to see that his archers were also at the ready. He was pleased to see that they had already organised themselves and formed up with Sir Hugh's retinue, but when he saw Peter scampering about with his eating knife in his hand, he was firm. 'Not you.'

Peter's face fell and for one moment Edwin thought he was going to answer back or disobey, despite the lesson he'd learned the other day. But he had no opportunity to do so: John scooped him up and carried him back to another cart that had caught them up. Alf and Dickon were there, having woken from their morning rest, and John deposited the squirming boy next to them. 'We all admire your bravery, lad. But let us have a go at the Frenchies first, eh? You can give Alf and Dickon your protection if we let any get through.'

Peter brightened and held the knife out in a rough approxima-tion of a swordsman's grip. John turned away and caught Edwin's eye. He cleared his throat. 'Well, I've already started on another knight, haven't I? Be a shame to waste it.'

Sir Roger nodded at the cook, who now had a vicious-looking meat cleaver in his hand. The knight had been wearing his mail and surcoat since the morning, but he now laced on his helm and accepted the shield that one of his men produced for him, and a lance. He made as if to head back up the column but Edwin grabbed at his stirrup as he went past. 'Sir Roger ... the lord earl.'

The knight was faceless under the helm, but he'd heard. 'I understand. I'll stay close to him. Brother William is there too.' He hesitated, probably looking at Edwin's awkward handling of the bow, and the muffled voice came again. 'Good luck.'

Edwin took a deep breath. 'And you.'

John's men were still forming up, so Edwin took the oppor-tunity to slip forward to see what was going on. Sir Roger had reached the earl and was now riding on one side of his litter; Brother William had dismounted and was walking on the other side, hefting the earl's shield. Sir Hugh was still semi-prone in one cart, his squire Alan riding next to it; Martin was now sitting more or less upright in the other, also with a shield, and manoeuvring himself so he could hold it over Adam, who was now stirring, thank the Lord. As Edwin watched, Martin ordered little Hugh off his pony and into the cart as well, tying the reins to the rail. Then he picked up something that lay beside him – his new great helm.

Edwin thought he would put it on his head, but instead Martin held it out to Alan. 'Here. Better protection for you. As you're riding rather than sitting in a cart like a woman.' He sounded dis-gusted with himself, and Edwin knew how disappointed he would be to miss his first real chance at combat.

Alan nodded his appreciation. 'My thanks. But this old thing has done me for years and will serve still, and besides, I like to see what's coming at me.' He rapped his knuckles on his own helmet, an older pot-shaped one that only covered the top of his head and his nose, not the rest of his face. 'And there's no shame in being ill, unless you're saying my lord's acting like a woman?' He gestured at the prone Sir Hugh.

'No, sorry, I didn't mean —'

Alan waved him away. 'Say no more. Look. I'll guard them all from this side; you stay ready in case there's a sudden attack and anyone gets past. You're sick, but you're in a better state than the others.'

Martin nodded and raised the shield again. There was nothing more Edwin could do for them, so he made his way back down the column. He joined the end of the line of Sir Hugh's and Sir Roger's archers and tentatively pulled at the bowstring again. It barely moved.

John was making his way round the group, and he stopped by Edwin. 'Been in combat before?'

'Yes. But I didn't enjoy it much.'

'You'll be fine. We don't know if there's anyone out there, anyway, but Louis's men hold all this land so there might be. Me, I'd wager on a party hiding out in those woods about half a mile ahead.'

Edwin followed his pointing arm and saw that although the road was on open ground as it ran between two fields, behind the one to his right was an area thick with trees. Any number of enemies might be hidden in there, unseen. Those in charge seemed to have reached the same conclusion, as some men, individually or in small groups, split off from the host and began to fan out across the field.

They were moving again, everyone on the alert. Edwin's heart was in his mouth. His knees felt shaky, but that was just starting to walk again after stopping, surely. John, on the other hand, looked more carefree than Edwin had yet seen him; he smiled as he nocked an arrow. 'Cheer up. We all have enemies.'

Yes, thought Edwin, *we have enemies*. But were they all out at sea and in the forest? Or were some of them much closer than that?

———•———

The first thing Edwin heard was a kind of whining, buzzing noise. The second was the shouts of alarm of the men all around him as they threw themselves to the floor just as the arrows fell.

Edwin slammed to the ground along with them – not because he had recognised the danger, but because John had pulled him. He closed his eyes in terror, breathed in the dirt and prayed as arrows slapped down around him, piercing both earth and flesh. He heard the first screams. He risked opening his eyes and then gave an almighty start as a last arrow with a vicious-looking point smacked into the road not three feet from him.

John, inexplicably, was grinning at him. 'No shields for us – just have to hope for the best.'

And then the hail was over and men were springing up and shouting. John was one of them. 'Who marked where they came from? Those trees there? Right, form up, damn you! Ready? Nock. Draw. *Loose!*'

Sir Hugh's well-trained archers had got off their first volley before Edwin had even picked himself up, and belatedly he realised he was supposed to be one of them. Hands trembling, he joined the end of the line and picked an arrow out of his quiver. He nocked it. No, that was the wrong way round – the marked cock feather needed to face outwards. *Concentrate*. He just about managed to get it in the right place before 'draw' sounded again and he hauled the string back as far as he could, muscles screaming.

He didn't quite get as far as 'loose' before he couldn't stand the strain any longer and had to let go, but his arrow only shot off a fraction before everyone else's, so in the heat of the moment he hoped nobody would notice.

Another return flight was heading their way so they all ducked and crouched again. But only one or two stray arrows reached their group – the rest were aimed further up the column. *At the easily recognisable and brightly coloured nobles and their horses, God help them.* More cries sounded.

But now there was action. The second volley had pinpointed the enemy's position, and now the mounted sergeants and the foot soldiers were preparing to charge. Edwin heard a huge 'After them, by God's blood!' from up the line, and then they were off, hooves ploughing through the earth and crops in the fields. Sir Hugh's sergeants joined them, and Edwin felt the steam of horseflesh and sweat as they passed.

John was nocking another arrow. 'Quick, lads – one more over their heads before they get there! Nock, draw, *loose!* Now, after them so we've got their backs!'

What? Surely he wasn't going to … but he was. The archers of both Sir Hugh and Sir Roger were pouring after the last of the spearmen and heading for the woods. There was no choice but to follow.

Once Edwin left the road the ground was softer. After all the wasteland they'd passed through during the last few days, this field was actually full of crops ripe for harvest; he found it harder going. But he was already right at the back so he had to keep up or risk being exposed. He pushed on through the thigh-high wheat, over the ridges and furrows of the strips, briefly wondering who would starve after he'd ruined their winter food. His feet thudded and slipped beneath him even as he strained his ears for the sound of more arrows. But there was only the odd one or two, thank the saints, and not near him. The horsemen had reached the woods and there were sounds of fighting, the clash of metal and the screams of men and horses. The spearmen caught up with them and joined the fray. Hopefully the enemy were now too busy defending themselves to worry about him.

He reached the edge of the wood and plunged in. The moment it took for his eyes to adjust to the reduced light could have been fatal, but the arrow that thrummed past him was wide of the mark and ricocheted off a tree.

Edwin looked about him. Dear Lord, what was going on, and what should he do? There were figures flitting everywhere in the shadows, in and out of the trees, caught in flashes of a grim dance. There were men fighting, bleeding and dying. Edwin was sure he had caught a glimpse of Philip, the Earl of Salisbury's squire, on horseback running someone down, but surely he wouldn't be here among the common men?

He nocked an arrow, but Lord, who was who? He turned around and about in an agony of indecision, unwilling to let fly if he risked hurting anyone on his own side.

There. That man was one of Sir Hugh's archers, hard pressed against two enemies. He was fighting hand-to-hand, his bow discarded on the ground. *I don't want to kill anyone*, thought Edwin, even as he drew back the string. Then the archer slipped on a root and fell back as he lost his balance. The others closed in. *I don't want to kill anyone, but he's going to die if I don't.* At this distance there was no need to aim upwards, just straight across. Panic gave him strength and he drew further than before, bringing the string back almost to his ear and loosing all in one smooth movement. Perhaps he had remembered something from the lessons of his youth.

The arrow thumped wetly into the chest of one of the men, who fell without a sound as blood spewed from his mouth. His companion was startled and paused long enough for the archer to lunge forward with a blade – Edwin wasn't sure whether it was a long dagger or a short sword, but it went into the man's stomach like butter. His gape of surprise turned into a shriek of pain, abruptly cut off as the blade jerked out and slashed again. Edwin averted his eyes just quickly enough to avoid seeing the man's throat cut, though he couldn't avoid the sight of the blood that splattered up on to the bark of the nearest tree.

The archer picked up his bow and ran over to him. 'Thanks. Come on, we'll find the others.'

They slipped through the woods, following the sounds of combat which were now becoming fainter and further away as the enemy fled. They caught up with a small knot of others – Edwin's companion recognised them as friends before he did, so he had the chance to pause and consider how hard his heart was thumping.

The fighting was over. Edwin was, somewhat to his surprise, still alive. So was John, who was now directing his archers to pick up anything they could find – discarded weapons and spent arrows. Edwin gathered a couple off the ground, but he wasn't yet ready, as others were, to rip them out of sprawled bodies.

The sound of hoofbeats came from behind them, and Edwin turned to see both Salisbury's squire and the man who'd stopped him back at the village. Philip looked down at him, faceless behind his steel mask and saying nothing, but Edwin knew he'd been recognised. *New business with you*, he remembered, but what could the man do to him here? He turned away to follow John.

Before long, everything had been dragged out of the woods into the light. A pile of enemy corpses, maybe a dozen or so. Four bodies from the host laid out straight – one of Sir Hugh's, and three others Edwin didn't recognise, though Salisbury's loud-voiced sergeant was crossing himself before one of them. Bows. Arrows, being hastily sorted by John and his archers into those that could be re-used straight away and those that were damaged. A few blades, but nothing special.

Philip, now helmetless and with sweaty hair sticking up in all directions, poked his foot at the heap of enemy dead. 'No leader. No man of rank. So where are the rest?'

The sergeant made his way over. 'Just a raiding party to distract us? Or maybe deserters? But never fear – there will be plenty more where they came from.' He turned to bellow at his men, telling them to bury their own dead, leave the others and bring the captured weapons back to the host. Then he and Philip remounted and rode off.

Edwin found John at his side. 'Still here, then? And Nigel says you saved his life.'

'I didn't …' he began. But he had, hadn't he? He'd killed a man in battle to save the life of a companion. Was this what comradeship was supposed to feel like? 'Anyone would have done the same,' he managed, aware of how lame it sounded.

John thumped him on the back. 'Good man. You're one of us now.'

Edwin followed the others back across the field, trying to trample on as little of the wheat as possible. He might, as John said, be one of the archers now, but his eye was drawn to the spot where he knew the earl was. There were men milling around, bareheaded now the combat was over, but still too far away for him to make out their faces.

He screwed up his eyes to look at the figures with the most colour. Green and yellow, flash of blond hair – that was Sir Roger, walking around unharmed, thank the Lord. And yes – blue and yellow checks: the earl himself, now upright.

But they were standing around a figure on the ground.

Edwin's instinct was to run towards them, but he stopped himself when he remembered it was no longer his place to do so. Instead he followed the others back to their own part of the column and then wormed his way forward through the press. A few casualties were being dealt with, here where the arrows had fallen thickest: a horse being put out of its thrashing misery, two bodies being carried off to be buried with the others, and some men groaning with wounds. The host had got off lightly, he supposed, for none of the enemy had got near enough to the column to strike a blow in person. Not that that would be much comfort to the agonised sergeant begging his friend to pull the arrow-shaft out of his bleeding thigh, or to the widows of the dead.

Edwin reached the outer edge of the earl's circle, checking off his friends as he saw them. Martin. Yes. Adam hadn't got out of the cart, surely? And that white robe over there could only be Brother William. Then who…?

The crowd of men parted as they began to drift away back to their duties. A body was just a body, and they were on campaign, after all.

Edwin peered through, trying to remain unnoticed. A final set of legs moved aside and he was able to see Sir Hugh's squire Alan, flat on his back, arms outstretched and eyes wide, with an arrow through his throat.

Chapter Six

Martin held on to the rail of the cart for support. It wasn't the sight of the body – of course not; what sort of knight-in-training would he be if he couldn't look at a man slain in combat? – but rather that he was still feeling unsure of his legs after his illness. That was it. Plus, there was an uncomfortable sense of guilt. Should he have tried harder to persuade Alan to borrow his great helm? And if he had, would Alan still be alive?

Sir Hugh, now upright although still not looking in the best of health, was gazing down at the body in stony silence. Everyone else kept a wary distance, and nobody spoke.

Martin wanted to say something, but he didn't dare break into the knight's isolation, and anyway he couldn't think of anything that wouldn't sound trite. He turned back to the boys still in the wagon. Hugh was crouched, gripping on to the side with both hands, his knuckles almost as white as his face and his teeth chattering as he shivered. Martin recalled that he'd been a bit older than seven when he'd seen his first violent death, so maybe it was harder for such a small boy.

'Are you all right?'

Hugh forced himself to nod, eyes still fixed on the body.

Martin tapped him on the shoulder. 'Stop looking at it.' He got no response. 'Look at me!'

Hugh dragged his gaze away. Huge eyes stared into Martin's, and he managed no more than a whisper through almost unmoving lips. 'I'm trying to be brave.'

What was the right thing to say? 'You'll be fine.' Martin hoped he sounded more encouraging than he felt.

Another voice croaked from deeper in the cart. 'You're braver than me.'

It was Adam. Thank the Lord, Adam had woken and was now trying to move. Martin scrambled over the tailboard and crawled to him, slipping an arm around his shoulders to help him into a sitting position. 'How are you feeling?'

Adam leaned against him. 'Better. I think.' He focused his attention on Hugh, who was close on the other side. 'You're a good lad. Brave.'

Hugh appeared to become a little more human, the first hint of colour returning. 'Me?'

Adam licked his cracked lips, and Martin groped around for the skin of watered wine he knew was lying about somewhere. He unstoppered it with his teeth and then managed to get a little of it into Adam's mouth so he could speak again.

Adam waved his arm in the page's general direction. 'Well, at least you were awake and paying attention through it all. And helping to protect me.' His eyes fluttered and began to close again. 'And my lord still lives, that's the main ...' He tailed off as he fell asleep.

Martin held him for a moment before lowering him back to the bed of the cart. He was surprised, overwhelmed even, by the emotion he was feeling. Was it because he was still frail himself? He'd only known Adam three months, but apart from the week he'd been away at the abbey they'd been together almost every moment. If something happened to him, there would be a big hole in Martin's life. He busied himself tucking the blanket around Adam so he wouldn't have to think about it.

The earl was now standing next to Sir Hugh. 'My condolences. But ... we'll need to get moving soon.'

Sir Hugh nodded, and then knelt down next to his dead squire. He placed his left hand flat on Alan's neck, where it met his shoulder;

Martin initially took this to be a gesture of affection or farewell, but then the knight grasped the arrow with his right hand and ripped it out in one smooth movement. The sound was unpleasant, but fortunately – Martin turned to check – Hugh was facing the other way, so he didn't notice.

Sir Hugh gestured to those of his sergeants who were standing a little further away in respectful silence. 'Take him over there with the others and see that he's properly buried.'

They murmured their assent and moved to pick up the body. The blood beneath it had already soaked into the dusty ground and was no more than a dark smear, soon to be scuffed and forgotten as the boots of hundreds of men passed over it.

But Martin didn't have time to dwell on that. The earl was up and about, and Martin was well enough to serve him. With a final look at Adam's swathed form, he descended from the cart, wobbled, waited a moment for his legs to become steady, and made his way over.

On his way he passed Humphrey, who had appeared from somewhere. He approached Sir Hugh, who was staring across the field with the bloodied arrow still in his hand. 'I heard. I just wanted to say I'm s—'

But he was shoved roughly out of the way, Sir Hugh not even meeting his eye. 'I don't care what you've got to say. He was a better man than you.' Sir Hugh thrust the arrow towards one of his archers. 'Here. Clean it up and you can use it again. Now, find my horse and get out of my way.'

Martin couldn't help noticing that the old knight was rubbing his face as he strode off.

Edwin stood back as Sir Hugh brushed past him without noticing. He needed to get back to his place in the host, his new station, but he also needed to learn more. Had that arrow been shot towards the host in general? Or had it been aimed at the lord earl and missed?

There was no doubt that this part of the column had been the focus of most of the arrow-storm. Brother William was holding up the earl's brightly coloured shield and making a jocular remark as he pointed out the number of shafts embedded in it – it looked like a hedgehog. But Edwin didn't know whether that was just because the enemy had noted the presence of so many nobles, or whether they were targeting someone in particular. He also didn't know whether it might have been possible, in the chaos of the fight in the wood, for one of their own men to have picked up a stray arrow and loosed it at his own army. And, to add to the things he didn't know, he didn't know how he would even begin to find out.

'You need to go,' said a voice in his ear.

Edwin jumped.

Thankfully, it was Sir Roger. 'The lord earl is up and about, and he will be angry if he sees you here.'

That was true, but what if —?

'Just go.'

Edwin couldn't disobey, so he made his way back through the press of men. John was ahead of him, and Edwin saw that he had the fatal arrow in his hand.

He jogged to catch up. 'Is there anything special about that?'

John looked at him with a puzzled expression. 'What do you mean, special?'

Edwin didn't know what he meant either, but he had to do something. 'I just … that is, is there any way to tell whose it is?'

Understanding dawned. 'Oh, I see. No, not really. If I was at home in my village shooting against friends, we'd all mark our own so we could collect them up. But for a campaign we get extra ones in because we need more. They're made … well, I don't know where they're made, but this looks like most of them, and I suppose the enemy ones are the same.' He held it up to examine it more closely, continuing to walk as he pointed. 'Bodkin head – better for going through mail. Very common. That blood'll clean off. Fletchings, just normal goose feathers, though it's either been done in a bit of a hurry or by someone new to the trade.' He pointed out some tiny imperfection in the way the cock feather was aligned, although Edwin couldn't see anything wrong with it. 'So, nothing special about it.'

They reached their part of the column and John pushed the arrow into a basket of assorted others. Edwin could see that none were particularly distinguishable, and he sighed. 'So, that could have been in anyone's quiver, and anyone could have shot it?'

'Aye.' John accepted a pie from young Dickon; Alf was taking the opportunity of the column's halt to pass out rations. 'Anyway,' John continued through a mouthful of pastry, 'like I said, once we make camp tonight we'll do some shooting.'

'He's already done some,' came the voice of the man Edwin had saved in the woods. 'And grateful I am. Here.' He was also holding a pie; he broke it in two and offered one half to Edwin. Edwin didn't really feel like eating, but everyone else was tucking in heartily, so he forced himself to take a bite and smile.

They eventually got moving again. Edwin looked over at the scar of fresh earth at the edge of the woods as they passed it, and winced at the damage they'd caused to the wheat-field, but after that he saw little of their surroundings, concentrating as he was on putting one foot in front of the other and trying not to think too much. Sir Geoffrey, Mother – and Father, God rest him – the earl, Alan, Martin, Alys … everything. It was all spinning around in his head too fast.

One thing at a time. There was nothing he could do about matters in Conisbrough just now, so he should put that to one side while he considered events here. Right. They were marching to war. Men were going to be killed, including perhaps the earl. But was there danger to the earl before they got there? Some things that had happened so far – the fire, the poisoning, the arrows – might just be accidental or a normal part of a campaign. Or they might not. And the thrown knife certainly wasn't.

Father had always told him: Look not just at *what* has happened, but *why*. Assume for a moment that somebody was trying to kill the lord earl. Why? Who would want him dead? Unfortunately, there were many possible answers, for the strange thing about this war was that it was difficult to know who was on which side. It wasn't the French against the English: the French were all enemies, of course, but there were English in both camps. Not to mention the fact that many of the 'English' lords were French or Norman anyway, and they certainly spoke French. In fact, the lords on both sides probably had more in common with each other than they did with the likes of Edwin. Which was interesting in itself, because …

Never mind that – concentrate. Many nobles, the earl included, had switched allegiance more than once. What if there was someone in the host who was pretending to be on their side but who was secretly on the other? That was certainly possible. And such a man would benefit from the earl being dead, because the earl was providing lots of men and money for the campaign. But so were the other nobles, so why attack him in particular?

Maybe it came down to his lack of an heir. The lord earl had no children and no brothers, so if he were to die then his lands would either be split between his sisters or go to the eldest sister, Edwin wasn't sure which. But in either case there would be confusion and it would all take a while to sort out, during which time the host would be weakened. Perhaps that was why he was being targeted, rather than Arundel or Salisbury or any of the others.

Salisbury. Now, there was a thought. Arundel seemed more closely allied to the earl – his former brother-in-law and the man to whom he had confided his son – but Salisbury was a different matter. He and the lord earl were cousins, sort of, and both linked to the king by blood, though their lines were tainted by illegitimacy: Salisbury's own, and that of the earl's father. But still, with the young king having so few adult male relatives, this put them both in a powerful position. Maybe Salisbury thought he would be better off without any rivals who shared the king's blood, however diluted? And, as Martin had pointed out, all these 'accidents' had only started happening once Salisbury had joined the host.

Martin. Now, there was another thing. What was going on between him and Salisbury's squire Philip? Why did they hate each other so much? Something must have happened before. They had certainly met each other previously, as their earls were comrades and peers of long standing, but Edwin knew nothing of their history.

He was getting away from his point again. Edwin wiped sweat and dust off his face as he trudged and tried to sink back into his thoughts. Was Philip's rivalry with and evident dislike for Martin enough cause for *him* to take action against the earl? Surely not. He could not possibly – but then again …

Edwin's concentration was broken properly this time as he walked into the back of the man in front, not having noticed that the column had stopped.

There wasn't another attack; it was the evening halt. Men all around him were putting down their burdens and sinking to the ground in relief. Edwin did the same, but he'd hardly taken the weight off his feet when John was there, dragging him up along with the other archers.

None of them had much to unpack and they had no horses to attend to, so once they'd piled some wood and left Alf building up his cooking fire, they made their way to the edge of the camp where there was some open pasture; hay harvest was over so the grass was short and the line of sight was clear. A couple of the men were carrying sacks of straw, and John instructed them to count out eighty paces and a hundred paces respectively. Edwin watched them get further and further away, wondering just how wide of the mark he was going to shoot, and how he was going to live it down.

John had removed his own bow from the bag and was stringing it. It was a monster of a thing, and Edwin hoped he wasn't going to be asked to try it out. There was a second bow in the bag, a smaller, slimmer one, and Edwin reached out without thinking.

'Don't touch that!'

Edwin withdrew his hand as though it had been burned, surprised at the vehemence of the tone. 'Sorry. I didn't mean ...'

John recovered himself. 'No, it's fine. Didn't mean to make you jump. But it's not in a usable condition: no string, and hasn't been bent for a while so it needs to be worked on. Try it now and you'll snap it.'

Edwin stooped to examine it once more, hands firmly clasped behind his back. It might not be serviceable now, but it had certainly seen some use in the past; the wood was worn smooth. Maybe it was the bow of John's youth, the one he'd grown up shooting with, and he was attached to it.

The other archers had by now all strung their own bows and were dividing themselves into two groups, the younger among them lining up to face the nearer target and shuffling arrows in their quivers. There were a few spare bows stacked up, and John considered them. 'How did you get on with that one earlier? Too strong? Hmm ...' He picked one out and held it up. 'Try this.'

The string was already knotted fast at the lower end of the bow, so it was a relatively simple matter for Edwin to step through and bend it around his thigh to slip the loop in place at the top. He gave an experimental pull – yes, much easier than the other one.

'Good. Now, let's see some shooting. At that eighty-pace target.'

Edwin positioned himself on the end of the line, planted his feet and took up an arrow. He didn't like being watched so closely and hoped that John wouldn't notice his fingers shaking as he nocked the arrow. Funny, he was more nervous now than he had been in the woods. But he managed to draw back the string to his cheek – *one finger above the arrow, two below, and keep your thumb out of the way*, he could hear the instructions from childhood echoing in his head – and let fly. The arrow hissed reasonably straight towards the target, but fell short. Edwin took a deep breath and tried again. This time he angled his shot further up, and was pleased to see the arrow land at a respectable proximity to the target.

He risked a look at John.

'Not bad. Reasonably smooth action, but keep your elbow down a bit more. Don't worry too much about accuracy – if there's a whole host of Frenchies coming at you, you're bound to hit one of them. What you need is to be able to shoot quickly, so you can get as many arrows off as possible before they reach you. Try again, and see how fast you can loose six arrows. Don't forget: start in the middle and push and pull at the same time so you spread out the strain.' He wandered off down the line to look at the other youngsters.

Left to it, Edwin did as he was bid, and the results weren't too bad. But his shoulders were aching by the time he'd finished – and that was after, what, eight arrows? He'd need more practice.

He was conscious of being watched, and turned to see Peter and Dickon staring, eager expressions on their faces like puppies.

John had seen them too. He laughed. 'Want to learn, do you?' They both nodded. 'All right, let's see what we can do.'

He hustled the other men off to join the group at the further target and had one of them move the second sack so it was now only about thirty paces away. He picked the smallest bow out of the pile and held it out to Peter. 'Here. This is still going to be too strong for you, but it's the lightest there is, so we'll have to manage and you can take turns.'

He was interrupted by a shout from behind them. It was Alf, who had managed to stump his way to the edge of the camp and was calling for Dickon. 'You get back here! You've got work to do. And you know you can't … that's not for the likes of you. Come on!'

Dickon looked up at John with a pleading expression, but it was no use. 'Oh no – I'm not going to get on the wrong side of him, not if I want to eat the rest of the week. And he's your father, so do as you're told.'

Edwin watched in some amusement as the child sulked his way back at a pace that was just slow enough to be rebellious but just fast enough to look like it might not be intentional. Then he took a rest while John went through some basics with Peter. He was right, the bow was far too big – taller than the boy – and he couldn't get the string even halfway back, but his technique looked sound and he was a fast learner. His arrows peppered the ground, and John joked that the sack was at least frightened by now.

Over to their left, past the rest of their group, another knot of men had formed, wanting to get some practice in themselves before dark. They were Salisbury's men, Edwin thought, a guess confirmed when he unexpectedly spotted the squire Philip in amongst them. He was more popular with the archers here than he was with his fellow squires, joking around with them as he watched them shoot, and then taking up a bow himself. Amid friendly catcalls he loosed off three arrows; Edwin saw, with some chagrin, that they all thumped into their distant target.

'You don't see that very often.' John was standing next to him.

'See what?'

'A noble being able to shoot straight. Normally they think an honest bow isn't good enough for them.'

Edwin opened his mouth but John had already turned back to Peter. 'That's enough for today. You might feel all right now, but your shoulder will be hurting tomorrow and best not to overdo it.'

Peter handed the bow back and John ran appraising fingers up and down the wood. 'We might be able to shave it down a bit. Most of my tools are at home but I've got one or two with me. No promises, mind.' He ruffled the boy's hair and sent him on his way, watching as Peter skipped off. 'A good lad, that.'

Edwin agreed, proud of his fellow villager.

John addressed his men, whose own practice was starting to wind down. 'Right now, lads! That'll do for today! Collect all the arrows and count them back in; the man who shot the worst brings back the targets.'

Edwin found himself surrounded by an affable crowd of men as they made their way back to the camp, where another appetising-smelling pottage was ready on the fire. He sat down with his new comrades and felt, for the first time in a while, as though he belonged somewhere. It was not to last long, though, for he soon caught sight of Sir Hugh sitting alone at the entrance to his tent. He was eating the same pottage as the others, but gingerly, and Edwin's mind turned back to the poisoning again. Lord, had that only been last night? So much had happened since then that it felt like a life-time ago.

He wondered if he should try to steal closer to the earl's camp in an attempt to spot or prevent any further attempts on his life, but as he made to stand he caught Sir Hugh's eye and the knight beckoned him over.

Edwin approached, unable to help noticing that, although the tent had been erected properly by the men, the belongings inside it were still packed up and the bags were strewn around untidily; the wooden bed remained in pieces.

He felt awkward, but the subject had to be broached. 'Sir Hugh, may I say how sorry I am for your loss.'

He half-expected to be angrily rebuffed, as he'd seen happen to Humphrey earlier, but the knight just nodded and gestured for him to sit. Edwin lowered himself to the ground, for there was no second stool ready placed, and waited.

Eventually Sir Hugh let out a huge sigh. 'All men reach their time eventually, and we are at war, after all. I'll get used to it.' He gestured helplessly, for once looking his age. 'But … thirty years he'd been in my service, so it might take me a while.'

'I didn't know him well, Sir Hugh, but he was a good man.'

The knight nodded. 'That he was.'

'Can I … help with anything?' Edwin looked pointedly at the still-packed baggage.

'That's kind of you, lad, but I'll leave it for now. I'm not too old to sleep on the ground for one night, and I'll try to get better organised tomorrow. I called his name, you know, once the tent was set up. I forgot. And I keep turning round expecting him to be there.'

Edwin thought that was probably fair enough, when a man had had another at his beck and call every day for thirty years, but he said nothing.

Sir Hugh tried to rouse himself. 'Anyway. Still plenty of the evening left, and I need something else to think about. I don't suppose you know how to play chess?'

———

Martin looked unenthusiastically at the bowl in front of him. He certainly felt much better than he had done earlier, but his stomach was still gurgling and – for once – food wasn't the most important thing on his mind. Still, in deference to everyone's continuing delicacy, Humphrey had had his men produce a very bland pottage, supervising them personally and not leaving the pot for an instant, so it couldn't do him much harm. The lord earl had managed some, and even Adam had pushed in a few spoonfuls. He dipped some bread into the bowl and lifted the dripping morsel to his mouth.

He was surprised to find that he felt better after the warm meal had gone down, and he began to look around him with a little more attention. The earl was in the pavilion's main space talking to Sir Roger, and had no need of the rest of them just now. Adam looked tired so Martin told him to go to bed; he was rewarded with a look of gratitude as he slipped away. Brother William was over in the corner, trying to make best use of a single candle as he wrote something, his pen scratching. Hugh had finished eating and was staring into space. Martin recalled the shock the boy had experienced earlier in the day – maybe keeping him busy would be a good idea?

'Hugh.'

The page sprang to his feet. 'Do you need something?'

Martin passed him the empty bowl. 'Take all these and stack them on the side table ready to be collected. Then go to the sleeping place, take the lord earl's sword out of the kist – Adam will show you if he's not asleep already – and bring it here. He'll need it tomorrow when we join with the rest of the army, so I'll show you how to make sure it's clean and sharp.'

Hugh's face brightened at the thought of such an important task, and he scampered off.

Martin unpacked the oil, a couple of rags and a whetstone, and when Hugh returned he busied himself demonstrating the basics – Hugh needed to be able to hold the weapon without cutting himself before he could start work on it, a task made harder by the fact that the sword was almost as tall as he was – and showing him how to sharpen the edge and then wipe off the residue before applying the oil.

He hadn't been going long when he heard his name being called from the other side of the hanging. Hugh was getting on well, but he wasn't sure he should leave him alone with the earl's precious sword, so he hesitated. Should he get Adam up again?

Brother William made a show of stretching his arms and needing a break from his writing. 'I'll keep an eye on him, if you like.' He was looking at the sword with something of a professional eye, and Martin wondered again about his past.

He ducked through into the main space. 'Yes, my lord?'

The earl pointed through the back wall of the pavilion. 'See if you can find out what that infernal noise is and put a stop to it.'

Martin had been concentrating so hard on his task that he hadn't noticed anything before, but now the earl mentioned it he could hear a groaning and crying. It sounded like a wounded animal. 'At once, my lord.' He exchanged a nod with Sir Roger as he turned away, knowing that he'd ensure the earl's safety in Martin's absence.

It wasn't quite dark, so Martin had no problem making his way through the maze of tent ropes and baggage as he followed the sound. It led him to Humphrey's kitchen area, where his men were busy, making use of the last of the light to scour pots and bowls.

The steward spotted him and hurried over. 'Is everything all right? Does the lord earl need anything else?'

'No, all is well. And thank you for the meal, by the way – we all feel a bit better now.' The worried expression on Humphrey's face lifted a little. 'No, my lord sent me to find out what that noise was and stop it.'

Humphrey's mouth set in a line. 'Come with me.'

He led the way to a canvas shelter that had four pallets crammed into it. A man was lying on one of them, groaning and crying, eyes closed. Even in this light Martin could see that he was soaked in sweat. He took a step back. 'Fever?'

'I don't think so, or everyone else would have it by now. He's one of the three who fell ill at the same time you did.'

'Ah. After they ate some of the meal that was meant for us.'

'Yes. Although …'

'What?'

'Well, he seems to be different. The other two admitted taking the food – I've set them extra duties as punishment – and they're both recovered. But Rob here seems to be getting worse, and on top of that he swears he never touched the earl's food, and that he was already feeling ill a few days ago but he didn't say anything. Before you got sick. Before the fire, even.'

'Well, he's disturbing my lord, so can you maybe move him further away from the pavilion?' Martin looked at the prone figure, writhing now and clutching at his belly. But for the grace of God, that could have been him. 'But … look after him. I'll see if Brother William can do anything.'

Humphrey organised a few of his men to lift the sufferer, pallet and all. As he was moved, the groans turned into a shriek of pain, and Martin winced. 'I'll find him now.'

He considered the situation as he made his way back. Had the man been poisoned along with them, or not? And why would anyone want to put something nasty in the food anyway? He needed to talk it all through with Ed—

Oh God. How was all that to be sorted out? The only person who was clever enough to see his way through all of this was Edwin, and Edwin was the only person he wasn't allowed to talk to. All he could do was keep his eyes open so he could try to prevent any physical danger to the earl.

He was brusque when he returned, asking Brother William to visit the sick man and telling Hugh to go to bed. The boy's face fell and Martin hastened to praise the work he'd done on the sword before packing him off.

Martin knew he should go to bed as well – he was exhausted after the day's events on top of having been ill. But he didn't want to rest, didn't want to lie down. Instead he sat on his own, watching the candle burn lower, until it guttered out and he was in the dark. He made no move to light another, enjoying the solitude.

The noise of the camp gradually slacked off, and silence reigned in the cool of the night. He belatedly wondered where Edwin was, and felt guilty that he hadn't tried to find out earlier, but there was no point blundering around now – he'd only cause alarm.

He enjoyed a few more moments of quiet before the sound of the conversation in the centre of the pavilion was replaced by that of men standing and taking leave. He sighed and made his way in, just in time to see Sir Roger depart.

'Ah, there you are. Good. I'll retire now.'

'Yes, my lord.' Martin carefully blew out all the remaining lights and waited a moment to be sure that they were all indeed extinguished before he followed the earl to the sleeping compartment.

Adam stirred as they passed him, and made as if to rise, but Martin poked him with one foot. 'Shh. Go back to sleep – I'll sort everything out.' Adam mumbled something incomprehensible and pulled the blanket back over his head.

Once he'd settled the earl, Martin found his own pallet, happy at least that he could finally remove his boots. He rolled himself up, thinking that he'd probably … lie awake … all ni …

———

The chess game was over. Edwin had lost, but it had been a close-fought battle. He flattered himself that he had perhaps the sharper instincts, but Sir Hugh had been playing the game since long before Edwin was born and could call on his reserves of experience.

The knight surveyed the final position of the pieces in the disappearing light. 'Not bad. But you were too cautious with your pawns.'

Edwin scowled at the board. 'How so?'

'In trying to keep them all you lost your knight and your bishop, which disadvantaged you. Keep your discipline: if you're faced with the choice of losing a pawn or a higher piece, always sacrifice the pawn.'

'I'll try, Sir Hugh.' Edwin replaced the pieces in their bag and packed them and the board back in the box where he'd found them, replaying the game and its moves in his mind.

'Good lad. Off you go and get some sleep now, for we'll be off again in the morning and we should reach the rest of the host by nightfall tomorrow.'

Edwin left the knight to settle himself on the floor of his tent and went back to the circle around the fire. Alf was still up, working at his oven, but most of the others were already asleep or at least wrapped up and dozing off. Edwin found himself a space where he could see the comforting glow of the fire, and lay down. Sleep did not come immediately, but he'd known that would happen. At least he wasn't walking, so he could tell himself to enjoy the rest. And it wasn't raining: it had been dry all the way from Conisbrough. Camp life would no doubt be considerably less pleasant in the pouring rain.

As he watched Alf limping around, putting loaves in his oven and sealing up the door, he recalled what the cook had said about men getting sick easily on campaign. They did, he'd heard that from other sources, but the incident with the earl just seemed too precise, too targeted, to be an accident. Someone had gone near the food while it was being prepared and had put something noxious in it. And who would best know what was poisonous and what wasn't? A cook.

But Alf couldn't have been anywhere near the earl's meal: he'd been here, cooking for the rest of them. And there was something … Edwin was getting dozy but he forced himself to think. Oh yes, his leg. Edwin silently cursed himself for not having looked at the ground near to Humphrey's cooking area. The earth was summer-hard but it was well trodden around that part of the camp, and with various liquids being carried and spilled, some imprints would have been visible. And Alf, of course, would leave distinctive imprints. But the whole thing was impossible: if he had been lurking around the earl's section of the camp, someone would have remembered seeing a stranger with only one leg and would have mentioned it. But anyway, he must ask Humphrey about it when he got the chance. Poor Humphrey. He'd looked bereft when Sir Hugh had publicly rebuffed him in the immediate aftermath of Alan's death. But there wasn't really anything Edwin could do about that, so he should push it away from his other list of worries.

He wondered what Alys was doing right now. Sleeping, of course: it was late. But in the morning she would get up and be about some work around the cottage. She would hum to herself and smile. She would think of him. And she would be there when he got back, so that was a thought worth holding on to through all of this.

Edwin's eyes were starting to close when he glimpsed more movement near the oven. Little Dickon was still up, sleepily fetching more brushwood from the pile so his crippled father didn't have to do it. It was a late night for a child, but he'd get to sleep in the cart in the morning, Edwin supposed.

Now the boy was looking round at the sleeping figures. Edwin didn't move: he was in a comfortable state of drowsiness and didn't want to be identified as awake and asked to do anything. Dickon seemed satisfied that he and Alf were the only ones stirring; he leaned over his father, who was sitting with his back against a cart-wheel and half-dozing in front of the oven, and whispered something in his ear. Alf nodded, looked around, and pointed off somewhere. He asked a question that Edwin didn't catch, and Dickon shook his head. A whispered 'Stay there, I'll be all right on my own and I won't be long' floated over to Edwin on the night air, and the boy was gone.

Where was he off to, at this time of night? Maybe the latrine pits, Edwin thought, and he paid it no more heed as he fell asleep.

Chapter Seven

It was late the following afternoon when they neared their destination, the town of Sandwich. Edwin thought that their host would be far too large to stay inside it, and he was right; as they crested a rise he could see a huge and well-ordered camp laid out, the town further off in the background. He supposed he should be awed at such a demonstration of power, but all he could think about was sitting down for a while. His feet hurt. They had trudged around the outside of the city of Canterbury that morning but, dulled as his senses were, he had barely looked up to see the walls or the top of the great cathedral within them. In the normal course of things Edwin did, he supposed, spend more of his time sitting down than most men, but he was still used to being on his feet for much of the day and he was surprised at how tiring, how energy-sapping, it was to walk at a constant but not particularly rapid pace.

Someone rode out to talk to those at the head of the column, and they were directed to a space at the far side of the camp, squeezed in at the edge of a field just inside a ditch and hedgerow. Edwin had to follow the rest of Sir Hugh's men, but he was disconcerted to notice that the earl was being pointed in a different direction, further towards the centre. Indeed, if his eyes didn't deceive him then that was the regent himself, accompanied by his nephew John Marshal, greeting the earl and Salisbury and Arundel. He would be in exalted company now, and Edwin would be nowhere near. How would he find them to keep an eye on what was going on? Would the risk to the earl lessen with so many people around, or would he be in even greater danger? Edwin could only hope for the former while fearing the latter.

He had no time to follow up, for he was soon embroiled in the setting up of their part of the camp. He joined the other men in erecting Sir Hugh's tent, and then unobtrusively started unpacking and arranging things inside the way he thought Alan might have done. By the time that was finished he was dragged off for more shooting practice; there were many archers in the host so a proper target area had been set up just outside the camp.

Edwin was not keen on having to demonstrate his skills – or rather, his lack thereof – in front of strangers from the rest of the army, so he stood to one side pretending to supervise Peter, who had tagged along, while he watched. There were some very talented marksmen in the host, and soon an informal competition had sprung up. He was pleased to see Sir Hugh's and Sir Roger's men making a good showing, and he cheered under his breath when John's arrow smacked into the centre of a target so distant Edwin could hardly see it, beating the only two men left in the round with him, one of the Earl of Salisbury's men and an archer Edwin didn't recognise from another retinue. It was all good-natured (Edwin involuntarily looked around to check that the squire Philip was not in attendance as he thought this to himself), as they would all be on the same side in any forthcoming combat. Once the shooting had stopped and the cry of 'fast' went up, Peter hared off to fetch John's arrow for him, returning it with the look of adoration he had previously reserved only for Sir Roger. John ruffled his hair and sent him off to tell Alf they were on their way back and hungry.

As they made their way back through the thicket of tents and carts, Edwin craned his neck to see if he could spot the earl's pavilion anywhere. But there were a number of similar large and colourful tents around, and he didn't see anyone he knew; he could hardly start blundering into the private and restricted camps of earls and nobles he didn't know, in a host full of armed and possibly suspicious men, so he followed the others back to their own area.

The meal was ready and waiting for them. Alf had once more managed to produce a surprisingly tasty dish with the limited ingredients and facilities available to him; a clue as to how he managed this was given when Edwin saw him call to Dickon and then send him off with instructions to glean the hedgerow for fresh herbs. Dickon was playing with Peter – Edwin couldn't help noticing that Peter now had a matching carved wooden knight, though John had said nothing – but he listened to some words in his ear and then trotted off obediently in the direction Alf indicated. Peter made to follow him but Alf waved him back. 'Let him get on with it by himself. He knows what to look for, and I'll wager you don't.' Peter sat down again and was soon engrossed in heroic imaginary action with his new possession.

Edwin wiped up the last of his pottage and then sat fidgeting. He was impatient to get on with two things: he wanted to go and find out where the earl was situated and what was going on there, and he wanted some peace to think in an orderly manner through everything that had happened and the possible implications. But there was little chance of either. The camp was huge and he didn't know his way around it; it would be the height of folly to start wandering around now it was getting dark. And quiet was certainly not available: hundreds of men were seemingly trying to forget their nervousness at the thought of impending battle by being as raucous as possible, and shouts and laughter floated across the evening air.

Edwin did have one further option, and a pleasant one it was too. He reached into the purse at his belt and drew out his letters; he put back the one from Sir Geoffrey and opened Alys's. Even with the poor light from the camp fire he would be able to make out the words 'most worshipful husband' and 'beloved wife', and he could stare at them as long as he liked.

But even in this he was to be thwarted, for Sir Hugh was calling him over. Grumbling under his breath, Edwin folded the letter with care and replaced it, but he brightened when he saw that Sir Hugh was lighting a lantern next to his chess board.

There was nothing else for it. Edwin gave up trying to think of other things and concentrated ferociously on the game. The noise around him receded; the world narrowed to the squares in front of him. This time he used his pawns more strategically to protect his higher pieces, and he soon had an increasingly disgruntled Sir Hugh backed into a corner. Belatedly realising that he might not want to antagonise his only benefactor, Edwin casually but deliberately slipped up with his next move, offering Sir Hugh an escape route if he could spot it.

He did, and Edwin had just started considering how he could lose gracefully but convincingly when Sir Hugh banged his hand down hard on the board, scattering the pieces and making Edwin jump. He waved an angry finger. 'Don't patronise me like that, boy. A man knows when he's got to fight for his life, and you're demeaning us both by making foolish moves.'

'Sir Hugh, I —' But there was no point denying it. 'I apologise. I won't do it again.'

The knight grunted. 'Good. Now, I can't remember where all the pieces were, so I resign. Be good enough to put them away for me.'

Edwin could have told him exactly where each piece had been standing on the board, but he decided to hold his tongue as he picked up the scattered knights and bishops, counting them back into their bag.

By the time he'd finished, Sir Hugh had regained his temper. 'Good man. And I suppose I have you to thank for making it a bit more organised in here.'

Edwin nodded and mumbled something non-committal about Alan, not wanting to upset the knight again.

He risked a direct question. 'Will you get a new squire?'

'I expect so. As you have seen, I can't seem to manage without one. I'm a bit old to be training a boy at my time of life, but I'll be able to find someone grown once this is over.'

'But where from? I mean, anyone who is going to be a squire will already be one, won't he? So you'll have to get a little boy like Hugh.'

Sir Hugh looked at him as though he'd just said something idiotic, and Edwin felt himself growing hot without really knowing why.

Sir Hugh spoke slowly enough to make Edwin wince. 'Think about it. We're at war. We will fight, and men will die. By the time we're done, there's going to be more than one squire in this camp looking for a new master.'

Chastened, Edwin bowed and withdrew. *Men will die.* He looked around him. All the others, except Alf and Dickon, who were hard at work, were sprawled in various attitudes around the place and snoring at different pitches. Who among them would survive? And who would leave desperate, weeping widows behind them?

He sat, wrapping a blanket around his shoulders. The camp fire had died down to embers, but Edwin thought he might just still be able to make out a few words, given that he knew what they said already, so he took out Alys's letter once more and smoothed it against his knee.

Edwin woke early the next morning; he still wasn't used to sleeping outside so the dawn light affected him more than the others, he supposed. He made his way to the camp's latrine pits to relieve himself; Lord, but they stank already – what would they be like in another few days, in the summer heat? He was half tempted to find somewhere else, but if everyone did that then disease would soon spread, so he tried not to breathe in too much of the miasma and hurried back as soon as he could while the next man in the queue took his place.

Alf and Dickon were fast asleep in the back of their covered wagon, but the rest of the men were stirring, breaking their fast on bread and pies, so Edwin joined them.

'No marching to do today – you'll be glad, won't you?' John looked up at the fresh morning sky. 'Nice day, though. Shame to waste it.'

'What do you mean? More shooting practice?'

John laughed. 'Ah, maybe later. Reckon we can find some different entertainment first though, eh lads?'

The others guffawed at Edwin's lack of comprehension.

Nigel leaned in. 'There's a town there. A whole town full of women, who might be interested in a little business transaction with some lonely soldiers.'

Edwin belatedly grasped the gist of the conversation. 'But I'm a married man!'

The hilarity caused by this statement was not the reaction he had expected.

'What I mean is, I haven't been married very long, and —'

He was drowned out by calls along the lines of needing plenty of practice then, and he could barely make himself heard. 'But what about Sir Hugh? He won't want us all to go off to the town, surely?'

John's face became more serious. 'He's not here. Got called to see your lord earl and they'll be busy at a council meeting all morning.'

Edwin felt a pang. He should be there. He should be listening to the plans, using the council time to observe the participants and to work out who was allied to the earl – and who wasn't. Was there any possible way he could smuggle himself in?

John misread his expression. 'You're right, though – work to do first. Lads, tidy up here while I go and check the bows and strings. Don't want to get shown up by Salisbury's lot if we're needed later.' He walked off in the direction of the camp's main wagon and baggage area, throwing a comment back over his shoulder as he went. 'Besides, let's give the ladies another hour to get themselves ready, eh?'

Edwin busied himself collecting and stacking dishes so they would be ready for Alf and Dickon when they woke up. He checked briefly in Sir Hugh's empty tent but all looked in order. Sir Roger's tent was also deserted, so presumably he had also been summoned by the earl and had taken Peter with him. If Edwin couldn't get near the council – and it was bound to be guarded precisely to stop unwanted visitors – then maybe he could ask Sir Roger about it later.

The other men were piling up blankets and bags, chatting among themselves.

Nigel turned to Edwin. 'Don't you worry about getting in trouble with Sir Hugh. He won't mind us amusing ourselves as long as we cause no trouble.'

One of the others stopped what he was doing. 'Aye, well, just remember what he *does* do if you cause trouble.'

Edwin threw him an enquiring look.

'In France, three years ago, he hanged a man for stealing from a church when we'd all been told to keep our hands to ourselves.'

This was a side to Sir Hugh that Edwin hadn't encountered, and he was taken aback. 'One of his own men?'

Nigel interrupted, a shadow across his face. 'Yes. But we were supposed to be fighting for the Church, see? Or something like that. Some deal the old king made with the pope. So pinching bread and the odd sheep was one thing, but stealing a plate from a church, – that was another. He had to make an example. Discipline, he said.'

'And you won't be doing anything like that today?' Edwin still had no intention of joining them, but he was starting to get worried.

'No, we'll be fine. Find a tavern, find some girls, back by noon and nobody will know we've been gone. Now shut up about it.'

As they completed their tasks and started to make noise about moving off as soon as John returned, Edwin slipped away. He didn't know quite where he was going, but he worked on the basis that the council was likely to be in the biggest tent, and the biggest tent was likely to be near the centre of the camp.

His theory was confirmed when he ran into a ring of armed men who stopped him going any further. He tried to argue, but it was useless: his looks, his clothes and his voice all stood against him. Claiming directly that he was in the earl's household would run the risk of someone from the retinue being summoned and telling them about his expulsion. Claiming to be Sir Hugh's advisor would probably land him in more trouble, and it would at the very least be a breach of the knight's hospitality.

Edwin was turning away in disappointment when he saw a face he recognised among those inside the guarded area. He pointed and addressed one of the sergeants. 'That's John Marshal, the lord regent's nephew. He'll vouch for me.'

The man laughed. 'Vouch for you? You think I'm going to ask one of them great lords to come here and talk to someone like you? Get away now.'

'But —'

The man put his face close to Edwin's. Too close: Edwin could feel the stubble brushing his own skin. 'Anyone might recognise him. You've seen him about the camp with the other lords, no doubt. Now, I tell you, be off before you get into trouble.'

He was holding a short spear, and Edwin noticed that his grip on it had become less casual. Several of his fellows were taking an interest in the exchange and beginning to drift in their direction. It was time to go.

'What's all this?'

The altercation had drawn the attention of John Marshal himself, and he was approaching with a couple of men at his back. Edwin straightened.

'Begging your pardon, my lord, it's this man here. Wants us to let him in and says he's one of your men.'

'No, I didn't —'

He had no chance to continue. John Marshal shot him no more than a cursory glance before giving a dismissive wave and turning away again. 'No. Don't know who he is, but not one of mine.'

Edwin watched his departing back, humiliated. It was not much more than three months since he had ridden to Lincoln with John Marshal, and the two of them had embarked on the extremely dangerous escapade of getting into the besieged castle at night under the noses of the enemy. Edwin had succeeded and then made it back to the main army with information that had materially affected the outcome of the battle. Fine, in the noble world that might not exactly make him a comrade, but after such a heightened shared experience he had expected that John Marshal might at least *recognise* him, might remember who he was. But he had looked right through Edwin as though he were no more important than a piece of furniture.

The sergeant gave him a shove. 'Claiming to be one of his men, indeed. Don't you know who he is? Not just the regent's nephew, but the man who saved us all at Lincoln. He got into the castle and back again, a hero. I've heard his men talk about it round the fire often enough.'

Edwin let himself be propelled away by the hand between his shoulder blades. Dazed, misery complete, he made his way back to Sir Hugh's camp and sat down heavily. He was alone: Alf was snoring in the back of one of the carts, Dickon presumably asleep on the other side of him, hidden by his father's bulk, and the others had all gone.

He was nobody. In the eyes of his fellows he was an outsider, a man trying to get above himself; he wanted to read and to play chess when others were content with dice and drinking. But in the

eyes of the nobles he was a nobody, a tool to be used and then discarded at will. They didn't see him as a person. How had he thought
that he might have any worth? How had he possibly come to the
conclusion that he would be allowed into the inner sanctum of the
army, with those who were far above him? He was a joke.

Edwin didn't know how long he sat without moving, but eventually he realised he had to do something. He was a common soldier
now, an archer, so perhaps he should start behaving like one. But the
others were long gone, and besides, he still didn't really want to join
them. If there was one person in the world who believed in him,
it was Alys, and he wouldn't dishonour her. But maybe he would
go into the town anyway and have a look around. There would be
shops, wouldn't there? Like the fair at Conisbrough but bigger. He
had some money; perhaps he could buy something to take back
to her once all this was over. Because he was going back to her no
matter what, no matter whether the earl forgave him, no matter
what his status was by then, and no matter if he had to walk for a
month to get home.

He stood up, brushed down his tunic and hose, checked his purse,
and set off for the town. The camp could manage without him for
a while.

———•———

Martin didn't think he'd had a moment to himself since they'd
arrived. First there was the pavilion and the camp to set up, then
there had been other lords to greet and serve while they spoke with
the earl long into the night, and he'd been run off his feet since not
long after dawn this morning. He had just sent a man to fetch Sir
Hugh and Sir Roger, and was himself on the way to tell Humphrey
that the earl was to attend the regent's council all morning, so his
dinner would need to be pushed back until around noon.

The kitchen area, despite being busy, exuded an air of calm and orderliness. Humphrey was in the middle of everything, directing matters, keeping a sharp eye on the cooks and their pots, and sending various milling boys back and forth on errands. He greeted Martin and didn't seem too overwhelmed by the message – a very different reception from the one Martin suspected he'd have got from the previous marshal, and a welcome relief.

'That will give me a chance to prepare something a little more elaborate than we've managed the last few days. Hmm, let me see, we have a couple of grouse hanging that should be ready …'

Martin let him ramble on for a while, glad of a few moments' rest, but was startled by a piercing shriek from nearby. Instinctively he reached for his sword – he had kept it belted on at all times during the last few days, just in case – but Humphrey shook his head. 'It's only Rob. He's still in a bad way.'

Martin judged that the unfortunate man was now far enough from the pavilion for the noise not to disturb the earl, but it must be unpleasant for everyone else around. He ducked under the canvas cover to see Brother William kneeling beside a prostrate figure. The sick man was rigid on his pallet, bathed in sweat and alternating between cries, groans and pleas to be put out of his misery.

Brother William said 'Amen', made the sign of the cross, and rose. 'I'll be back later, whenever I can get away. Trust in the Lord until then.'

Martin followed him back through the kitchen area towards the pavilion. 'How is he?'

The monk shook his head. 'I've seen something like this once before. The pain, the fever, and the hard, unyielding stomach.'

'Can anything be done for him?' Martin felt his luck at not having eaten too much on that fateful night. 'Can I help?'

'You can pray for a swift end.'

It could have been him. It could have been the lord earl. It could have been Adam. Martin wanted to hit something. Specifically, he wanted to hit whoever had tried to poison them all, but to be honest he had so much bottled up inside him that battering anyone – anything – would do.

As if in answer to his prayers, he noticed a couple of squires in full training gear passing by. As his gaze followed them he spotted more, heading in the same direction.

'You go back. I'll only be a few moments.' He parted from Brother William and followed the boys. Sure enough, they were on their way to spar: a training area had been fenced off within the camp. There wasn't enough space for riding, but there were a number of boys and young men engaged in foot combat.

Martin didn't stay to watch – he needed to get back to tell his lord of this and to beg leave to go and join in. The earl wouldn't need anyone to attend him while he was in council, would he? They could all go.

He lengthened his stride and was back at the pavilion in short order, to find the earl inside with Sir Hugh and Sir Roger. Martin reported on the training area and was pleased to see the earl nod.

'Adam, find some gear and take Hugh there. Start him off with a few basics so he knows one end of a sword from the other by the time he gets back to Geoffrey.'

Adam did as he was bid, and Martin was halfway to following when the earl spoke again. 'Not you.'

Martin pulled back in surprise. 'My lord?'

The earl was looking him up and down. 'You're the senior. You need to start learning, so you can come to the council. You can stand with Sir Hugh and Sir Roger, and later on you can tell me what you've picked up. I don't have … well, anyway. Make yourself ready.'

Martin knew better than to argue, but his disappointment was extreme. Finally, to have the prospect of action and exercise dangled in front of him, and he was going to have to spend the morning in a stuffy tent listening to men talk *politics*? And he knew what his lord had been about to say. *I don't have Edwin any more.* As if Martin could possibly pick up on even half what Edwin would have done. Edwin could listen to a conversation about beans and then tell you ten important things about the speaker that nobody else had noticed.

But there was nothing for it. He checked that Adam and Hugh had everything they needed, tried to mask his jealousy, made sure he had nothing spilled down the front of his tunic, and followed the earl and the knights out of the pavilion.

They arrived in the regent's command tent a little ahead of everyone else, and even the lord earl was forced to wait while the regent finished the conversation he was having with another.

'Sheffield? But didn't he –?'

'Yes, my lord. But the boy has now died too, so the uncle is seeking advancement to the earldom.'

Martin watched as the elderly man's face wrinkled even more in thought. 'No. He shall not. That was a new creation anyway so there is no hereditary right. Tell him he'll be allocated five manors to keep himself, but the earldom will go into abeyance.'

'Yes, my lord.'

And that, thought Martin, pleased with himself at having picked up the nuance, is how much power the regent has. He stands in for the king and can abolish an earldom at will. The king, he recalled, was nine years old, so all power in the realm rested with the man in front of him.

He knew some of what was what, after all. He was cheered a little by this reflection as he watched the lord earl greet the regent. Sir Roger and Sir Hugh were moving towards the rear of the tent, so Martin followed. He would have no problem seeing what was going on, and at least if he stood right next to the back wall, fewer people would stare at him, and there might even be the chance of some fresh air.

The great men of the kingdom – or those of them who supported the king, anyway – entered and the tent filled up. Some of them were bishops, but Martin paid them little heed. Instead he looked at the noblemen: he recognised many devices and nodded to himself at each one. Hubert de Burgh. John Marshal. Richard Fitzroy, who wasn't much older than Martin was. The Earl of Albemarle.

Martin tensed as he saw Philip enter along with the Earls of Salisbury and Arundel, but fortunately he stationed himself well away from Martin. Arundel moved to stand with some other lords; Salisbury strolled up to the command table and inserted himself casually at a place nearer to the regent than the lord earl, which caused Sir Hugh, just in front of Martin, to whisper something in Sir Roger's ear. Neither of them had happy expressions on their faces.

Martin tried to concentrate on the talk, he really did. But he knew he wasn't taking all of it in. Edwin would be soaking this up. But two interesting pieces of information did make him prick his ears. One: tonight they were all going to embark on ships and spend the night there. And two: unless he'd heard wrong, the admiral of the expected French fleet was a monk.

Nobody was looking his way, so he risked bending forward and speaking as quietly as he could into Sir Hugh's ear, his hand cupped around his mouth. 'A monk?'

Sir Hugh, after a cautious glance of his own around the tent, whispered back, and Martin listened. Apparently, the man they all spoke of as Eustace the Monk had been committed to the cloister as a boy, but had escaped – and who could blame him, thought Martin – and had then embarked on a life of piracy. He'd raided towns around England's south-east coast and had recently, with an eye to further gain, put all his ships at the disposal of Louis as he sought to become king of England.

That reminded Martin of the other thing. He bent his head again. 'And what's this about us getting on ships? I thought we were here to fight them when they got here, to prevent them getting to London. Are we going to France?'

Martin felt Sir Hugh's beard scratch his face as the knight sought to answer without drawing attention to their conversation. 'Not quite. We're not going to stop them *when* they land – we're going to stop them *before* they land.'

Martin worked his way through the implications of that.

Chapter Eight

It was only once he was inside the walls of Sandwich, traipsing through the unfamiliar streets, that Edwin realised it might not have been a particularly good idea to come out alone. The shops were closed and shuttered; groups of locals who were gathered on street corners stopped talking and stared at him, only resuming their conversation once he had passed. They recognised, presumably, that he was from the host that was there to protect the town from the French – otherwise Edwin wasn't sure he'd still be in possession of life or limb, never mind his purse – but it was an unpleasant experience nevertheless. He berated himself for his naivety.

The taverns were open. Edwin approached one, but a single look at the riotous interior, and at the vomiting drunks outside – it was only the middle of the morning! – convinced him not to bother. But he didn't want to go back to the camp yet, either, so he wandered, aimlessly, simply following his feet. He was soon met with the comforting sight of a church, so he removed his hat, smoothed down his hair and entered.

As he adjusted his eyes to the gloom, he looked about for a quiet corner where he could kneel or sit to pray and collect his thoughts. But he was greeted by frightened cries and squawks: there were a number of women and children huddled together who evidently didn't like the sight of a strange man with a dagger at his belt entering their sanctum. As he stepped in and away from the door they fled out of it, giving him as wide a berth as possible.

'No, wait, I —'

But they were gone. This is what he had become: a nameless soldier who represented danger to innocents.

He followed them out, in case he could call after them, but there was no sign and he didn't want to call attention to himself by shouting down the empty street.

As he stood, uncertain, outside the porch, a strange odour came to him on the breeze. He sniffed. What was it? Something tangy, salty? His interest piqued, he left the church behind. He rounded a corner and was met by the sight of – nothing. That is to say, the town simply ended: a great cobbled space with no houses on the other side, just an open expanse of water.

The sea! He'd been told about it, of course, but he'd never seen it. He hurried across to lean on the low wall and look out at it. The water immediately below him wasn't blue, as he'd been led to expect – it was brown, sludgy and filled with all kinds of muck. But the further away he looked, the more beautiful it became. And endless: the white-topped waves stretched as far as he could see. France was over there somewhere. He drank it in, unable to take his eyes off the swaying, mesmerising sight.

Of course, it was dangerous as well as beautiful. He couldn't swim, or at least not very well; he could manage to splash about a bit in the shallows of the river at home, but anything more than that was beyond him. When other boys his age had been teaching themselves, he'd been hard at work with Father Ignatius learning to read and write, skills he would need in the career mapped out for him. They had teased him, of course, but he had enjoyed his learning so he didn't really mind when they all swam off into the middle and he stayed by the bank; he had the best of the bargain. One or two of the poorer boys were quite strong swimmers: the river was full of eels, but if you didn't own a boat the only way to catch them was to dive down and place the baskets on the riverbed, and then go back to pick them up the next day. Those families who needed the eels to supplement their diet encouraged their sons to swim as much as possible, and, barring the one or two who had drowned over the years, they did themselves and the village a good service. Fortunately, Edwin's father, being the estate bailiff, didn't need to resort to such actions, for Edwin didn't much like the taste of eel anyway.

He should gather his thoughts. Anyone who saw him here day-dreaming would think he was some kind of halfwit. He dragged his eyes away from the sea and looked along the dock. He was standing next to the only free stretch of water that there was; the rest was ships, ships everywhere. Their round bellies moved up and down with the swell; masts rose into the sky; ropes ran from every conceivable point to every other point. Edwin stood engrossed. How did they work? Those rolled-up bits were sails, so if you untied those ropes there, they would unfurl and catch the wind. And then if you pulled on those ones *there*, you could maybe tilt the sails, depending on which way the wind was blowing? And those ropes at the side must be for –

'Are you going to stand there all day, or are you going to help?'

Edwin turned. The man addressing him was carrying a large bundle on one shoulder, and simultaneously rolling a barrel with his foot. As he saw Edwin's face he realised his mistake. 'Oh, sorry mate – thought you were someone else.'

'Not to worry, I can help you anyw— You're in the lord earl's service!' The man had a small chequered patch of blue and yellow on his tunic.

'Aye, Earl Warenne. That's his ship there.' He gestured with his head, not having a free hand.

'What?' Edwin gaped at the vessel in surprise, stopping only when the loose barrel rolled into his leg. 'Let me help. That looks heavy.'

The man nodded his thanks. 'Just take it to the bottom of the gangplank, if you would.'

Edwin rolled the barrel, trying not to let it bounce too much on the stones. 'I didn't know the lord earl had his own ship.'

'You're in his service too, are you?'

'I —' It was going to be too complicated to explain. 'Yes, yes I am. I'm from Conisbrough.'

'Never heard of it. Up north, is it? I know he's got lands all over, and you don't sound like you're from round here.'

'Yes. We've been on the road for over a week to get here.'

'I'm Stephen. From Winchelsea.'

It was Edwin's turn to be flummoxed. 'Is that near here?'

'Two, three days' travel down the coast by land. Quicker if you sail.'

They reached the ship and Edwin stopped rolling his barrel before it could fall into the water. Seen this close the vessel was huge, wallowing up and down and making him feel quite queasy just looking at it. The movement didn't seem to be bothering the sailors on board, though; they hurried easily round the deck, and some were even high up in in the labyrinth of masts and sails. The ship was fastened to the dock by several thick, wet, green ropes; a single narrow board came down from the side and stopped near his feet. He was glad when one of the sailors came down to take charge of the barrel, as he was fairly sure he would have rolled it straight off the plank and into the water if he'd tried to push it up there.

'Edwin!'

The shout from behind was from John and the others. They strolled across the open space of the dock, ignoring the busy, running, loaded, cursing men all around them.

'Got another job, have we?' joked Nigel as they reached Edwin and his companion.

'No, but – did you know the lord earl had a ship of his own? This is it.'

John looked it up and down. 'Didn't know it was his own, but we went on one like this when we went to France three years ago.'

Edwin was curious. 'What was it like?'

Several of the men shuddered in response. John shrugged. 'It wasn't pleasant, but it's part of the job, so we got on with it. Glad we had time to get our legs back before we had to do any shooting, though.'

Stephen had taken his own package on to the ship and was now descending, the plank bowing and bouncing under his feet. 'You lads offering to help too?'

There was a general murmur of disagreement, and the men started to back away, but John clapped Edwin on the shoulder. 'If he can, we can. Won't take long if we all carry something each.' There were a couple of groans and John's voice hardened. 'Jump to it, then. Sooner it's done the sooner you'll get back for your meal.'

With all of them helping it only took a couple of trips from the ship to a warehouse a couple of streets back from the dock. As they went there and back Edwin found out a little more about Stephen's home, and was glad that he didn't live on the coast. Apparently raiding parties led by someone called Eustace the Monk (who wasn't really a monk, as far as Edwin could make out) made frequent attacks, sailing in under cover of darkness to raid, steal and even murder.

'But does nobody stop them? You have no garrison?'

Stephen made a derisive noise, struggling under the weight of a bale of something. 'If they tried to attack any of the noble folk I expect they'd get short shrift, but taking our food and our women, that wasn't worth their while to defend.'

'Women?'

They reached the ship and Stephen gladly dropped the bale, putting his hands to his back as he straightened. 'Aye. I had a girl I was going to marry – pretty little thing, biddable, good cook, and all sorted out with her father as well. Then while I was away on a run up the coast they came. Found her and a couple of others out combing the shore, nobody else around, and … well, what they did to them was …' He tailed off and shook his head.

Edwin thought of Alys, of all the girls in his home village, and he felt sick.

Stephen prepared to hoist the weight once more in order to carry the bale up the gangplank. 'Couldn't marry her after that, of course. Absolutely ruined. So I gave the dowry back and her father made no fuss. But if I ever see that whoreson of a monk, I'll know what to do about it.'

He made his way up the plank, and then others came down to pick up the goods Edwin and his companions had carried. There were still a few bits and pieces left in the warehouse, but it was nearing noon, the time they'd agreed to be back in the camp, so they had to go. Nigel in particular seemed quite anxious about it. As they all dropped their last boxes and prepared to leave, Stephen said they'd have to get together for a drink sometime; the other sailors shouted out their thanks and said they'd see them later, which Edwin assumed to be a general farewell. He waved, but he wasn't sure he'd see them again, for surely the host was going to form up somewhere ready to fight off the French when they landed. Perhaps these ships would sail behind to capture the French vessels while they were empty.

As they walked back from the town to the camp, Edwin realised he didn't know what he was going to do when he got there. Hours of boredom certainly weren't going to do him much good, not in noisy surroundings, anyway.

He skipped a few steps to catch up with John. 'Have you got time to give me another shooting lesson?'

John was pleased. They fetched their bows and a sheaf of arrows, and left the others lounging around while they made their way through the camp. They had to pass through it to get to the area where the butts had been set up, but not so near to the big central pavilion that they were stopped. They found themselves at a fenced-off area where some squires and pages were being put through their paces; Edwin started to follow John around the outside of it, but stopped when he noticed that one of the boys there was Adam. He dawdled, hoping to get the chance for a brief word.

Adam was accompanied by the tiny new page, who was carrying a wooden sword; they were both wearing their padding. Edwin watched as Adam showed Hugh how to hold his sword up and how to place his feet while he was doing so.

John had walked on a few paces before realising he was on his own; he returned to join Edwin and leaned on the rail. He gestured. 'Are we so desperate that we're training tots now?'

'No, he's seven, apparently – that's Hugh, the lord earl's new page.' Edwin tried to catch Adam's eye; he was concentrating on his teaching, but eventually he looked up. Leaving Hugh to practise waving his sword in the air in various manoeuvres, he came over.

Adam nodded, looking more uncertainly at John. 'Edwin. Are you all right? Should you be here?'

'I'm fine. But how is the lord earl? Has anything else … happened?'

Adam shook his head. 'Not since we all recovered our stomachs. Or at least, not that I know of.'

'Good. But —' Edwin was interrupted by John nudging him. 'What?'

John pointed. 'That little lad's one of yours, you say? I don't know who they are, but my gut says there's about to be trouble.'

Back in the training area, little Hugh was still swinging his sword with intense concentration in the moves Adam had told him to practise, but he had drawn an audience: Salisbury's younger squire and his page. They were standing watching Hugh, the elder with some hilarity. Edwin noted with relief that Philip wasn't there. 'It's all right. They're not exactly friends, but Adam was kind to —'

He stopped. To his astonishment the page Matthew, the one who was bullied by his elders and who should have known better, stepped forward to shove Hugh and send him sprawling. Gregory laughed louder and made some comment, of which Edwin only caught the word 'nursemaid'.

Adam's mouth set in a line. 'Excuse me.' He went over, picked Hugh up and addressed Matthew. 'We don't do that in my lord's household.'

Matthew initially looked cowed, but Gregory stopped sniggering long enough to answer on his behalf. 'Well, the rest of your household's not here now, so what are you going to do about it?'

'I don't want to fight you. Just leave us alone to get on with our training.'

Adam started to turn away, but this seemed to increase Gregory's confidence, and he pushed Hugh again. 'Well, what if I say different?'

Edwin wasn't sure whether to be worried or not. The boy was full of swagger, but he was no bigger than Adam, who was regarding him with quiet assurance. Adam sighed. 'I told you, *we don't do that*. So, if we have to fight about it, then fine. But if I win then you both leave him alone.' He raised his fists.

Gregory grinned and they started to circle, gathering an audience of other squires, but they got no further before another voice froze them all.

'Oh, what have we here? A challenge?'

It was Philip. He made his way through the rapidly evaporating crowd of boys, thrust Gregory out of the way without a word, and faced Adam. 'You want to fight one of my lord's squires, do you? Well, let's try that, shall we?'

His voice was malicious, loaded with menace, and Edwin knew quite suddenly that this was going to be Philip's way of taking his revenge on Martin. And it was going to be bad.

He turned to John. 'I have to go for help.'

John looked puzzled. 'Help? Ah, it's just boys. A few fisticuffs and they'll call it a day.'

Edwin shook his head. 'It's not – he isn't – you don't know – look, I'm going to find Martin. Promise me you'll do something if it looks like it's getting serious.'

John was still focusing on the altercation. 'Isn't he the one whose lord wanted me hanged? Might be best if – oh no, wait, *that* isn't fair.'

Philip had ordered Gregory and Matthew to hold on to Hugh, with the promise that 'it'll be his turn when I've finished with this one', and Edwin saw the little boy squirming, frightened but unable to escape his captors. He tried to whack Gregory with his wooden sword but merely had it wrenched out of his hand; Gregory threw it on the ground and cuffed him around the head. Adam, meanwhile, had turned completely white, but he hadn't moved.

Edwin wasted no further time and ran. How long would it take to find Martin? How long could Adam defend himself against a trained and vicious young man some five years his senior?

He reached the earl's pavilion, but as he made to rush inside he was grabbed and prevented from entering by Turold, who was on guard outside it. 'Sorry Edwin. My lord's orders.'

'But you don't understand!'

'I understand well enough that I have orders and I have to follow them. So just go, and don't make me stop you.'

He was now standing firmly in the doorway and Edwin knew he wouldn't get past. But what was happening back in the training area? He hadn't wanted to make a scene, but there was no choice. 'Martin! MARTIN!' Please God he was inside and would hear.

Turold tried to herd him away. 'Stop that!'

But Edwin kept on shouting as loud as he could. Men all around were stopping to look. After what might have been ages but might also have been mere moments, Martin ducked out of the doorway. 'Edwin? What —'

Edwin opened his mouth, but oh, dear Lord, the earl was also stepping out, a furious expression on his face. 'What is all this —' His eyes fell on Edwin and his voice rose. 'You!' He started to gesture to Turold, who took hold of Edwin by the shoulders.

Edwin looked only at Martin. He didn't have much time before he was dragged away. 'It's Adam. In the training area. Philip is —'

Martin had only to hear the name before he started forward, but he was called back by the earl. 'Stop right there! What is this?'

Martin was torn between urgency and obedience. Obedience, as ever, won. 'My lord, please. Philip, my lord Salisbury's squire – if he's left with Adam he will give him a beating.' He turned to Edwin with a sudden look of panic. 'Where's Hugh?'

Edwin was in the process of being hauled off, his feet scuffing along the ground, his arms pinned behind his back, but he managed to wrest himself round so he was at least facing in the right direction. 'He's there too. Philip's going to start on him next. Adam's trying to stop him. Hurry!'

The earl, despite his anger, sensed some of the urgency. He addressed Martin. 'Explain.'

'My lord. Philip is – you don't know him, my lord. He's vicious – he will beat them both.'

The earl began to turn away. 'Is that all? Boys fighting? Adam can take care of himself, I'm sure.'

Martin was so panicked that he went as far as to place himself between the earl and the pavilion. 'Please, my lord.'

The earl stopped.

Martin's words were spilling over themselves in his anxiety. 'My lord, you don't know him. If he's threatened to beat Hugh then you can be sure he'll make no allowances for size – he'll cripple him. And if Adam is trying to stop him then it will be worse. He won't stop, he'll beat Adam to a *pulp*, maybe even kill him. And Adam won't give up, he won't back down, he will stand there and he will take it because he knows it is *right*. Please, my lord. You have to let me stop him.' For a moment Edwin thought Martin was going to fall to his knees, but he didn't. Instead he waited for the earl's reply, desperation radiating from his every fibre.

Edwin belatedly realised he had passed on his message and could do no more here. He was better off getting back to the training ground to try and stave off the worst. He extricated himself from Turold and ran. Behind him he just about caught the earl saying Martin could go, and something along the lines of how he'd better be right, but he didn't stop to find out.

He was breathless by the time he got back, stooping to inhale as he tried to take it all in. Hugh was still in the grip of the two bigger boys. John was still leaning on the rail. And Adam was …

'He's still on his feet – just,' were John's words, but he sounded less relaxed than he had earlier, and his hand was gripping the wood. Edwin could see Adam staggering, holding his ribs, blood trickling down his face as he sought to remain both upright and in between Philip and Hugh. But then Philip's fist caught his bruised and battered face once more and he fell. Edwin cried out and made to climb the fence as he saw Philip settling himself down in triumph astride the fallen figure and landing thump after sickening thump on his body and head.

But before Edwin could scramble over, there was a roar from behind him. Martin, unencumbered by any heavy armour or padding, six-and-a-half feet tall, charged straight past him and vaulted over the fence in one bound. He was upon the attacker in two strides, grabbing Philip's shoulders, wrenching him off Adam and throwing him bodily to one side.

Philip skidded away on his back in the dust before he realised what was going on. Then he smiled. Taking his time, he brought himself to his feet. Martin, Edwin couldn't help noticing, stood aside to let him get up. Was that wise?

Martin was more furious than Edwin had ever seen him, his face distorted. 'Why don't you pick on someone your own size?'

'Well, there's no one your size around, you misshape, but I'll teach you a lesson just the same. Or have you forgotten?' He made a show of dusting down his gambeson.

Martin was not to be drawn. He said nothing and simply raised his bunched fists.

Philip prowled around him on light feet, taunting him, and Edwin wondered if everything was about to go terribly wrong. He scrambled over to their side of the barrier and tried to prepare himself in case he had to throw himself between them.

He therefore had the perfect view of what happened next, although, try as he might – and he was asked to recount it more times than he could remember, afterwards – he couldn't quite explain exactly what had occurred. Philip moved in to try and land a punch, but instead of stepping forward to meet him or back to get out of the way, Martin merely planted his feet, drew back his right arm in a kind of twisting manoeuvre, and then brought it lashing round faster than Edwin's eye could follow, to land it on a precise point on the side of Philip's head. The *smack* noise of his knuckles connecting with flesh and bone echoed all across the space and outside it, where a crowd of curious onlookers had gathered to view the entertainment.

One thing Edwin did see very clearly was Philip's eyes rolling back in his head as he flew backwards, and one thing he heard very clearly was the thump of him hitting the ground like a sack of grain, already unconscious. Incredibly, Martin had knocked him out with a single blow.

Martin made no move to hit his fallen opponent again, but instead turned to Gregory and Matthew, who were still holding Hugh and twisting his arms. His voice came out in a low snarl that Edwin hardly recognised. 'Anyone else?'

Edwin didn't really think that he'd hit two smaller boys, but he was glad all the same when they dropped Hugh and fled without a word.

Martin stood alone in the space, the focus of all eyes, his chest heaving. Then he slowly uncurled his fists and dropped his arms, before shaking his head like a dog coming out of water. He moved to kneel beside Adam.

Edwin remembered to breathe. He clutched at the rail for support, realising he was still on the inside – the wrong side – of it.

Next to him, John gave a whistle. 'Well, I'll tell you one thing.'

'What's that?'

'I'm bloody glad he's on our side.' John patted Edwin on the shoulder. 'Go and help him – we'll have our practice later.' He moved off.

Edwin watched him go, still struggling to take it all in. He hurried over to crouch on Adam's other side and to help him up. He was battered and bruised but still coherent, thank heaven. As they hauled him to his feet and put his arms around their shoulders, Edwin glanced back to where Philip was still lying. He was showing signs of coming round and would presumably recover, which was good in that Martin wouldn't get into trouble for killing him, but which was otherwise very, very bad. Philip had been utterly humiliated in public. He would be a laughing stock throughout the host once word got round, and that would make him more dangerous than ever.

Chapter Nine

They arrived back at the earl's pavilion, although Martin wasn't quite sure how they got there; he had no memory of walking through the camp. As they drew near he summoned one of the sergeants to help him, and then sent Edwin on his way. No point in complicating matters further.

When the lord earl saw them he said nothing, but his lips set in the thin line that meant he was seriously displeased. Not with them, fortunately; he barked at Hugh to follow him and stalked out, but not before casting a glance at Adam that betrayed some sympathy and telling Martin to lay him down on his pallet.

Martin and his helper dragged Adam into the sleeping area, and Martin then sent the other man off to find Brother William. While he waited for the monk he laid Adam down and put a rolled-up tunic under his head – lying flat might make him choke on the blood streaming from his nose. He spied the cloth and basin that the earl had used for washing that morning and knelt down to try and get the worst of it off Adam's face.

'How do I look?'

It was just a croak, but if Adam was alert enough to worry about such things then he couldn't be all that badly hurt, could he?

He dipped the cloth again, turning the water pink. 'Actually, not as bad as you did the first time I met you. You must be tougher than you look.'

Adam managed a weak laugh. 'He thinks he's hard. He wouldn't have lasted an hour with my old master.'

Martin recalled the events of early May – only a few months ago! – and shuddered. Adam had never spoken of the time before he'd entered the earl's service, but Martin knew that he'd been mistreated by both his lord and his senior squire. Well, the lord was dead and could do Adam no more harm, and if he ever saw the other squire again then Martin would know what to do. He still felt the energy coursing through him, could feel again and again the sensation of his fist hitting Philip's face, and the satisfaction it had given him to see his enemy sprawling in the dust at his feet.

He busied himself cleaning Adam's face. 'I think your nose has survived intact again. How do you do it?'

'It's a talent. Or he can't aim properly.' His voice sounded slurred, but he remained lucid. 'To be honest, I was more worried that he'd keep hitting me in the gut. It's still not right after the other day, and …'

Martin contemplated for a moment the image of Philip being vomited on as he fought, but, cheerful as the idea was, he was glad it hadn't happened in case it caused anyone to laugh at Adam for weakness.

He'd cleaned as much as he could, but he had no salve or anything, and he wasn't happy with the way Adam was wincing and holding his side every time he moved. Where was Brother William?

Eventually the monk arrived, breathing heavily. 'Sorry. Came as fast as I could.'

'Where have you been? Adam needs you.'

'So did Rob, Humphrey's man.'

Martin recalled the tortured figure. 'Oh yes, of course. How is he?'

'He's dead.'

Martin crossed himself. It could have been any of them.

Brother William examined the cuts and bruises on Adam's face and pronounced them not serious. Then he ran his hands down

Adam's left side and watched him for signs of pain. 'Hmm, ribs, I think. Help me get this off him.'

Between them they managed to remove Adam's gambeson and his shirt. There was no cut – thank the Lord Philip had attacked with his fists rather than with a knife – but there was a nasty bruise forming.

Martin watched anxiously as the monk poked his fingers into Adam's side, making him flinch, although he kept his teeth gritted and didn't cry out. 'Anything broken?'

Brother William sat back on his knees. 'I think the padding saved him from the worst of it.' He looked down at the pale boy. 'Plus, of course, Adam's too hardy to let a little thing like a grown man punching him cause any damage.' Martin was pleased to see Adam smile. 'I think we'll still bind it up, though, just to be sure.'

Once Adam had some strips of linen wound tightly around his body, and had taken a draught of the earl's own wine – Martin didn't think he'd grudge one small cupful, under the circumstances – they left him to rest.

As they sat down in the pavilion's service area, Martin realised how tired he was. He hadn't done much, to be sure, throwing that one punch, but now the exhilaration of the event had worn off he felt drained. He poured himself some ale and sat in silence while Brother William busied himself with some pieces of parchment.

After a while the monk looked up. 'So, I heard of your victory.'

'What? Who from?'

'Are you jesting? It was all over the camp by the time I got here. You've got yourself something of a reputation.'

Martin considered that. 'Good … I think?'

He knew that the monk had sensed his indecision. 'How so?'

Martin wiped his face as he was forced to confront the reality. 'I don't think he'll bother me again. But he'll want to find a way of getting back at me, and now I'm worried about the others.'

'Well, that does you credit.'

'It does?'

'Of course. When you're knighted you'll have men under your command, and if you care for their welfare, as well as what they can do for you, you have the makings of a good leader.'

Martin said nothing, but he felt himself slumping less and sitting a little straighter. 'Adam is … I haven't got a younger brother, but if I did then I'd want him to be like Adam. And Hugh is – well, I don't know him that well yet, but I think he's going to be all right.'

Brother William laughed. 'I hope so, though we might have to feed him a bit more.'

Martin forced his mind to keep working. He had other things to worry about. One he didn't want to mention to anyone, especially not a monk, but the rest … 'Edwin, though.'

He heard a sigh. 'Yes. Whatever is happening in Conisbrough, he's innocent of any wrongdoing, I'm sure.'

'And my lord needs him.' *As do I*, Martin added to himself.

'We must work on a way to get him back into my lord's good graces.'

'I suppose finding out who's trying to kill him would be a good start.'

'Agreed. Whoever he is, he hasn't succeeded so far, but he has two deaths on his conscience already.'

'Two?' Martin struggled to think for a moment. 'You mean, Alan?'

The monk shrugged. 'It's possible that he was just unlucky, as were others during the skirmish. But he was riding close to the lord earl's litter, so I don't think we can rule out the possibility.'

Martin was considering this when the sound of the earl's voice came from the main space. Martin ducked through to find that he and Arundel had both arrived, young Hugh and Arundel's squires trailing behind them.

The earl saw him. 'Good. Now, plenty to do – the lord regent has ordered us all down to the dock to embark. The French ships are expected tomorrow morning, and we must be ready to sail out and meet them before they can reach land. It will take some hours so we need to get going.'

Martin snapped to attention. Action at last. Proper action. 'Yes, my lord. Do we strike the camp?'

'No. All tents to be left here, along with non-combatants. The rest of us to be prepared and on the move as soon as possible.' He turned to bid farewell to Arundel with a curt 'Godspeed', and then there was a whirl of activity to take Martin's mind off everything else.

Martin fetched his lord's armour from the sleeping area and laid it all out in the main open space, where there was plenty of room. Adam was dozing, so Martin let him lie for now. He had been arming the earl for most of his life and could easily manage, not needing anyone to help with the weight, and Hugh could pass him bits and pieces as required.

But it was not needed, or at least not yet. The earl broke off a conversation with one of his messengers to turn to Martin. 'I'll have my own cabin on the ship so you can have it stowed there and I'll put it on later.'

Martin sighed and started to put it all back in the bag, but the earl, dismissing the other man, shook his head when it came to the spurs. 'No need. We'll be on a ship, not on horseback, so you can leave those here.'

That gave Martin pause – he'd been on ships, of course, but he'd certainly never fought on one; how was that going to work? – but he swallowed his misgivings.

The earl gestured. 'Get yours too. You're plenty old enough to come, but you'll need to be properly armed.'

Martin's heart leaped and he started to move off to get his own things. Then he stopped. 'What about the others, my lord?'

The earl looked down at his page. 'Hugh will certainly stay here. How is Adam faring?'

'He's resting, my lord, but he's not seriously hurt.'

'Get him to help you and we'll see. If he's fit then he can come

– the experience will be good for him. If he's not fit then he'll be a liability and he can stay here.'

Martin knew what Adam's answer was going to be, so he rushed to shake him awake. As he expected, Adam's face lit up. He tried to get up too suddenly, though, and groaned. Martin put a hand over his mouth. 'Shh! Don't let my lord hear that or he'll tell you to stay here with Hugh.'

Adam nodded and raised himself more carefully. They carried Martin's mail, rather plainer than the lord earl's, into the main space and Adam helped him into it, on the basis that it would be easier to wear it than carry it. Other than during his sojourn at the abbey he'd made a point of putting it on for at least some part of every day since midsummer, and the weight felt familiar and comfortable. He took his helm out of its bag.

Adam wrestled himself back into his gambeson and belted a dagger around his waist. Martin made sure his own sword and dagger were loose in their scabbards and felt his excitement rising. He exchanged a glance with Adam. They were going to be in a real battle!

Martin sent Hugh out to fetch some men to transport the lord earl's armour. When the boy came back, Martin noticed how woebegone he looked.

He put his own excitement to one side for a moment and crouched. 'Hugh. You must know you're too small.'

'But —'

Martin shook his head. 'Never mind "but". My lord told you to stay, and his orders must be obeyed without question. Always. Do you understand?'

Hugh nodded, but his lower lip was still wobbling.

'Besides …' Martin cast about for an idea. He saw the white robe on the other side of the pavilion. 'Besides, you have to stay here and protect the other non-combatants, like Brother William.'

Fortunately, the monk got in on the act. 'Of course. And between us we will keep the lord earl's domain here safe, won't we? It's an important task.' He slid his eating knife out of its sheath. 'Here. This is probably more use in a fight than yours.'

Hugh's eyes were wide. 'But won't you need it?'

'Tsk, boy, don't you know that monks aren't allowed to "smite with a blade"? I'll just have to defend myself as best I can with my cudgel, so it's a good thing I've got you to look after me.' He winked at Martin.

The earl was already outside, and it wouldn't do to keep him waiting. Martin and Adam made to move after him but paused as Brother William raised a hand; he murmured a blessing and made the sign of the cross over them both. Martin said 'Amen', crossed himself, put his hand on his sword hilt and stepped outside.

———

The order to move out had reached Sir Hugh just as Edwin got back to the camp. There would be no time for more shooting practice; this would be the real thing.

Sir Roger was already armed, but Sir Hugh wasn't, and Edwin felt guilty for not having arrived in time to offer to act as squire. It was too late now: they were already forming up, so the knight barked at one of his sergeants to bring the bag and he'd arm himself as soon as he could once they got there. He saw Edwin and thumped him heartily on the back. 'Bound to be some time between us embarking and them getting here. Let's go to it!'

Strange how the prospect of imminent bloodshed and danger had a different effect on different men, thought Edwin, as he tied the proffered quiver to his belt and tried to hold on to the contents of his stomach. He had one final decision to make: everything else must stay here, but should he bring his letters with him? If he took them, he ran the risk that they would get sweaty, dirty or otherwise smeared, but if he left them … no, they had to come with him. If he was going to die today then he wanted the words 'beloved wife' next to his heart. He darted to where he'd left his scrip and extracted the letters, pushing them down inside his shirt before he turned to face the rest of the camp.

Sir Roger was looking about him in consternation. 'Has anyone seen Peter?'

Edwin moved over to him as a chorus of negatives sounded. 'When did you last see him?'

'Earlier. I didn't know we'd be moving out so soon, so I told him to go and play. I thought he might be at the butts but the others have come back without him.'

He looked worried, and despite his own fear Edwin hastened to reassure him. 'He'll come back to find you gone, but at least he'll be safe here.'

Sir Roger nodded and called over to the fire. 'Alf! If he turns up, can you keep him here?'

Alf, with Dickon next to him, was busy wrapping and distributing various foodstuffs, but he managed a nod and a quick 'of course, my lord' as he went. He'd have to stay here – a one-legged man would be little use in a fight anyway, never mind one on a ship – but the rest of them would still need to eat, so Edwin accepted his share and bade them farewell.

Then they were off. The town of Sandwich was eerily quiet as they marched through it: every street empty, every house shuttered. The people were right to be frightened, thought Edwin, recalling what he'd seen at Lincoln, but hopefully they would be able to defeat the enemy out at sea so that they never came rampaging through the town. Please God.

The thought gave him a little more strength, and he tried to hold on to it as they neared the docks. Alys wasn't here, but somewhere in Sandwich there would be a newly married young woman of her age. There would be mothers and children. They needed protecting, and he could help.

They reached the docks, a scene of growing confusion as men had to wait to board the ships while others arrived behind them to crowd the space still further. There were even a few horses: it was beneath the dignity of the higher nobles to walk from camp to ship, so they had ridden and were handing reins over to grooms. Edwin spotted the Earls of Arundel and Salisbury among the others, the latter with Philip close behind him, not looking his best but, alas, seemingly otherwise recovered from the incident earlier. The two younger boys followed, and Edwin was close enough to see that they both had swollen faces that were starting to bruise. They certainly hadn't looked like that earlier, and Martin hadn't touched them: Philip must have taken out his frustration at being humiliated on the nearest and easiest targets. They both looked sullen rather than frightened, but Edwin worried for them when he saw them embark on the largest ship along with Salisbury and Philip.

After watching Philip's back disappear, Edwin looked for Martin; thankfully he was heading on foot for a different ship, clearing a path through the press for his lord. Edwin and his companions would surely be going there as well, as it was the ship that belonged to the earl, the one they had helped to load earlier. And indeed, the tide of men was carrying them that way, though it would no doubt be a while before they got near to it, never mind on it. Edwin watched as each craft took on its load of men and weapons. There were – Edwin ran his eye along the dock – twenty smallish ships and sixteen larger ones, of which one, the vessel Salisbury had boarded, was really huge. It was sitting very high up out of the water, although Edwin supposed it would sink lower once hundreds of armed men were on it. The most impressive things to him were the great wooden castles built up at the front and the back.

Any archers positioned up there would be able to shoot downwards at their enemy, a significant advantage.

Edwin still hadn't reached the earl's ship, and the crowd appeared to have come to something of a standstill. He occupied his mind while he was waiting by looking out for, and checking off in his head, the coloured devices he had learned by heart from Sir Geoffrey's lessons. Salisbury and Arundel were easy, of course; and there was John Marshal, the regent's illegitimate nephew who had so easily forgotten Edwin and his actions at Lincoln. The royal arms of red and gold, but with only two lions instead of three, would be Richard Fitzroy, another bastard but the son of King John himself and therefore an older half-brother of the young king. Fortunately, for his own sake, not old or influential enough to be involved in any struggle among those with royal blood. And there, flying from the mast of the furthest ship, was the red cross on a gold background of Hubert de Burgh, the most important man in the kingdom after the lord regent. Edwin hadn't seen him before, for he'd been resisting Louis at Dover while Edwin was at Lincoln, and he looked with interest at the man who was in charge of the kingdom's administration. What a job that must be!

But there was one coat of arms Edwin couldn't see anywhere – the red lion on a green and gold shield. He slipped his way through the stationary throng to reach Sir Hugh and managed to attract his attention. 'Is the lord regent not here?'

The knight shook his head. 'No. He's an old man, don't forget. Fighting on a ship isn't for him.'

Edwin was mildly amused by the grizzled Sir Hugh, who must be well over sixty himself, describing the regent as an old man, but the smile was wiped off his face by the knight's next words. 'Besides, if they get past us then someone needs to be on land to co-ordinate the second line of defence.'

Sir Hugh turned away to speak to someone else, and Edwin

shrank back into the crowd. He had considered the possibility of his own personal death, of course, probably more times than was good for him. But he hadn't thought too deeply about what might happen if the host as a whole failed in its purpose. For how could it? With all these nobles and men? But now the spectre of the French wading ashore over their bloody corpses reared its head; they would join forces with those already on English shores, and then make their way northwards to devastate the land and burn the villages ...

If he hadn't been thinking of Conisbrough, he might not have noticed that the small boy weaving in and out of the ever-thickening crowd was Peter. He wasn't cut-pursing, as he might once have done, but was rather slipping his way towards the earl's ship. Edwin followed, but a grown man couldn't slide through the thicket of elbows and weapons quite so easily, and they were almost at the water's edge before he could reach out and catch the boy's arm.

Peter was startled and his initial reaction was to hit out and try to squirm free, but he relaxed a little when he saw who it was.

Edwin tried to keep his voice low. 'What are you doing here? You know you're supposed to be back at the camp.'

Peter shook his head. 'I'm not disobeying his orders. I said I wouldn't, remember?'

Realisation dawned and Edwin sighed. 'You were hiding, weren't you? So he wouldn't tell you specifically to stay there.'

Peter scowled. 'He's mine and I need to look after him.'

Now was not the time for a complex discussion about the dangers of Peter investing his whole life in one knight, a knight who was master, father-figure, brother and saviour all in one. Now was the time to get the child out of this crowd of armed men preparing for battle. 'What if *I* tell you to go back?'

'You can't give me orders.' And then he was away, twisting out of Edwin's grip and disappearing expertly into the crowd.

Damn! Edwin tried to force his way through, but the men around him didn't take kindly to being shoved, and he was awkward with the bow on his back and quiver at his belt, so he got nowhere.

He was by now almost at the edge of the dock, near to where the gangplank led up to the earl's ship, and he felt himself being pressed back as those around him made room for the earl and his knights, who were pushing their way through to board first. There were many men close around him, their voices loud and their breath sour. He was starting to get carried along despite himself, but he felt a hand on his back, stopping and steadying him. Once he had regained his feet he turned to see John.

'Still looking out for your precious earl, are you? You're supposed to be with us now.' He jerked his head to where the rest of the archers were forming a solid and unmoving group about ten yards away.

'No, I was – oh, never mind.'

He watched as the earl, Sir Hugh and Roger reached the bottom of the plank. Martin was a few paces behind, making sure that the crowd didn't rush forward at them while they were at the water's edge. The earl turned to speak with someone, indicating that the other two should go ahead, and Sir Hugh stepped on to the gangplank.

When Edwin had seen it before it had bowed and bounced a little under the weight of men and baggage, but it had still seemed secure. But now …

'Is it supposed to bend as far as that? It looks like it's about to crack.'

John shrugged. 'I've been on a few ships before and getting on and off them is always the worst bit. You worry too much – keep your voice down or you'll draw their attention, and that's never good.'

Edwin knew the shame of public embarrassment, and he had no desire to experience it again, so he said nothing. Sir Hugh was now nearly at the top, anyway; Sir Roger was behind him and the earl was just stepping on to the plank.

A loud, sharp report rang out, causing exclamations all around.

Edwin watched in horror as the plank snapped in two, dropping without warning the three men standing on it.

Sir Hugh just managed to grasp something on the side of the ship and was left dangling, his feet kicking in the air.

The earl fell into the water near the dockside, shouting and flailing.

Sir Roger, too far from either shore or ship to reach anything, and heavy in his armour, splashed into the water and sank like a stone.

Chapter Ten

There was uproar. Edwin somehow found the strength to shove aside the shouting and gesticulating men in front of him so he could reach the water's edge. An enterprising foot sergeant had reversed his spear and reached out the butt end for the earl to catch hold of; he was hauled back towards land and Martin extended a long arm to seize a fistful of his tunic and heave him up out of the water.

Edwin wanted to feel relief, but the real tragedy was unfolding further out: he could see nothing breaking the surface of the water where Sir Roger had gone in.

Behind him were two soldiers he didn't know. Their voices sounded detached.

'They never stand a chance if they've got their armour on.'

'But it's not that deep there, is it?'

'Deep enough if it goes over your head. A halfpenny that he never comes up.'

'It's a shame about the boy, though. What did he think he was doing? Fool.'

Edwin was out of his mind with worry already, but the words sent ice through his blood. 'The boy' could only be …

The men behind him were thrust aside by a frantic John, who grabbed hold of Edwin's arm. 'The lad! Get him out of there! Can you swim?' He pointed at a stream of bubbles.

'Hardly at all. You?'

'No.' But John was unslinging his bow and untying his quiver. Edwin looked round helplessly for something – anything – that might help. Oh dear God, why hadn't he said something? Why hadn't he shouted a warning when he had had the chance?

It felt as though an age passed, but in fact, as Edwin was to realise later, it was only moments before there was a huge upheaval in the water and Sir Roger's bright blond head broke through the foaming surface. There was a huge shout, and a man who had had the wit to tie a rope around his waist jumped in. He reached the flailing knight, caught hold of him, and was pulled back to shore by many willing hands.

Behind Sir Roger was a smaller figure, paddling, gasping now with the effort and in danger of going under again.

'Here! Quick!' John was holding out his bow. Peter took an unsuccessful swipe, eliciting groans from the spectators, but he managed to clutch it at the second attempt, at which point John towed him in and Edwin hoisted him out. One of the men now trying to help was the one who had wagered on Sir Roger's death, and Edwin elbowed him angrily out of the way.

Peter was alive. John was thumping him on the back – had he gone mad? Edwin tried to stop him.

'No, leave me – dirty water – he needs to spit it all out or he might die anyway …' he continued the sharp blows between the boy's shoulders until he was satisfied that it had all been choked up.

Sir Roger was lying face down on the cobbles, likewise spewing up brown filth, but as he drew near, Edwin heard him take in a rasping breath of air. Thank God and all the saints.

Once he'd finished retching, Sir Roger managed to turn over and he saw Edwin. He didn't even have time to frame the question before a small figure shot through the crowd and flung itself at him, wrapping its arms about him and sobbing as it buried its head against his chest.

Sir Roger gripped Peter in a tight embrace, crushing him against his mail, tears in his eyes.

Edwin rubbed the back of his hand across his own face. A few moments only and he'd nearly lost two of the only people he'd known since before all this madness started.

The crowd around them was packed, noisy and intense. Edwin tried ineffectually to move them away but they were yelling, waving their arms and paying him no attention. It was good-natured – they all wanted to congratulate the boy on his efforts and the knight on his escape – but it was too much.

Martin suddenly appeared. Oh Lord! The earl! Edwin had nearly forgotten him. But Martin wouldn't have left him unless he was all right … and yes, there he was over there with Adam and some other men.

The crowd recognised Martin's authority – and his huge fists – and, aided by John's brusque shouting, he managed to clear a space.

Edwin knelt by the two soaking figures. He was wet through as well by now, but he didn't care. He looked from one to the other, trying to reassure himself that he wasn't imagining the incredible good fortune.

'Sir Roger! Are you – and Peter, how in the Lord's name did you do that?'

Despite the warmth of the day, Peter's teeth were chattering. 'S– s– swimming. Did a lot of it. Sometimes those eels were the only thing we had to eat.'

Edwin knew what he meant, even if Sir Roger didn't. But that still didn't explain … 'But the weight! His armour!'

Someone had found a blanket from somewhere, and it was passed to Sir Roger. He wrapped it around Peter as the boy continued. 'Not that deep. Father sh– showed me what to do if you got stuck. Push up. Thought it m– might be … same.' He burst into tears and buried his face in the knight's chest again.

'It's all right, Peter, it's all right.' Sir Roger murmured soothing words into the top of the boy's head before lifting his face to Edwin's. 'Help me up.'

Edwin put out a hand and hauled him to his feet as he clasped Peter in his arms. Once the sobs and the shaking had subsided a little Sir Roger put the boy down.

'Peter. I owe you my life.'

Peter scrubbed at his face, angrily. 'I told him,' he gestured at Edwin, 'that you have to have someone to look after you, and he didn't believe me.'

Edwin had the sense not to interrupt.

'I believe you. I believe you now.'

'So I can stay?' Peter looked up at the looming ship.

But the knight was shaking his head. 'I'm sorry, Peter, you must go back.'

Peter looked like he was going to cry again, reaching out his hands to hold tight to his lord.

Sir Roger crouched so they were eye to eye. Water was still dripping off him and pooling on the ground. 'You can swim better than me. Better than anyone. And you're brave. But the battle will be full of armed men, blades, arrows – I owe you my life, and I won't see you die out here on the sea. We still have too many adventures to look forward to.'

Peter opened his mouth but Sir Roger held up one finger. 'Orders.'

There was a moment of silence before Peter nodded, looking at the floor now. Sir Roger stood again and looked around him. 'Now, how to –?'

John stepped forward. 'Begging your pardon, sir, I can take him through the town and put him in the care of one of the grooms to take back to the camp. You'll need to stay here.'

The one person, thought Edwin with relief. The one person he respects almost as much as Sir Roger. He watched as they parted, the knight folding the child in an embrace one more time before he watched them go.

Edwin caught some of the conversation as it floated back to him. 'Come on, you. Brave lad you are – the camp will need you to protect it.'

'But what about you?'

'Don't worry, I'll be straight back here. Don't want to miss …'

They passed out of earshot, and Sir Roger finally turned his attention to Edwin. His eyes looked even bluer than usual, reflecting the afternoon summer sun, and they almost bored through him. 'I swear to you, Edwin, I swear on the cross and on everything I hold dear that I will guard that boy and keep him from harm until my dying day.'

Edwin nodded, feeling choked by all he'd just witnessed. He was saved from replying by the arrival of the earl; he melted back into the crowd to avoid confrontation.

The earl looked Sir Roger up and down. 'Glad we didn't lose you.'

'Likewise, my lord, I can assure you. And Sir Hugh also.'

Edwin had almost forgotten about Sir Hugh, but there he was, safe and dry on board the ship and watching as the sailors laid out another gangplank.

The earl was continuing. 'Get on board, then, and get out of those wet things. That mail is going to be hell to clean, but I'm sure I can find you a volunteer.'

They were both standing at the bottom of the new plank, and there was the barest hesitation. Then the earl seemed to remember that they were in full view of a crowd of men, so he spoke loudly. 'Onwards, then, to defeat the enemy!' He strode up the plank and on to the ship without looking to either side.

Edwin realised he was holding his breath; very slowly, he exhaled.

Martin followed the earl up on to the deck of the ship and then down inside it, to the one private space it afforded. With two knights and two squires in the cabin as well as his lord it was overcrowded, but the others wouldn't stay long.

He had managed a brief exchange with Sir Roger, and as he searched through a couple of stacked boxes for dry clothes, Martin heard the knight broach the all-important subject.

'My lord, may I speak?'

'You may. Adam, help him out of that mail before it rusts solid.'

Sir Roger's voice was muffled as he tried to continue from halfway out of his hauberk. 'My lord, I – we – think you might be in danger.'

The earl looked nonplussed. 'Danger? Of course I'm in – no, not that one; I'll keep that for after the battle. See if there's a plainer one in there.'

There was a thump of mail hitting the floor, and Sir Roger straightened and continued. 'No, my lord, if you'll excuse me – we think it's possible that someone on our own side has been trying to kill you.'

The earl was in the act of holding out his arms ready for the tunic, and he stopped. 'Say that again?'

The sopping gambeson had now joined the hauberk on the wooden planking, and Adam passed Sir Roger a cloth to dry himself. Like all knights he had a brown neck and forearms, and a pale body. 'My lord, with everything that's happened in the last few days – the fire, the thrown knife, the poisoning, and now this – we think there might be a traitor in the host.'

Martin had finished adjusting his lord's tunic and was now stooping to attend to the belt buckle. The voice, coming from close above his head, was sceptical. 'So who is this "we"?'

Sir Hugh broke in for the first time. 'Both Sir Roger and I think the same, my lord. And so does … well, never mind that.'

'Seriously? You both consider this a real possibility?'

They murmured assent.

'Then who?'

'That we don't know, my lord, but I've been on campaign often enough to see when "accidents" are too frequent.'

'Hmm.' The earl gave them both a hard stare. 'All right, you may go, both of you. Get something to eat and some sleep – we'll be sailing before dawn tomorrow.'

Martin watched as both knights left the cabin, shutting the door behind them. That created a little more space and air, but it was still very close in here. And the ceiling was too low.

There was one folding chair, and the earl now sat in it. He drummed his fingers on the arm. Martin and Adam waited.

'Right. Adam, get all that wet stuff cleared out of here and find someone to dry that gambeson and oil the mail. He'll need it tomorrow.'

'Yes, my lord.' And Adam was gone, leaving Martin alone with his lord. He busied himself repacking the extra clothes.

'So, what is your opinion of all this?'

Martin dropped two shirts and jumped upright too suddenly, just remembering at the last moment to keep his head down before he cracked it on a beam. 'Me? You want to know what I think, my lord?'

'Yes. Come now, you're not far off becoming a knight and you need to get used to the idea. What do you make of Sir Roger and Sir Hugh's assertions?'

'I —' This was such an unfamiliar situation that Martin didn't know how to respond. Should he say what he really thought, or what he thought the earl wanted to hear? 'They are both loyal to you, my lord, and I don't think they would say such things to you unless they really thought they were right.'

The earl grunted. 'Agreed. But *are* they right, though? Or are they just worried about a lot of hot air? Yes, accidents have happened. But nothing you might not see on any campaign.'

He was still looking at Martin, still seeming to invite his opinion, so Martin risked continuing. 'You're right, of course, my lord. But I think it's more that so *many* of these "accidents" have happened, and so close together – all within the last few days. And it's difficult to see how the knife could have been an accident at all.'

'Could have been. Men making sport in camp, that kind of thing. Not noticing I was there.'

'Even so, my lord, we should remember that we're in a host that contains men who have changed sides before.' Martin winced at his own audacity, for of course his lord had been one of those men himself, talking to Salisbury on that very subject on the night of the fire.

But fortunately the earl didn't seem to be thinking of his own action, only those of others. 'Well, yes …'

'And, my lord, Edwin thinks —'

Damn, it had slipped out of his mouth before he could stop it, and it was too much. The earl became curt.

'Enough. I don't care what he thinks – nothing that isn't to do with his own advancement, I'll wager. Get me a drink now and see about something to eat.'

'Yes, my lord.' There was wine in a little niche in the corner, the jug stoppered to prevent it spilling as the ship moved. 'Sorry, my lord.'

He expected a further outburst, but the earl relented. 'All right. You mean well, I know. But look: whether someone means me harm or not, there's nothing he – or we – can do about it now. I'm here in the heart of my own ship, surrounded by my own men, and nobody else will get on board before we set sail. And after that we'll all be too busy fighting the French. If necessary we can return to the subject after all this is over.'

'Yes, my lord.' Martin could do no more, say no more. At least Salisbury was on another ship and could get nowhere near. But there were many soldiers above decks, and Martin didn't know all of them by sight. What if one was a stranger who had been sent by the earl's enemies?

He looked about the cabin. He could make this secure, surely.

The walls were of wood so nobody could cut their way in from the back; he could sleep across the doorway. His sword would be of little use in here – he'd already unbelted it and stood it in the corner near the earl's armour – but he would keep his dagger. And he'd be up before dawn to arm his lord, which would help to protect him against any direct attack. It was the best he could do, for now.

———

Edwin found himself a space on the crowded deck. He and John had rejoined the rest of Sir Hugh's men, and between them they formed a solid and somewhat belligerent block that managed to carve itself a distinct area. He let everyone else around him talk as they would; he wanted some time to himself to think.

The plank had been fine when he'd seen and helped with the loading of the ship. The plank had snapped when three men stood on it several hours later. It could be just the difference in weight. But some of those barrels had been quite heavy, and he certainly recalled that several burdened sailors had been on it simultaneously. Therefore, the plank had, at the later time, failed to carry the same weight as it had earlier. But was this natural, some fault in the wood that had been worsened by the earlier load and had just happened not to break until later? Or had someone tampered with it? Had anyone pulled the broken pieces out of the water? Maybe he could look at it.

He half-rose from his position, but Nigel, who was next to him, pulled him down again. 'I wouldn't get in the way of the sailors if I were you.'

Edwin looked about him and noted that all the fighting troops were packed in specific spaces – away from what he supposed were the important ropes and workings of the ship – but that the sailors themselves were swarming all over the place.

'Are we going to sail now?'

Nigel shook his head. 'Don't think so. They're just …' he floundered, presumably having as little sea-going knowledge as Edwin himself. 'Just getting things ready. I heard someone say we'll be off on the tide just before dawn.'

'What's a tide?'

Nigel gave him an incredulous look. 'A tide. You know, when the water pulls either into shore or away from it?'

'Really? But how?'

'How can you not know what a tide is?'

'Oh, leave him be, Nigel. He's not stupid, he's just never seen the sea before.' This was John, who then started digging in a bag for his rations. 'Eat up, both of you. Line your belly now – you probably won't want it in the morning just before we fight.'

The reminder of why they were actually there formed a stone in Edwin's insides once more, and he stared unenthusiastically at his bread. He'd need his strength, though, wouldn't he, so he'd better force it down.

As he ate he saw Sir Hugh and Sir Roger come up on deck, the latter now disarmed and dry. They moved to a position near the ship's mast to join several other knights. Edwin was impatient to hear their views on the accident, but there was no way he could get across to them – the press of men formed a physical barrier and the circle of knights a social one. He would just have to work it out on his own and hope that they all lived long enough tomorrow for it to be resolved.

More movement from the sailors distracted him, and he nudged John. 'What are those?'

John surveyed the clay pots and canvas bags being carried with extreme and exaggerated care. 'No idea. Something important, though, I reckon.' One of the sailors laid down his burden near them and then paused as he straightened, so John took the opportunity to hail him and ask.

'Lime,' came the short answer.

John whistled. 'Nasty.'

'Lime? You mean, like they use in building?' Edwin was confused.

'Yes, though you can use it in fighting as well. Comes as a powder, horrible stuff that burns on your skin and in your eyes if you get on the wrong side of it. Let's hope we've got all of it and the Frenchies none, eh?'

The sailor was about to head off again but he paused. 'Oh, it's you.' It was Stephen, the man Edwin had met that morning. 'I owe you thanks for all that help earlier – we wouldn't have done it half so fast if you hadn't come back.' He looked around, perhaps expecting to be reprimanded for slacking, but when he wasn't, he leaned comfortably on the rail.

He nodded at the lime. 'The most important thing is, make sure you've got the wind behind you.'

It didn't take long for Edwin to work that one out. 'Of course.'

'It's light, like dust, so it gets everywhere, right inside armour. And like John here says, you especially don't want it in your face. If you throw it wrong it'll come back at you.'

A shout from the other side of the deck recalled his attention and he nodded to them both. 'Remember.' He picked his way back through the crowd.

With even more to worry about, Edwin settled himself down as best he could on the deck. Darkness fell, the only light coming from the lantern burning at the top of each ship's mast, a long line of glimmers spread along the wharf. Edwin had been concerned that he might suffer from sickness, as several men had warned him about the movement of the ship on the water, but actually he found the rocking quite soothing, at least here in the port. Maybe it would be different out on the sea, but he didn't want to think about that just now.

As men around him slept, he forced himself to go back over the details of every event of the last few days, checking it off against his recall of who had arrived with the host and when. The earl's own household and others from Conisbrough had been there all the way, obviously. As had Sir Roger – not that he could possibly have anything to do with it – who had been there the night of the fire to help him. They had picked up other retainers such as Sir Hugh on the way. Now, Sir Hugh had arrived *after* the fire but before the poisoning and everything else. The Earl of Arundel even later than that, so surely he could be counted out as well, unless he had managed to infiltrate someone into the host before he arrived himself, in order to allay suspicion. And the same went for those whom they had only joined at the main encampment: the regent, John Marshal and the others.

Arundel. Consider Arundel. But he was a close ally of the lord earl – his sister had once been the earl's wife and he had even now given his son over to his care. Why would he want the earl dead? Would he gain anything?

Unless there was something going on that Edwin was completely unaware of, and unless Arundel had laid extremely specific plans, Edwin couldn't see that that particular thread was going to lead anywhere. So he went back to the man who had loomed large in his thoughts all along: the Earl of Salisbury.

The fire had started on the night Salisbury arrived, and all the other incidents had followed in short order. He was another ally of the earl – supposedly – but they were two of the only close male relatives of the young king and could thus perhaps be considered rivals for power. But was that enough to suspect Salisbury of repeated attempts at murder? And if so, how had he managed it? A peer of the realm did not steal about the camp putting poison into cooking pots, and nor did he tamper with a ship's gangplank. But he had many servants, of course. Servants and squires.

Squires and pages could go anywhere; it was accepted that they were continually being sent on errands, so nobody would be surprised to see them. With the possible exception of Martin, who stood out due to his unusual height, they tended to fade into the background. Could any or all of Salisbury's servants be involved?

What was most frustrating about all this was that he hadn't seen most of the incidents with his own eyes. All he could do was to put together information from what others had said, but that was not nearly as useful, for people always thought they were telling the truth when in fact their recollection was coloured by their own feelings: they told the truth, but only the truth as they saw it.

He shifted on the deck; the wooden boards were less comfortable than the ground he'd been sleeping on recently, and he suspected he'd be as stiff as one of them in the morning. He rolled over on to his back and looked at the sky, unimaginably far above him. God was up there somewhere, looking down on the deeds of men – did He know or care what Edwin was thinking about?

Edwin paused in his thinking in case divine inspiration was going to strike, but it didn't. Instead he set himself to list and compartmen-talise in his mind everything he knew about each incident, trying to cross-reference it with what he knew about people's whereabouts.

He didn't remember falling asleep, but he must have done at some point because Nigel was shaking him awake. He sat up, stretched and then winced as he cricked his neck. It was still dark, but there was a very faint pre-dawn glimmer in the sky, and all around him men were stirring, shaking their own stiff necks, and moving to relieve themselves over the side of the ship.

'Is it time?'

'It is. The tide's turned and we're about to sail.'

Any remaining sleepiness dispersed on the fresh breeze. Edwin watched the sailors untying and coiling ropes, heard them calling to each other, and felt the surge as their ship moved away from the dock. It was soon out of the shelter of the port, and Edwin turned to face the wide grey expanse of the open sea.

The camp was too quiet. Peter awoke and was at first confused at the canvas above him; this wasn't Sir Roger's tent. Then he heard the snoring and recalled that he was in the stores tent with Alf and Dickon; Alf had insisted he come with them so he wouldn't be alone. As if he could possibly be frightened in a place that was as near to home as anywhere he'd ever been.

When his barely remembered parents, his little sister and his baby brother had all died within a year of each other he'd been properly alone, sleeping wherever he could find shelter and stealing or begging for food. A few people had been kind to him – Edwin was all right and his mother was a nice lady – so he didn't starve, but he'd been isolated, forlorn, until the blessed day Sir Roger had come for him. Peter considered that his life had really begun on that day in the stable; he'd been born again. Now he was warm, he was fed, and his life had a purpose. He slept on a pallet near Sir Roger at home and on the road, always at hand to make sure his master had everything he needed, and in return he was well treated. More than that: he was trusted, he was *respected*. And even with Sir Roger gone, the tent still smelled of him, still contained his things, and Peter would have been quite happy in there guarding it all. But of course, Alf didn't know any of this, and Peter didn't have the words to explain it all properly. So he kept his mouth shut and did as he was bid.

The others were still asleep. Alf took off his wooden leg at night, and there it was in the corner; Peter was careful not to touch it, in case it brought bad luck. He couldn't imagine going through life with only one leg, and the thought made him shudder. And wouldn't it hurt terribly when …? But anyway. He gave it a wide berth as he crept out of the tent without waking either of the others.

The camp was strange and quiet as he walked through it; there were a few men around, grooms and servants and so on, but none of the knights or the fighting men who had filled it and given it such life. The ground was dusty under his bare feet after being trampled so much in the last few days. He owned a pair of boots these days, thanks to Sir Roger, but he was used to going without and he hadn't thought to put them on as he left the tent.

He reached the edge of the camp, bare earth making way for cool, dewy grass, and stood on the rise overlooking Sandwich. The sun wasn't up properly yet, but he could see the town well enough, and the smoke from cook fires smudging the sky. And beyond was the water. His eyes prickled as he saw the ships making their silent way out to sea; it was so unfair that he'd been left here while the others all went! He could fight as well as anyone, he was sure. And who was going to watch his master's back while he wasn't there?

He stood unmoving as dawn broke and the ships became smaller and smaller, eventually disappearing from his sight.

———

Martin had been awake since before dawn. There had been no alarms in the night, and he had safely roused his lord, found him something to eat and then armed him. The earl had gone up on to the deck to speak with his knights, telling Martin to follow once he was armed himself. Adam had helped him into his mail and now he stood, shrugging his shoulders, shaking his arms and bouncing on his feet, making sure that everything was in the right place and all the ties were fastened correctly.

Adam himself had only a gambeson, no mail, and he was under strict instructions to stay back from the main fight, guarding a spare sword and shield for the lord earl in case he needed them. He looked pale under his bruises, but Martin was pleased to see the set line of his mouth. He wouldn't fail in a crisis. And even wearing his padding he was still quite obviously a boy, so he shouldn't be targeted by any enemy with honour. There was no place of absolute safety here, but Adam should be as well protected as he could be.

No such courtesy would be extended to Martin, of course: squire or no, he was armed and ready to fight, and once his helm was in place men would be able to judge him only by his size, not his age. He would be a target, and to be honest he felt he would welcome that. If he really started fighting, it would give him no chance to worry about the knot in his stomach.

'Are you sure you don't want that lace on your coif a bit tighter? You don't want it slipping down over your eyes once you've got your helm on.'

Adam was fussing around him, but Martin guessed it was his way of dealing with his own nervousness, so he let him get on with it.

Once everything had been double- and triple-checked, there was no excuse for staying in the cabin any longer. Martin took a deep breath. 'Bring my lord's spares, then, and let's get going.'

Adam started to move and then paused. 'Before we go, I just wanted to say ...' He tailed off as they looked at each other in silence.

Martin nodded. 'I know. Me too.'

He could feel the sweat starting to pool under his arms and run down his back. The cabin was too small. He had to get out, into the air. 'Come on then.' He checked the buckle on his sword-belt for the fourth time, picked up his helm and made his awkward way up the ladder, trying to convince himself that his feeling of nausea was due to the movement of the ship.

The fresh, salt air hit him in the face as he emerged into the light of day, and he recovered himself a little. *You're going to be a knight, and this is what knights do.* He glanced around him; Sir Hugh was here so Edwin must be on board somewhere, but Martin couldn't see him in the press of men. He sent up a brief prayer that Edwin would survive the day – he wasn't exactly a fighter, after all – and then moved to take up a position behind his lord.

They all stood to hear a brief blessing from the one priest aboard – the bishops all having remained on land with the regent – and a plea to St Bartholomew, whose feast day it was, to watch over them. Then he administered a general shriving, forgiving them their sins in case they should die today. Martin wasn't really taking it all in, but he mumbled 'Amen' at the end and then turned his attention to more practical matters.

The group of knights were discussing tactics, but there didn't seem much to it: archers as soon as the enemy came in range, then waiting until the ships came close enough to each other to board for hand-to-hand fighting. There was no terrain to consider, no possibility of an additional force appearing from behind a hill or out of a forest.

Martin steadied himself as the ship rode up and down in the waves. How close would they get before they attempted to cross from one ship to another? How would it be done? Would he have to jump? Fighting was one thing, but the thought of falling into the bottomless depths of the sea was another. No dock nearby, no solid ground a few feet down, nobody to pull him to shore. To fall in the water out here would be certain death.

Think of something else, damn you! The talk had now turned to the possibility of taking prisoners for ransom. Sir Hugh turned from the general conversation to address Martin. 'If my lord captures anyone and passes him over to you, make sure he's disarmed and then secure. And if you fight directly, remember: the richer his armour and surcoat look, the harder to try to capture him rather than kill him.'

Martin nodded. A tiny thought uncurled itself in the corner of his mind. Prisoners meant ransom; a higher-ranking prisoner meant more money; more money meant that he could put it away against, say, the purchase of a horse of his own ... the forthcoming battle suddenly seemed a little more like an opportunity than something to be afraid of. They had thirty-six ships packed with armed men – surely no boats carrying troops from France could stand against them? He stood a little straighter and loosened his sword in its scabbard.

The noise on the ship had abated. Everywhere, men were looking out over the sea, straining their eyes for the first sight of the enemy, who should surely be close by now. The captain of this ship had explained to the lord earl last night about what time they would have left French shores in order to make best use of the tides. They would sail across the Channel to a point further south than here, but all were agreed that they would not attempt a landing there, as the mighty fortress of Dover defended the coast. Instead they would come up the coast and round the Isle of Thanet, aiming to sail right up the Thames to where Louis himself waited in London. And if they reached London and were able to join forces –

'There!'

Martin jumped and looked about him in confusion before realising that the cry had come from above him. Heavy in his mail coif, he managed to lean his head far enough back to see one of the sailors perched up towards the top of the mast, pointing. He followed the direction of the outstretched arm and waited a few agonising moments as the sea remained empty. Then a roar went up as those on deck spotted the first ship.

He felt himself joining in, cheering until his voice was hoarse at the thought of the fight, at the relief that at least the waiting would soon be over.

The first ship was followed by another. And another.

And then another.

And then more.

The shouting on deck subsided and then died down completely as the scale of the enemy fleet became apparent. For, heading up parallel to the coast, so close together that the water between them could hardly be seen and their sails made one solid mass, were at least eighty ships.

Chapter Eleven

Edwin watched as more and more ships appeared. There were mutterings all around him, but Nigel spoke up. 'Lots of them, yes, but look properly: most of them are tiny. Won't that make a difference?'

It was true: when Edwin forced himself to examine the oncoming fleet more calmly, he could see that no more than ten of the ships were of a comparable size to their own, and none of those was as large as the great ship with the castles. The rest were much smaller vessels. He was muttering a prayer of thanks when he noticed something else.

'We're going to miss them.'

'What?' John and Nigel were both next to him now.

'Well, look.' Edwin pointed southwards, which was to his right. 'We're coming out from the shore, and they're running along it sideways, but they're going so fast that they'll have gone past us before we get there. We'll end up going behind them.'

John scratched his head under the filthy cap. 'You might be right.'

A thud sounded next to them on the deck: Stephen, jumping down from the rigging that was fastened to the ship's side rail. He grinned. 'They'll probably think that too, but we're far more manoeuvrable. Watch and learn.' He hurried to join a group of other sailors who were doing something to some other ropes, shouting back over his shoulder. 'And remember what I said about the wind!'

Edwin tensed, his strung bow in one hand and the other hovering over the quiver at his belt. He also had his dagger, but nothing else, and no armour. But the knights and the armoured sergeants, they'd do the bulk of the hand-to-hand fighting, wouldn't they? If they were anything like the ones he knew, they'd certainly want it that way. But it was no use wondering. He was in God's hands now and there was nothing he could do except deal with events as they happened. He forced out a breath and tried to stop his hands from shaking.

He was right about one thing: they were going to pass behind the French fleet. Their ship was second in the line, behind that of Hubert de Burgh, and they were heading south-east and into the wind. It was strong and Edwin had to screw up his eyes as it pummelled his face. That meant that they were slow and laboured in the water. The French fleet was now almost directly ahead, passing from right to left as it sailed northwards up the coast. They had the wind at a sort of diagonal angle to them, so they were making better speed. Oh Lord. They'll escape us, they'll reach London, *they'll march north.*

As his ship continued on its course Edwin saw the vessel that was at the back of the French fleet. It was the largest of the enemy and was flying many flags and carrying a great number of brightly coloured knights. The command vessel, surely, although if that were true then why wasn't it at the front?

The answer to that was immediately obvious, even to someone who knew as little of the sea as Edwin. The French ship was so low in the water that it was wallowing through the waves like a pig in mud. What could they possibly have on board to make it do that?

Nigel must have had the same thought. 'Horses, maybe? All those knights won't want to be walking when they land.'

Edwin looked more closely, straining his eyes. 'And what's all that wood stacked up there?' He was reminded of something he'd seen at Lincoln. 'Are those pieces of a siege engine?'

'Looks like it. Long beam, a sling there, look.' Nigel turned to John. 'What do you reckon, a trebuchet? We saw some of them in France before.'

John nodded. 'Seems like it. Better get that sent to the bottom before it can land and cause trouble. But that wouldn't account for all that extra weight.' He scanned the great ship. 'There's just too many of them, I think. If he's the one in charge' – he pointed to a bright figure standing on the high part of the deck towards the front of the ship, who seemed to be issuing instructions to someone more drab – 'then they'll all have wanted to be on the same ship as him. Makes them feel important.'

That seemed logical, and his theory was proved correct, in Edwin's mind at least, when howls started to sound from the sailors on his own ship: the drab figure had been recognised as Eustace the Monk himself. It would seem that many of the crew had suffered at his hands.

But they were going to get away! Both Hubert de Burgh's ship and their own were past the French now, heading out to sea.

And then, at a word from the ship's captain, there was a sudden frenzy of activity, sailors swarming everywhere … an unexpected lurch that threw Edwin and his companions to one side. They had turned around.

Edwin staggered and tried to re-orient himself. The sun was … yes. They had turned almost back on themselves, and now they had the wind directly behind them so the ship leaped forward at a great speed, the sail filling fit to burst. They were heading directly for the French command ship, and gaining.

The sailors cheered and John gave a whoop. 'To the rail now, lads, and arrows ready!'

Edwin followed the crowd and planted his feet to steady himself. They were going to reach the enemy first; Hubert de Burgh's ship, which had been in front of them on the way out, had overshot and was having some difficulty in turning. What had Stephen said about being more manoeuvrable?

The gap was closing. Edwin's heart was beating faster. This was it. He pulled a first arrow out of his quiver. Would he be able to do it?

To kill again? He had taken two lives in the past few months, and he had done both almost without thinking, as a reaction to an extreme situation. Would this be the same?

To start with he wouldn't need to find out. At this extreme range all he would be able to do was shoot high in the air and aim in the general direction of the enemy ship, with no specific target. The real test would come later.

'Nock!'

'Draw!'

'*Loose!*'

The flight of arrows went singing into the air, the wind helping it on its way. Some fell short; others reached the ship but they were almost spent and did little damage. But by the time everyone nocked a second arrow, they were closer.

Edwin tried to get himself into some kind of rhythm, but it was difficult with the target ship moving up and down and the ground bucking under his feet. He was shooting successfully – in that the arrows had left the bow and joined the rest of the flight – but he wasn't sure he'd hit anything. He didn't want to know.

His attention was distracted by a man further down the line who had rigged up some kind of sling and was attempting to throw a pot of lime. It splashed into the water well short of the French ship, and Edwin heard someone curse the man for wasting the stuff. Edwin looked at the crate. Some of the powder was in pots but there were also some more simple balls where it had been wrapped in a twist of fabric and tied off. He looked at the arrow in his hand.

'John!' He had to shout several times before he could get John's attention; he'd stopped shouting orders for each volley now and was just concentrating on his own efforts. He was barely looking down at the quiver as he reached for each successive arrow, knowing exactly where to put his hand from long years of experience, and drawing smoothly time after time.

Eventually Edwin got through to him.

'What?'

'The lime! The balls – can we shoot them?'

'Can we …? Wait.' John left his place in the line and strode to pick up one of the fabric twists. He weighed it in his hand. 'Maybe if –'

'Stop!' Edwin put out his hand. 'Turn around so it's downwind of you before you do anything.'

John faced out to sea again, riding the movement of the ship. The French vessel was now no more than a hundred yards away and the men on it were readying themselves for combat. He took an arrow. 'No … bodkin will just slide out again …' he replaced it in his quiver and selected a different one, with a larger triangular broadhead. He held the lime away from him, over the rail, as he pushed the sharp arrowhead with care through the fabric of the bag and twisted it. He gave it a slight shake. It held.

He shrugged. 'Here goes.' He nocked, drew back the string, and released.

Encumbered by the extra weight, the arrow did not fly as true as his others had done, but it traced an arc into the blue sky before landing squarely on the deck of the French ship. The bag burst, spraying powder at all those nearby. Even at this distance and upwind, the cries of alarm and pain could be heard.

Cheers sounded from their own ship and men jostled around the crate. Within a few moments many more of the poisonous shafts were on their way.

They were now only some twenty yards from the ship. They would hit it somewhere near the back, at an angle, and soon.

Along with the other archers Edwin found himself being pulled back away from the ship's rail as armed men took their place, ready to board and start the fight as soon as they were able. The enemy deck was full of staggering, choking, screaming men barely visible among the white clouds, the lime driving into their eyes as they sought to stand into the wind in order to face the oncoming enemy.

There was a crash and a judder as the two ships struck. Sailors, light on their feet, leaped across with ropes to lash the vessels together, and as soon as the gap was firmly sealed the horde of heavy, armed, jagged, yelling men poured over.

Edwin stood on the deck, catching his breath as he watched. The earl, unmistakeable in his blue and yellow checks, was safely over. So were Sir Roger and Sir Hugh, the former putting one foot on the rail and jumping to land on light feet, despite his armour, and the latter clambering over more heavily. And the tall helmeted figure behind them could only be Martin. *God and St Bartholomew keep them all safe this day.*

But there was no time to rest. The clash of weapons and the first screams of the wounded and dying had hardly started when John and Nigel were urging their fellows over too. 'Quickly now, and then get up somewhere high. Pick them off as you can. Go!'

Edwin was carried along in the rush, over the rail, on to the heaving enemy ship, and into the battle.

———◦———

Peter was playing with his toy knight. Up and down, up and down it rode, engaged on a heroic quest. And, of course, the knight had a boy with him, sharing in his adventures. They were going to go on a crusade together, to fight the devil and to see the fabulous wealth of the East, where the sun always shone and the streets were made of gold.

He was waiting for Dickon to come back, and then they were going to take some food to Sir Hugh's grooms, over at the picket, and look after Sir Roger's horse. He would want it when he came back, and Peter was determined to make sure it was well fed and that its coat was brushed until it shone. His lord would be proud of him.

Dickon skipped back into the camp area and Alf reached for a parcel of food. 'It's just bread and cheese, some dried meat – not much point cooking properly for so few of us. But we'll get the fire going and make sure there's something in the pot for later, in case they all get back before dark.'

He was in the act of handing over the pack when he stopped, his body stiffening. 'Listen.'

Peter heard it too. Shouts in the distance, the sound of metal clashing on metal. The neighing of frightened horses.

Alf was angry. 'Bastards. While the fighting men are away.' He turned to Dickon, his face grim. 'Fetch me my cleaver. And then hide, both of you.'

Peter watched as Dickon rummaged about in the stores wagon and then came back with the large, square blade. Yesterday Alf had hacked right through a leg of pork with it, bone and all.

Alf tested the edge with his thumb. More cries and the sound of fighting could be heard, louder now. He looked about him. 'Not the wagon or the tent – they'll search those for anything they can steal. Try and find a hole in the hedge, or a tree to climb. They might – they might leave you if they're only after thieving.' He didn't sound convinced.

Peter looked at Dickon. Dickon just stared at Alf, who grew more urgent. 'Quickly now. Run!'

A shake of the head. 'No.'

'You do as you're told!'

Dickon's voice was firm. 'No, Father. You brought me with you so we could stay together, so I'm not leaving you.'

'But you're all I've got! I have to keep you safe!' Alf was starting to panic, his voice sounding agonised as he tried to push Dickon away.

'And you're all I've got. I'm staying right here.'

'But —'

'No.'

With a cry of desperation, Alf gave up. 'Dear God, you sound just like your ...' He glanced at Peter. 'Never mind.'

He had a look of resignation in his eyes. Peter knew it well; he'd worn it himself often enough. It was the look you had when you'd tried everything you could to get out of an unjustified beating, and then realised there was nothing you could do so you'd better just brace yourself and take what was coming.

Alf was talking to him now. 'And I suppose it's no use telling you, either?'

Peter shook his head and drew his knife. His eyes met Dickon's. 'I have to look after you. My lord taught me that.'

He could see the surprise. 'Why?'

'Because you're my friend. And because ... well, you know why.'

Dickon nodded, slowly, and looked up at Alf. 'I didn't tell him, honest.'

Alf's face was sad now, and he sighed. 'All right. Too late for anything else, anyway.' He laid his hand briefly on each of their heads and then took a step so he was in front of them, steadying himself with care. Peter could see his broad back, his good leg and his wooden one standing firm as he sought to do the last thing a father could for his beloved child. Peter thought of Sir Roger, far away on the sea, fighting his own enemies with determination and bravery; he raised his chin and gripped the knife harder.

Alf looked over his shoulder. 'Courage, then. We'll all stand together.'

The screams and the clash of weapons came closer.

Martin felt himself yelling as he followed the earl and the knights over on to the enemy ship. He had no idea what the words were, but the very act of shouting helped him as he charged on.

His first and most important task must be to track and protect his lord; anything else relating to his own safety or anyone else's must be suppressed. Given the restricted vision afforded by the eye-slits in his helm, that meant that he needed to keep the earl more or less directly in front of him.

There he was. And what a sight! Martin spent almost every waking moment – and most of his sleeping ones – in the earl's presence, and he had become accustomed to seeing him as a figure of authority, of justice, of power wielded with the flick of a finger or a wax seal. He had, of course, also seen his lord in training, but somehow he had forgotten that as well as an earl, he was also a *knight*. And what a combatant he was proving to be today; if he hadn't been in the middle of the battle himself, Martin could have sat back and simply admired.

Despite the weight of his armour, the earl had cleared the lashed-together rails easily. Those on the enemy ship were unsteady on their feet, seemingly disoriented, which Martin put down to the clouds of white powder blowing into their faces. Nevertheless, no fewer than three armed knights made straight for the earl as he crossed, doubtless hoping to catch him while he was still off balance.

But the earl saw them coming. He used one of them to break his fall as he jumped from the rail, managing to twist in the air so he kicked out and landed on the man, bowling him over in the process. As he crouched and regained his balance he aimed a well-timed thrust at the second, using his low position to slide his sword in under his opponent's shield and hauberk. The sword came away bloodied and the man cried out and fell back.

The earl was now back on his feet and trading blows with the third assailant. Belatedly, Martin remembered his instructions about prisoners. The man who had taken the sword blow was bleeding copiously from his wound, which must be in the thigh or groin area, so he wasn't a great bet – he'd be dead before the fighting was over.

The first knight seemed only dazed; he was in no particular state to defend himself, and others were now closing in on him. The earl would not be pleased at losing such a prize when he'd been there first, so Martin drove forward, shield first, forcing lesser men out the way. The knight was wearing a proper great helm not dissimilar to his own, which would have plenty of padding underneath, so Martin took the simplest path: he walloped his sword into the back of the knight's head as he tried to rise. That knocked him flat again, allowing Martin to drop his shield, grab a fistful of his surcoat and drag him at swordpoint back out of harm's way – and away from any other grasping hands.

There were supposed to be words to say, proper words, but he couldn't remember what any of them were. Besides, between him trying to shout through his helm and the other trying to hear through his, not much of it would get through. So he just yelled the earl's name and rank as loudly as he could and pushed his captive backwards into the waiting arms of a group of the earl's men, who took his sword and bundled him back towards the other ship.

The shield was hanging awkwardly from the guige around his neck, so Martin took a moment to push his left arm back through the enarmes and settle his grip before he stepped into the fray again. More men were coming at him now, lightly armed sergeants and unarmoured sailors as well as proper combatants. He swatted them out the way while he tried with his limited vision to see the earl.

There he was, thank God, just despatching the third of his attackers after what had evidently been more of a fight. This would be no prisoner, though. As the knight yielded and stepped backwards, his foot hit the fallen body of a sailor and he tripped; he blundered back into the ship's rail and, unbalanced and top-heavy in his armour, fell backwards into the water. His despairing cry floated up to Martin before it was cut off short.

They were winning. Weren't they? The earl was driving forward, Sir Roger was over there fencing with a French knight, and Sir Hugh was barrelling through opponents as he roared like an angry bull, his sword arm rising and falling as he hacked his way through the press at the earl's shoulder. But the supply of knights and combatants on this ship seemed to be endless – where were they all coming from?

Crouched behind his shield while he continued to slash and thrust with his sword, Martin came to the realisation that he was now standing still as he fought, as was the earl up ahead. Their progress was slowing against the mass of opponents, and they were becoming mired. Soon they would be completely surrounded.

———·◦·———

Edwin's feet hit the deck of the enemy ship and he tried to regain his balance as the men around him poured forward into the crowded and hellish space. He had his bow with him but there was just too much confusion – he didn't want to shoot for fear he would hit someone on his own side.

But he must keep pressing forward. To turn and go back would mean facing into the wind, with the lime still flying around. To be blinded by that would be to invite death, with all these blades flashing around him.

What had John said? Yes – a vantage point, that was it. He scanned the deck. The fighting was mainly in front of him as the earl's men pressed forward and he had been left behind by his hesitation. The deck immediately in front of him was clear except for a few groaning wounded and a dead knight who lay in a spreading pool of blood. But it was all flat, except for …

Did he dare? And would it be any use if he did? The ship was heaving up and down on the waves, he was carrying an awkwardly long bow, and the netting ladder formed by the rigging attached to the side of the ship didn't look terribly steady. But it would make him that little bit higher than everyone else, so he might just be able to shoot over the heads of his own side and at the enemy beyond.

He slung the bow over his shoulder and made for the ropes. At least this was one advantage of wearing no armour – he managed to clamber up a few steps without too much trouble.

But of course, it wasn't as simple as that. He was riding up and down with the swell; as he tried to unsling the bow again he got himself tangled up in the ropes. Once he extricated himself, he had to let go of the ropes with both hands in order to nock an arrow, and then it was all over. A zinging noise, like a hornet, went past the side of his head and he realised with terror that he had narrowly missed death by having his brains scattered by a crossbow bolt to the head. Then the ship gave another lurch and he felt himself falling, and knew that he was going over the side …

Martin could make no move further forward. He was standing still, with hardly enough space to wield his sword as the press grew thicker. The men all around him had ceased to be men and had turned into a mass of separate arms, legs and weapons that flew about him in no kind of order. It would never stop. The earl was fighting on, Martin could see him, but he couldn't get to him. It was like a dream he'd once had where he wanted to run forward but found that his feet were stuck in mud and he was sinking.

He brought his sword crunching down on an armoured wrist that came too near him and used his superior size to push his shield hard against an opposing one, feeling it give under his strength as the man was forced back. The deck was now slippery with blood, and he had to fight hard just to keep his footing. His opponent flicked a sword out from behind his shield, but Martin kept him at arm's length – *his* arm's length – and the blow got nowhere near him. Then the Frenchman disappeared in a fountain of red as Sir Hugh's blade hacked into his neck.

That gave Martin a tiny breathing space, and he gasped in as much air as he could inside his suffocating helm. There wasn't enough of it; he couldn't suck it in fast enough. He would give the rest of his life to be able to take it off and gulp in some cool air ... but of course that was exactly what he would be risking. So he took in what little was available, damp with his own sweat, and gestured to Sir Hugh that they should try to force their way forward together in order to get closer to the earl.

Then there was some kind of movement behind him, some sort of momentum, and the press was suddenly carried forward. What —?

More shouts filled the air. Martin saw the lions of the Earl of Salisbury's surcoat as a fresh influx of men appeared and swarmed into the fray. Of course: the other ships had caught up and now they had boarded too. Surely now they would carry the day.

But the new influx of men made it even more congested on the deck, and Martin was mired again. And – oh dear Lord, what if the new group of men included some who were trying to kill not only the enemy, but the earl as well?

He shouted louder at Sir Hugh and they fought on. Martin had no idea where Adam was, or whether he was safe, and he hadn't seen Sir Roger in what seemed like an age either. But he had only one aim in mind, one purpose to his life at this moment, so he slipped and pushed and hacked and slashed his way towards his lord.

Edwin's flailing arm managed to hook round a rope, but the bow was gone. He couldn't hold on to it all at once, and his instinct for self-preservation hadn't allowed him to think. He clutched at the rope and watched as the weapon bounced off the side of the ship and hit the water. But he was alive, and he managed to swing himself around so his feet were safely over the deck before he let go. A sudden rush of men came towards him and for a moment he thought it was all over, but they were coming from the other direction; they charged past him to smash into the main hand-to-hand fight. Reinforcements. Thank the Lord.

There was no point in continuing to encumber himself with the quiver dangling from his belt. He fumbled at the ties for a moment and then drew his dagger and cut them. Then, blade in hand, no idea what he would do when he got there, he slid across the bloodied deck towards the melee.

John and Nigel were still shooting. They were standing together by the side rail of the ship and – as Edwin had unsuccessfully tried to do – were aiming over the heads of their own men. As Edwin watched, John lowered his arm and let fly straight at an enemy rushing towards him. Such was the force of the arrow at short range that the man was sent flying backwards as the arrow thumped into him, landing like a crumpled doll.

But others were upon them now, and John had no chance to nock another arrow. One of the onrushing men paused, and Edwin thought he'd been scared off – until he noticed the crossbow being brought up to its release position. He couldn't miss from here. *This was it.* Edwin closed his eyes and prayed, but felt nothing. Nothing, that is, except the spray of hot liquid as Nigel screamed in agony beside him. The bolt had taken off half his face and Edwin wanted to vomit as he saw his companion shrieking and clutching at what was left of his head before he fell. *You saved him in the forest just so he could die more painfully here.*

Edwin lunged forward with his dagger and stabbed the crossbow-man, causing him to fall back, although he wasn't dead. A sergeant brandishing a hatchet was bearing down on John, but Edwin had been carried too far forward by his own stroke and couldn't recover in time to put himself between them. He cried out a warning.

John should surely drop his bow and draw his own blade, but he didn't, preferring instead to use it as a stave as he whipped it around and hit the enemy in the face. But it was no good; the man was barely scratched and came again at John together with another; a third screamed obscenities at Edwin from a twisted, inhuman face as he raised a blade. They were going to die.

It was then that an armoured figure in a green and gold surcoat – Sir Roger, said the part of Edwin's mind that was still functioning – appeared from nowhere and slashed at Edwin's opponent, not pausing to see his relief or hear his incoherent words before his sword bit into the neck of one of John's attackers, sending blood high in an arc over them all. The axe fell to the floor and Edwin stooped to pick it up. It would be better than his knife.

But in the time it took for him to turn on John's remaining assailant, it was too late. Edwin could only watch helplessly as the Frenchman barged into his friend, and they both fell back and over the side of the ship.

Martin's single-minded determination to reach the earl faltered as he caught sight, through his narrow eye-slits, of the device. The lions of Salisbury, but not the full-size ones of the earl himself: the smaller emblem worn by his squire. The man fighting not two paces away from him, his attention focused on those in front, was Philip.

In the heat of battle, anything could happen. Men could be killed by chance, by accident … or by design. And who would know the difference? When this was all over and the bodies were counted, one more with a sword wound would not be conspicuous. And even if the wound were to the side or to the back, who could guess from that the identity of the attacker? The melee was so confused that men were being turned about all over the place – although those who faced into the wind were faring worse, so Martin had tried to avoid it.

His inattention almost cost him his own life. His left arm had slackened ever so slightly, and a dagger found its way behind his shield. He saw it just in time to shift backwards, causing only a glancing blow that slashed his surcoat without damaging the mail, or at least he couldn't feel anything. He thrust his sword forward and was rewarded by feeling some kind of hit; he couldn't see what or to whom, but the arm holding the dagger fell back.

Philip was still there. He could be dead in moments and nobody would know. Martin went as far as shifting his weight a little in preparation.

But you'll know, said a voice deep inside him. *You'll spend the rest of your life knowing that you murdered a fellow squire.* For murder it would be: to stab a man in the back, knowingly, when that man was on your own side in the battle. He couldn't do it. He wouldn't.

A bellowing Frenchman, drenched in blood, had killed the sergeant in front of Martin and he now aimed a blow at Philip while Philip's attention was engaged elsewhere. Without thinking, Martin ran him through, kicking him off the end of his sword before stepping away so that Philip would never know who had saved his life.

They were moving again now. The impetus provided by the new men had forced the French to give ground, and they were clustered towards what was the front of the ship, on and in front of the steps that went up to the higher part of the deck.

Sweat was pouring into Martin's eyes. He had no free hand to bring up to his face, and the gesture would have been futile anyway given the helm. He shook his head as best he could. The earl was still fighting ferociously, and Martin was proud. Everyone would know how courageous his lord was, for he stood out clearly in that checked surcoat. Salisbury and Arundel were both near him.

But the French had one final throw of the dice. Along the higher part of the deck, a line of crossbowmen had formed. They were aiming down into the thick of the press. Dear God, no – surely they wouldn't shoot while their own men were there?

'Shoot them down, by God's blood!' came a cry from somewhere off to Martin's right, but the resulting volley of arrows was feeble – either the archers of his own side had run out of arrows or they were all dead.

One or two of the crossbowmen did fall, and some sporadic arrows continued, but the line was still firm enough for them all to raise their weapons to their shoulders on command.

Panicked warnings sounded from the fight below, but there was nowhere for the knights and men there to get out of the way. Damn it, why couldn't he get there, why couldn't he *move*? He redoubled his efforts, almost crying with the effort of the repeated blows, the shrieking of his muscles.

The warning had got through, and some of those in the press managed to raise their shields to protect themselves from the deadly rain of bolts. Martin, a head taller than those around him, could see it all clearly. But in raising them they left themselves exposed below, and opponents without shields took full advantage, diving and thrusting and hacking. Martin heard himself screaming at the top of his voice as he watched the earl fall.

Chapter Twelve

Edwin rushed to the side of the ship. The Frenchman was gone, given up to the hunger of the sea, but John had managed to grab something – some protruding bit of wood, Edwin didn't know what it was – and was gripping it with the fingers of one hand. They were turning white with the effort of holding his entire weight. His bow was still clasped in the other and his feet scrabbled, dangling above the waves as the ship rode the swell.

Edwin dropped his weapons on the deck and leaned over as far as he could, clutching at John's arm and shoulder. He had him. He had handfuls of his tunic. But —

'I can't pull you up! I'm too far over!'

John tried to heave himself up with his one hand, but he couldn't, not even with Edwin's help.

'You'll have to drop the bow! If you use both hands you can climb up over me!'

John shook his head. 'Never.'

'For God's sake – you'll die!'

John stopped struggling. He hung as a dead weight. 'Let me go, then.'

'What? No!'

'Plenty of others have died – one more won't matter. And you can't stand there with your back to it all.'

Edwin could hear Sir Roger still fighting behind him, so he was safe from direct attack for a few moments, but even the knight couldn't stop a crossbow bolt reaching him, and he felt how broad a target his back must seem. He tried to pull, but John was heavier than he was, and his arms were already tiring from holding the weight, feeling as though they were stretching longer and longer. They were pulled so straight that he couldn't bend them, and they would surely be wrenched from their sockets soon. He couldn't lift. And he was so far over the rail, almost upside down and looking at John's face and the churning waves below, that he couldn't get enough purchase with his feet to try and inch his way back. They were stuck.

John's voice was level. 'Let me go. You don't need to die with me.'

Tears welled in Edwin's eyes as his fingers dug further into the fabric of John's tunic. They were weakening and he could feel them beginning to slip. He spoke through clenched teeth. 'I've seen too many friends die to lose another one now.' But the strain was too much. His arms were screaming, his fingers starting to open of their own accord …

There was a rush behind them and Edwin thought, again, that his last moment had come. Was it to be a stab in his unprotected back? His body was under such tension that he couldn't even flinch. *Please let it be quick.*

But he heard Sir Roger's voice. 'Help him, quickly – I'll hold them off!'

And then men were around him at the rail, hands were pulling him back, arms were reaching down to John, the weight on him was lifted; John was hauled up and they were both back on the deck.

It was Stephen, the sailor, and some of his companions. Edwin started to gasp out thanks but John was on his feet again immediately, bow still in hand. He grinned at Stephen. 'I owe you. Let's kill some more of them.'

Stephen raised empty hands. 'Love to. But I'll have to bite them.'

Edwin had by now picked up both his weapons; wordlessly, he handed the axe to Stephen. It was better than the dagger, but he couldn't part with that. Besides, his arms were so sore he didn't think he'd be able to swing it anyway.

Sir Roger had moved a few paces away, his opponents beaten back, and Edwin could see the main press ahead. It looked brutal. It was then that he saw the line of crossbowmen on the high front deck and he cried out to John in a panic just as he heard the shouted order to shoot.

John said nothing, taking aim and bringing down one man, but very few other arrows followed, and the volley of bolts was still going to happen. Edwin started to run but John seized him, pulling him back. 'Oh no. Not right into the middle, not with no armour. Stay round the edge and see who you can pick off.' He nocked another arrow and searched for a likely target.

Edwin didn't know what to do. He was dazed, at once confused by everything that had happened, exhausted from his efforts, weak with the relief of being saved from the water, and stunned by the savage violence around him. If someone had asked his name, he'd have been hard-pressed to answer.

He stood next to John, dagger drawn. *Think.* Yes, John was right: diving headfirst into the melee in nothing but his tunic would be certain death. And, heroic as it might be, it would serve no purpose. He would be more help fending off any direct attack at John, who was still shooting with steady hands.

So he stood. And thus it was that, for the second time in as many days, Edwin saw clearly actions that would be the subject of ale-soaked reminiscence among the earl's men for years to come.

He and John were not the only ones to be standing off from the main press awaiting their opportunity. Hovering behind and around were a number of boys and youths, squires who were ready to re-arm their lords if needed. One of them was Adam – alive and unharmed – but Edwin had no time to let the relief soak in before he saw the boy fling himself into the crowd of noise and men and blades, carrying the earl's shield.

What in heaven's name? But there was the earl, lying on the deck. Edwin could catch only glimpses of him as others shifted their positions. He was alive, but men were closing in, hacking down at him ...

And there was Adam, his slight frame dodging through the press and miraculously avoiding death and injury. He had no weapon, but as he reached his lord he flung himself across the prone form and held the shield up with both hands. Swords slashed down; axes and maces battered; he held it firm.

Edwin's attention was diverted by an attempted attack on John, but Stephen finished the man off before Edwin could react, hacking the axe into his chest. He held up the dripping weapon and grinned at Edwin. 'Nice! Just wait until I see that monk.' He stepped forward to engage another. Lord, he looked like he was *enjoying* himself.

He couldn't be, of course, not really. But he was carried away by the moment, as were men all around them. They had become less than human. Those faces Edwin could see were contorted, snarling masks of hate and violence, while between them stalked the grim and faceless knights and armoured sergeants, masked harbingers of pain and death.

Helms covering faces ... Martin! Where was Martin? Edwin scanned the melee, sure he'd be in the middle of it all. And there he was, laying about him wildly as he sought to get nearer to where the earl was lying. And that shorter, burlier figure hacking its way through the press next to him had to be Sir Hugh. They were gaining, only yards away now. Closer ... Edwin couldn't see Adam, but the shield was still up. *He will stand there and he will take it because he knows it is right*, echoed in Edwin's head. How long could he hold before Martin got there?

Edwin grabbed at John's arm as he reached for one of the few remaining arrows in his quiver. 'Can you get any of those men there? The ones attacking my lord earl?' He pointed.

'Are you mad? Nobody could …' But one knight, suddenly rearing above the others to raise his sword as high as possible, fell back with an arrow in his chest. Even mail wouldn't stop a bodkin at this range.

Martin was there now, so Edwin shouted at John not to loose again. The sight was both awe-inspiring and terrifying. All the other combatants, all the surrounding confusion, seemed to fade away as Edwin focused only on his friend, watching and praying and willing him on. Martin planted his feet and stood astride the earl's fallen form so none could reach him while he still stood. His sword whirled almost faster than Edwin could see, slashing, crunching, forcing enemies back, while his shield took blow after blow after sickening blow. Armed French knights clustered about him, although whether they wanted to test themselves against such a great fighter or whether they were simply yelling at him to yield and surrender, to give up himself and his fallen prize, Edwin didn't know. But Martin paid no attention to any of them and Edwin knew that he was – temporarily at least – not the Martin he knew, but rather a ferocious instrument of violence and death.

The press was thinning. Shouts and cheers started to sound. Edwin thought at first that they were something to do with Martin, but either he couldn't hear or he was ignoring them, for he still stood tall, streaked in blood that Edwin hoped belonged to others, and with a growing pile of bodies around him.

John seized Edwin by the shoulders and shook him. 'Look!'

He was pointing at the high deck, where the Frenchman they'd identified earlier as the one in charge was holding up both his arms. He shouted something that nobody heard, given that he was still wearing his helm, and then in an unmistakeable gesture he reversed his sword and handed it to the Earl of Salisbury, who was opposite him.

The cheering grew louder, and John was thumping Edwin on the back. 'We did it! We won!'

Edwin almost staggered with relief. The French were surrendering.

Free from the danger of attack, he could now sweep his gaze along the carnage that covered the whole ship. And beyond: for the first time, he realised that other battles had been fought on other ships, and that they too were yielding.

Thank the Lord. The French fleet would not reach London. They would not march north to destroy everything Edwin loved. And here, as well, the bloodshed would be over.

But he was wrong. Still feeling the exhilaration of the fighting, of their dances with death, the soldiers and sailors of his own side were whooping in triumph and whirling their weapons. As Edwin watched in horror, they began to massacre their surrendering opponents, cutting and slicing and hacking even as they held up their arms or fell to their knees, and throwing the bleeding and dismembered bodies over the side into the sea. The white foam turned red as the waves lapped against the side of the ship.

Edwin cried out in despair, but there was nothing he could do against such bloodlust. He couldn't stop them; he would only invite his own death or injury if he tried to get in the way. He watched with a numb mind as several shrieking Frenchmen threw themselves into the water, where they would surely drown, in order to save themselves from the bloody slaughter.

Still not sated, the howling mob advanced on the group of French knights now clustered on the high deck, but here they were pushed back by a more disciplined guard of armed troops from their own side. Of course, thought Edwin, those nobles will want to save their prisoners for ransom, not lose their chance of gain. And besides, half of them are probably related to each other.

And then, somewhere, a cry went up that Eustace the Monk had not yet been found. Immediately the rabble was off like a pack of hunting dogs, swarming all around the ship, up and down ladders and in and out of all sorts of spaces and holes that Edwin hadn't even known existed.

Eustace was an enemy, but Edwin found himself praying that the man was already dead, terrified of what might be his fate at the hands of the blood-crazed horde ... and of what he himself might be forced to witness.

It wasn't long before the pack was in full cry after sighting its quarry; three men were dragged up from the bowels of the ship. They were all gabbling, pleading for their lives. But was one of them Eustace?

'That's him!' It was Stephen, pointing with the axe Edwin had given him, the blood on it now starting to congeal. He strode forward. 'That's the bastard.' He walked up to the man in the middle and spat in his face.

'Please, please ... I'll give you anything. Ten thousand marks of silver!'

The mob hooted and howled with derision. Stephen played up to them, shouting as much to them as to Eustace himself. 'I'll tell you what – I'll give you a choice!'

The ghost of hope flitted across the man's face, and Edwin felt sorry for him. *Please, don't be too cruel.* But then he remembered what Stephen had said about the girl he was going to marry, and her friends.

Stephen continued. 'Your choice! You can have your head cut off on that machine there,' – he pointed to the timbers that would be used to construct the trebuchet – 'or right here on this rail!'

Eustace's reply was drowned out amid raucous cheers, as was any attempt by the nobles to pause and see if his ransom offer was serious. Edwin tried not to look but he saw the axe rise and fall, heard the wet thump and the huge cheer, and then – oh God – saw the dripping head borne aloft as it was thrust on a stick. Suddenly the heaving of the ship was matched by a heaving in his stomach, and he retched over the side before collapsing to huddle in a corner away from the blood that slicked all over the deck, closing his eyes to shut out the sights all around him.

———•———

Martin woke up.

That was the only way he could describe it to himself; he had almost no recollection of what he had been doing, except that he had needed to protect the earl. And this he had done, and this he had continued to do, unaware of how much time had passed, until he realised that there was nobody left in front of him.

He sucked in more sweaty, fetid air as best he could from inside the helm and peered out through his eye-slits. Nobody in front, nobody attacking from the side … the battle was over. The French knights around him had fallen back and were surrendering to eager takers. There was nobody left to fight, and he was still standing.

But there was something else. The men around him were pointing at him, whispering, talking behind their hands. What …?

He tried to move and found to his surprise that he couldn't. Dear God, had something happened to his legs that he hadn't felt yet? But they were still there; the reason he couldn't take a step was that he was knee-deep in bodies. Some were wounded, stirring and groaning; others were dead, the victims of horrific injuries. It was a scene of utter carnage, and it would appear from the evidence and from the attitude of those around him that he had caused most of it.

Martin looked at his sword, still clenched in a right hand that didn't feel part of him. It was glistening red from the point to the hilt, as was his mail glove and sleeve. More blood was splattered all over the front of his surcoat. What had he *done*?

There was some kind of commotion behind him, howls of pain and splashes, but there was no accompanying clash of weapons, so he didn't bother looking round. He remained motionless, bloodied sword in hand, waiting for his mind to re-inhabit his body.

The earl! Dear God, what was he doing standing around when he should be helping his lord?

Casting his sword to the deck – *don't sheathe it or it will stick and you'll never get it all clean again*, said the voice of his long years of training – Martin slid the stifling helm off and enjoyed the sudden hit of fresh, salty air to his face and his wet hair. He took in several gulps. A drink would be good, but that would have to wait. He knelt and began to roll bodies to one side. That arm sticking out of the bottom of the pile, on the deck, surely that was …? Yes, it must be – he recognised some small repairs to the mail on the back of the hand. And the hand itself was moving. The earl was alive. Thank the Lord.

The corpses had some terrible injuries, wounds he could hardly bear to look at now, in the clear light of day and with unrestricted sight. Surely he, Martin, hadn't caused all this? He couldn't have. Why, that man there was almost – but never mind that now. He had to put such thoughts away for the present, had to push them down and hide them until he had the time to go over them in peace. For now he had to get the earl out, had to move the heavy weight of men and armour off him before he suffocated.

He neared the bottom of the heap, and a shield came into view. Blue and gold checks – his lord's.

No. A flash of recollection hit him without warning, and he saw again the picture of Adam flinging himself into the fray with the spare in order to protect the earl until Martin could get there. Good lad.

He shifted the shield, which was lying over both of them together.

'Come on then, up you get. You've been through it in the last few days, haven't you? You'll need some time off.'

Adam didn't move, limp and face down over his now-stirring lord. 'Come on now. Get up.' Was that his own voice, sounding so unsteady? His mouth was dry as he reached out to shake the younger boy by the shoulder. 'Adam?'

'Adam?'

———•———

Edwin gripped the rail as the dock came into sight. He was back on the earl's ship now; half of the sailors and men had made their way back before the ties that bound the two vessels were loosed, with the rest staying on the great French ship to guard the prisoners and to take over the sailing after the massacre of the French crew. Edwin would see their faces all his life, watch over and over again as their eyes opened wide with terror at the sight of the blades swinging towards them; he would hear their screams as they died or flung themselves into the water to face a different kind of death. The sea had swallowed them all, the living and the dead, and their cries were heard no longer.

Nigel was among the fallen, as Edwin already knew; his shattered face had howled and shrieked its agony for some while before the sound broke off abruptly, and Edwin wondered whether he had died from the injury or whether a comrade had put him out of his misery. John had remained on the French ship, filling his hands and his tunic with coins as they were plundered from the heavy kists dragged out on to the deck. The nobles had found out what was going on and put a stop to it, wanting the hard silver to go along with their rich ransom promises, but Edwin had no doubt that John and many others would find a way of keeping some of their booty.

On the subject of booty, now he had leisure to look about him Edwin couldn't help noticing that Hubert de Burgh's ship, having finally managed to turn around, had sailed in at the very end of the engagement and had claimed two French ships as prizes. Edwin had spotted John Marshal on the deck and he rather uncharitably wondered how long it would be before tales spread through the host about him winning the battle single-handed.

He returned his attention to their own ship. Sir Roger was standing next to him. He had saved Edwin's life, surely, by protecting his back when he was hanging over the side of the ship; he had taken no prisoners himself and seemed glad to volunteer to make his way back to a deck that wasn't smeared and soaked in blood. He had assured Edwin that he had seen both the earl and Martin upright and seemingly unharmed. Now he stood staring at the open expanse of the sea, saying nothing, his lips moving in silent prayer.

As they approached the town of Sandwich, Edwin could see the dock lined with men. Some were holding the reins of horses – of course, they'd have been able to see them coming and would have brought mounts for the nobles. Others were simply waving.

But something wasn't right. Obviously, news of the victory could not have reached the town, for theirs was the first ship back and they would share the happy tidings themselves. But the cheerful waving from the mast and ropes, and the fact that a French ship was limping in behind them, must surely have given a clue? So why did the gesticulating seem so urgent, why were the men cupping their hands around their mouths and shouting themselves hoarse in an attempt to make their voices heard over the wind?

Sir Roger picked up on the atmosphere. 'Something is wrong.'

They continued on their way, nearing land no faster or slower than they had before, but Edwin was tense. He willed the wind to carry them on.

Finally they docked, ropes being thrown across and made fast, a gangplank laid. Edwin was one of the first down it. He ran straight for a man he recognised as being a groom in the earl's household, but by then he'd already heard the shouted news: there had been an attack on the camp in their absence.

Sir Roger was just behind him, and Edwin heard him gasp as though he had been struck. The groom knew only that the raid had been swift, some horses and goods stolen, some casualties sustained, before the attackers had fled back the way they had come with their gains. Men loyal to Louis, no doubt, hoping to cause some damage.

Edwin had heard little past the word 'casualties', and neither had Sir Roger. The knight was now on the move, but Edwin called him back – there was no way he could run all the way back to camp in that heavy armour. He scanned the dockside. The man he'd been talking to was holding the earl's own horse, and it would be more than their lives were worth to take that. But …

He seized Sir Roger's arm. 'There! That's the horse Martin rides, that tall one. He won't mind.'

The knight nodded and commandeered the animal. With an astonishing energy and agility, given how long he'd been armed and how arduously he had fought, he sprang into the saddle. He held out a hand to Edwin.

Edwin took it and hauled himself up behind – the horse was big and could surely manage both of them over a short distance. And then they were off, bowling their way through the crowd on the dock, past startled onlookers who had begun to trickle out on to the streets of the town as news of the victory had filtered through, and out the gates. Sir Roger put his heels to the horse's flank and they gained speed as they galloped up to the camp. Edwin held on to his belt and prayed, trying not to imagine the sights that might greet them when they got there.

Chapter Thirteen

Sir Roger threw himself off the horse as they reached the earl's pavilion, and Edwin tumbled after him. *Oh please, Lord …*

In front of the doorway stood Brother William and Humphrey, both labouring for breath but upright and alive. Edwin spotted little Hugh inside, looking unhurt, thank God.

Humphrey was pale and bleeding from a gash to his forehead, but he held a bloodied sword in his hand and there was a body at his feet.

Brother William was the spectre from a nightmare.

He was surrounded by sprawling figures, some dead, some groaning and twitching. His white robe was sprayed all over with blood and drenched in it from the hem to the knee; the loose sleeves were dripping red and the cudgel in his hand was covered in gore and bits of things Edwin didn't want to think about. He also had a crossbow bolt embedded in the upper part of his left arm, a fact of which he seemed to become aware only when Edwin pointed wordlessly at it.

The monk's voice came out in gasps. 'We're fine – never mind us – some got past – check on the others – servants – boys …'

Sir Roger was already off, sprinting as fast as his armour and his exhaustion would allow, and Edwin followed him. They dodged through the labyrinth of the camp, tripping and skipping over tent ropes, scattered baggage and bodies.

Without warning, Edwin thumped into the knight's mailed back: he had stopped dead. Edwin peered round him and felt the ice close around his heart.

Alf was on his side by the ashes of the fire, his wooden leg smashed and his entrails spilling out of a gaping wound in his stomach. He was still alive, trying to drag himself nearer to Dickon; the dark, slick trail of blood across the earth showed that he had somehow made a yard or two from where he had originally fallen. It was no use, though: Dickon lay unmoving, wide eyes staring at the bright afternoon sky. A crossbow bolt through the heart pinned the body to the ground, and the expression on the small, pale face was one of surprise rather than pain, so Edwin hoped at least that it had been quick.

And there, in front of his friends, lay the body of little Peter.

His death had not been so easy: his lips were drawn back in a snarl and his chest was covered in vicious stab wounds. A knife was gripped tightly in his right hand, and his left arm was flung out wide as though he had tried to protect Dickon to the end.

Sir Roger had been standing in stunned, disbelieving silence, but now a howl escaped him and his knees buckled.

Edwin wanted to join him by Peter's side, wanted to cry his eyes out at the sight, wanted to kick and smash things to overcome his sense of powerlessness, wanted to rail against the absolute futility of it all, the tragedy, the *waste*. But a groan from Alf stopped him, and Edwin hurried to kneel at his side. He was aware of other men arriving behind them, exclaiming at the scene of horror, but he had no mind for them. He gathered Alf in his arms as best he could, trying not to hurt him even more. He looked around for something he could press over the wound, but there was nothing and he could do nothing. They were all dead and dying, these men and boys who had been ordered to stay away from the fight, and he could not help.

'Dickon …' Alf's lips hardly moved.

'I'm sorry, Alf, so sorry, but he's dead.'

A bloodied hand clutched at Edwin's tunic. 'Don't let them …'

Edwin tried to comfort him. 'They're all gone. Nothing will happen to him now.'

Alf grimaced with pain and tried again, his breath coming in shallow gasps. 'You don't understand ...'

Perhaps. Perhaps there was one thing Edwin could do for the dying man. His suspicions had been growing for some while, and the desperation in Alf's voice now made him sure he was right. He bent his head close to Alf's ear. 'Listen to me. Know that nobody has touched ... *her.* A crossbow bolt to the heart, a quick death, no fear, no pain. She is with the Lord and at peace. She is safe. *Nobody knows.*'

Alf's eyes were becoming unfocused but Edwin thought he had understood. He may as well keep talking if it was bringing him a crumb of comfort. 'Your daughter? And you didn't want to leave her behind.' There was blood everywhere, black blood, bright red blood and the grotesque blue inside parts of a man dying in agony. But Alf was still aware of him. What else to say? 'You're a fine father. She loved you, she saw you every day, you took care of her.'

Alf moved his lips once more, and Edwin caught the last whispered words. 'Until now. Couldn't protect ... forgive ... bury us together.' He swallowed. 'Please.'

'I will.' There was no point trying to give false hope about survival – no man could live through such a terrible injury. Indeed, he would not last more than another few moments. But one more thing ... 'Alf. Alf, can you still hear me? What was her name? Her name, so that I can say it over the grave. Alf?'

Alf opened his eyes wide. 'Edith,' he said, quite clearly.

And then he died.

Edwin sat for a long moment, his eyes and mind blank, then he laid the cook down with care. He went over to Dickon – for Dickon the name must remain to all except Edwin and the Lord – and picked up the child. He held the body for a moment and then placed it next to Alf. He would ensure they remained together, come what may.

Finally he was able to kneel next to the grieving Sir Roger, whose eyes were still locked on the small, twisted body before him.

'I sent him away. I said I would keep him safe. *Safe*!'

What was there to say? There was nothing, so Edwin gripped the knight's shoulder in sympathy and watched the tears – of sorrow, of pain, of anger, of guilt – course down his face. His own eyes were burning.

Voices sounded from behind them. Those men who had followed Edwin and Sir Roger had, after their initial shock, moved on through the camp, and Edwin could hear various shouts and cries for attention for wounded men and boys. The group now approaching was more measured, and Edwin turned to see the regent himself, surrounded by several lords and bishops. The old man was pristine in his bright surcoat, no blood or sweat or other men's entrails on him.

Edwin scrambled to his feet and hauled Sir Roger up with him. The regent looked from one to the other and then at Peter's body. 'Your boy?'

Sir Roger, incapable of speech, nodded.

The regent clapped him briefly on the back. 'My condolences.' He gazed down at Peter again and nodded. 'There's blood on his knife, and all his wounds are to the front. He would have made a fine knight.'

His companions murmured assent and they all moved on, their interest in one dead boy fading. Edwin removed his foot from on top of Sir Roger's, where he had pressed it in an attempt to stop the ill-advised retort of a grief-stricken man.

Once he was sure that the lords were out of earshot he spoke, urgently. 'A fine knight. Just think about that. How proud he would have been.' Sir Roger made no reply. 'You and I know he was a servant, not a page, but the lord regent judged him by what he saw, judged him by his actions. And he died bravely. *A fine knight.*'

Was Sir Roger just starting to turn that over in his mind? What else could he say? 'And … it's not a bad epitaph for a starving beggar boy who never thought he'd leave Conisbrough.'

A huge sob escaped the knight. After a few moments those piercing blue eyes met Edwin's. 'He – he did seem to enjoy these last months.'

'He did. I know he did. He spoke with such pride of serving you, and it meant so much to him. You did a good thing when you took him on.'

Sir Roger rubbed his gloved palms over his face. 'I felt the Lord telling me to.' He looked at Edwin with eyes that were still red but no longer dripping. 'But as the Lord gives, so does He take away … I won't be able to take him all the way back to Conisbrough to lie with his family, will I?'

'No. But perhaps we could bury him along with Alf and … Dickon. They were friends, after all.'

'Very well.'

Sir Roger knelt once more. Gently he opened Peter's fingers to remove the knife and tucked it in the boy's belt. 'A knight should be buried with his sword.' He reached out and closed the eyes, muttered a brief and heartfelt prayer, and slid his arms under the body. 'I'll lay him next to the others. See if you can find something to cover them with, and I'll have the men start digging.'

Edwin nodded and started to move away. Then he stopped to pick up the broken figure of a toy knight. 'Sir Roger?'

'Yes?'

'I've never felt more like killing anyone than I do now.'

Sir Roger turned to face him, the dead boy cradled in his arms. 'I know. Curious, then, that we should now finally be at peace.'

Martin looked down at the silent figure on the cot. He was still alive, but he would be dead in a matter of days, if not hours. Nobody could survive wounds like that; the only thing Martin could do for him was to pray that death would come swiftly so as not to prolong the agony. He'd helped to carry him off the ship, load him on a litter slung between two horses, and transport him back to the camp; he'd stood by while an attempt was made to treat the horrific injuries. But it was to no avail, and now he wondered if it might not have been more merciful just to –

A murmur. He was not quite conscious, eyes closed but the lids fluttering as he drifted on a sea of pain. Bandages covered his chest and stomach, but blood and other noxious liquids were already seeping through. Martin didn't like to touch them for fear of making things worse, so he knelt to wipe the beads of sweat away from the forehead. As he did so, he leaned in to whisper 'I'm sorry.'

Brother William entered the tent. His left arm was tightly bound: he'd made Martin pull the bolt out, a sickening act he'd never forget as he remembered the sensation of the flesh tearing under his hand. At least it had been a bolt, with its square, armour-piercing head, and not a broadhead arrow that could have caused unimaginable damage – it had come away almost cleanly. Men did still die from such wounds, though, and Brother William, walking and talking now, might be lying on a cot of his own tomorrow, screaming in agony as he turned black and poisonous. Even he let out a grunt of pain during the removal process, but he hadn't been too bothered by the subsequent copious bleeding, which he said would help, although Martin couldn't work out how that might be. Still, bleeding was the recommended cure for many things, wasn't it? Then, bizarrely, the monk had told Humphrey to pour a cup of the earl's best wine over the wound before binding it, which must have stung to high heaven.

He should probably be resting, letting the unscathed such as Martin care for their wounded, but there were many and he was a monk, so he'd hefted a bag of salves in his good right hand and said it was his duty. He was still wearing the gore-soaked robe in which Martin had first seen him after the battle; there was no point changing it before dealing with bloody slashes and cuts or he'd only sully another. As he neared the cot, Martin could see that the stains had soaked into the unbleached wool and dried out, making the garment stiff and crusty.

The monk knelt and spoke a brief prayer. Once his eyes were open again he took the cloth from Martin's hand. 'I'll stay here. You'd better go and see to Adam.'

Martin nodded and stood, taking a silent and probably final farewell of Sir Hugh. He ducked out the doorway and stood for a moment, rubbing his tired eyes. The survivors from among Sir Hugh's men were sitting about in a loose and silent circle, with Edwin and Sir Roger among them. Martin had heard about Sir Roger's loss, but he had avoided speaking to him about it as he just didn't know what to say. There were only so many times in a day a man could say 'I'm sorry' about a violent death.

He was glad when it was Edwin, rather than the knight, who made his way over. Edwin had a look of enquiry on his face and Martin shook his head. 'I'm sorry.' There it was again.

The men about him continued to stare at the ground. But another was approaching: to Martin's surprise, it was Humphrey. Had he come to summon him back to the lord earl? But Humphrey gave him only the briefest nod before entering the tent. Martin heard him speak to Brother William. 'Perhaps you'd better go. There are others you might be able to save. I'll stay here with him until –'

Brother William murmured something and issued forth from the tent. He moved to place a hand on Sir Roger's shoulder and offer what comfort he could before heading off.

Martin stood with Edwin, who seemed as loath to break the silence as he was. He could hear Humphrey moving inside the tent, perhaps settling himself on a stool for his vigil. Martin's dazed mind couldn't connect the two men, couldn't work out why the earl's marshal should want to sit with the dying knight, so the word, when it came, hit him hard.

'Father. Father, can you hear me?'

Martin looked in astonishment at Edwin, who shrugged. 'Didn't you know?'

'How could I possibly …' Everything was taking its time to sink into Martin's mind this afternoon, and this was no exception. 'You mean, you did know?'

'Of course. They're not actually that different when you think about it.'

Martin couldn't process that. The tough, bluff, bellicose old knight and the smooth steward who was … well, Martin wouldn't go quite as far as calling him 'effeminate', but still.

Edwin was shaking his head. 'If I'd known you didn't know, I'd have said something. They have different paths in life, yes, but the same determination to do things right, and to serve the earl. And if Sir Hugh shaved his beard off, or Humphrey grew one, you'd see they look quite alike. I can't believe you never noticed.'

Martin was trying to force himself to think clearly. 'He's Sir Hugh's heir?'

'No. He has an older brother who is a knight and who will inherit, so he had to make his own way in the world. Sir Hugh wanted him to train as a knight anyway, to get a place in someone's household, but Humphrey preferred something different. They argued about it.'

Martin stood in silence, but he was too close to the tent. He could hear Humphrey continuing, sounding agonised as he poured out words into the ear of a man who in all likelihood couldn't hear them. 'Father, I know I've always been a disappointment to you, but …'

Martin didn't need or want to hear this – it was between the two of them and he had no place intruding. Instead he took Edwin by the elbow and steered him away to the edge of the camp. 'I probably haven't got much time, because I need to get back to my lord and Adam, but I just wanted to say …' he trailed off.

'Yes?'

'I…' But now it came to it, he couldn't put it into words. If he could, then Edwin was the right person to talk to, Edwin was the one who might understand, but he couldn't. Not today. 'It doesn't matter. You go back and stay with Sir Roger, and I'll try to find you later.'

Edwin was looking at him in the way that he had – a shrewd glance that probably saw straight through him. But he didn't push the matter. 'All right. Talk to me when you're ready. And look after Adam.'

Martin made his way back through the camp. It should have been full of raucous man celebrating their victory, celebrating their survival, their life, their new-found riches; but the attack on the camp that had cost the lives of servants, children and even some women had dampened their enthusiasm. The men sitting around fires and drinking hard were doing so to toast absent friends and to forget, not to celebrate.

He slowed his pace, wanting a few precious moments to himself. The jumble of things that he'd wanted to say – to confess – to Edwin were distilling themselves into separate thoughts. The first was that, now he looked back at the event as a whole, he'd been nervous before the fighting began, but once it had started he had – there was no other word for it – enjoyed himself. While he was fighting he could feel his strength, feel that he was doing something he was good at, feel that he had untapped reserves that could go on forever. He had lost himself in the sensation, and crucially he had been able to forget everything else. All his worries about his lord, about his own life, about Joanna … all had disappeared. They had been replaced with something wonderful, something pure, and he wanted to feel that way again. He craved it.

In some ways there was nothing wrong with that – he was going to be a knight, after all, and a lord had no use for a knight who was afraid of battle. But there was more to it. When he had come back to himself, it was like he was falling, crashing down, and the feeling had been made ten times worse by seeing the havoc he had wreaked. The death, the agony … all down to him. And not just enemies, either: Sir Hugh had been at his side as they had powered their way through the press to reach the earl; Sir Hugh had also stood and defended his lord. But Martin had forgotten him. As the red mist had descended, as he'd come to see nothing except the enemies in front who must be cut down, he had lost any awareness of a comrade by his side, and he had left the old man to fight alone. One of the thoughts that would torture him from now on was the question of whether, if he'd kept his head a little more, one of the lord earl's most loyal retainers and bravest warriors might not now be leaching his lifeblood away in a close and stinking tent.

And that, of course, led him on to the second thought that would plague him in the darkness of the night. He had seen the unprotected back of a man he loathed and had felt the urge to stab it. A man fighting on the same side. In the back. He had managed to stop himself, but only just. And when he replayed the incident over and over, he knew in the depths of his soul that if he were put in the same situation again, *he might not be able to hold back.*

He had reached the earl's pavilion. It was now imperative that he appear normal, so he took a moment to compose himself.

Martin entered and was immediately thrown off balance by the sight of the Earl of Salisbury. Startled, he looked about him for Philip, but the earls were alone. There was some movement off in the service area to his right, but Martin couldn't face going in there. Instead he went to the sleeping area to check on Adam.

He was asleep, but it seemed to be genuine sleep rather than unconsciousness. He had been knocked out while he sought to protect the earl; he had been holding the shield over his lord rather than over himself as the blows rained down, and one of them had caught him on the back of the head. He'd only been wearing a pot helm, but that and the padded coif beneath had saved the worst of the damage: he had a lump on the back of his head but no cut, no bleeding. Remarkably, he had suffered no further injury while lying prone: whether this was because the men about him thought him already dead, or whether they recognised – even in the heat of their own moments – that he was a boy wearing no mail, Martin didn't know, but he thanked God and all the saints for it.

Adam had been among those who were transported back to the camp, amid all the rumours whirling about an attack on it during their absence. Martin had walked by the side of the litter as he couldn't find his horse, and he was too big to ride pillion with anyone else. Adam had regained consciousness on the way, seeming dazed but knowing who he was and who Martin was, so that was a good sign. By the time they'd reached the camp the raid was all over, though it was clear from the evidence that there had been casualties. Martin had at first no mind for them: he could think only of those close to him. He'd seen Edwin alive after the end of the combat, clambering back over to the earl's ship along with Sir Roger; he knew that Adam was injured and Sir Hugh was dying. And the lord earl was unscathed: those who had knocked him to the ground and surrounded him were intent on capturing rather than killing him.

Martin sat in silence next to the younger boy, listening to his steady breathing, and counted his blessings. All he wanted, for now, was to sit here in silence for a while longer. But he couldn't, of course; the lord earl had seen him come in and would be expecting him to organise things. Wearily, Martin stood and made his way back into the main space.

The earls were now accompanied by three figures, flitting round placing drinks and bowls of washing water, and picking up discarded pieces of armour. Little Hugh was one of them, and he looked uncertainly at Martin for approval. Martin managed a nod before he could face the rest of the room. The other two were Gregory and Matthew; Philip was nowhere to be seen.

A feeling of relief washed over Martin, but of course it would only be temporary. Philip was no doubt on some errand and would be back soon. Martin would have to face him and his malevolence in the full knowledge of his own feelings of guilt. He would have to push it all down even further so as not to give himself away.

But he didn't come. During a lull, Martin took the opportunity to pull Gregory to one side. 'Philip?'

The boy looked up at him with a face that was black and blue. Lord, had he been in the thick of the battle as well? 'He's dead.'

Martin gaped. Some sort of feeling swept through him from head to toe, but he couldn't have put a name to it if he had tried. He just stared.

Gregory took his silence as a request for further information. 'He went over the side of the ship. I … saw him fall.'

His eyes, as Martin looked into them, were bottomless. He noted in passing that Matthew, who was surely too young to have taken part in the battle, was also sporting a bruised face. What must it have been like to live under Philip's rule every day and night, with no escape? But he couldn't … surely …

For the last time that day, Martin said it. 'I'm sorry.'

Gregory kept his gaze locked with Martin's for a moment longer. 'Don't be.' He turned away to serve his lord.

The grave was a little way apart from the others.

A long trench had been dug outside the camp, in which the bodies of those who had died in the raid and those who had been brought back from the ships were laid. Side by side, head to toe, all very neat. Dead men, dead women, dead children. Edwin could have counted the corpses if he'd wanted to, but he didn't. Instead he exchanged a glance with Sir Roger, and the two of them moved further away to a patch of ground on the slope overlooking the town and the sea, where the fresh breeze fluttered the grass.

They began to dig, being joined in their task by others, for the grave needed to be large: three of Sir Hugh's foot sergeants and four of his archers, including Nigel, lay shrouded alongside Alf, Dickon and Peter. Edwin was glad that Nigel hadn't gone into the sea with the French corpses; he would rest better here.

The work was hard, for the earth was summer-hard, but between them, amid the sweat and the dust, they completed their task. They climbed out of the grave and began to lower the bodies in – with care, for these were their comrades and friends. Two or three men at a time handled the eight larger bodies; Edwin made sure that he and he alone carried Dickon, tucking the small form next to Alf and leaving space for Sir Roger to place Peter on the other side. He touched Dickon's head briefly, murmuring 'Go with God, little one,' and silently added a thought to Alf that he had kept his promise. He – she – would lie safe.

A priest had been found from among those in the camp, and he gabbled his way through the words with little interest or enthusiasm, having no doubt reeled off the same service many times that day. The earth was replaced, the turfs stacked on the mound. A wooden cross was hammered in. Then the men drifted away, leaving Edwin with John standing next to the kneeling Sir Roger. They waited until he finished his fervent prayer and stood for a final look at the grave.

John took a deep breath and addressed him directly. 'Sir. I'm not a man of many words, but I want to tell you how sorry I am about your boy. He was a lovely little lad. A good archer, willing learner, and he loved you like a father.'

Sir Roger took a moment to compose himself. 'Thank you. And my condolences to you on your own loss.'

John nodded. 'Aye, well. Nigel was a friend, and I'm sorry to lose him. But a grown man in battle is one thing; killing boys and crip-ples in cold blood is another. He – both of them – should have had the chance to grow up.'

His voice choked, and Edwin recalled his own tale of the wives and sons lost in childbed.

Unwilling to display any further emotion, John changed the subject as they began to walk back to the camp. 'And … Sir Hugh?'

Sir Roger sighed. 'Not long for this world, I'm afraid. To be honest it's only his stubbornness that's kept him alive this long.'

'No hope for him, then?'

'Only that his suffering might be short. Just keep him in your prayers.'

They reached their depleted area of the camp. One of the other men had made an attempt at cooking a meal, and Edwin looked at the unappetising mess that was presented to him.

He stirred it round as he allowed thoughts to wash over him, trying to work out who the victors in this war actually were. He himself had lost friends, but he was now more confident that his wife and family would be safe. The lord earl was alive and would no doubt be richer by the sum of several ransoms, but was he trusted by his peers, and did any of this make him happy? Peter had lost his life because he'd come here with Sir Roger, but if you asked him, Edwin reckoned he'd probably choose the same path again. His months with Sir Roger, following as they did his aimless and hungry existence as a ragged beggar boy, had been the happiest of his short life. Alf was dead, and so was his only surviving child, but they'd stayed together. Was that better or worse than Dickon starving in the streets as another orphan?

Edwin allowed himself a rueful smile, inwardly at least, about how stupid he'd been not to see the truth about Dickon earlier. And he called himself observant! All those trips off alone to 'pick herbs', the waiting to leave the camp until after it was dark – all to avoid having to go to the latrine at the same time as the men, of course. Along with everyone else, Edwin had been thoroughly misdirected about Alf and his 'son'.

He stopped stirring.

Misdirected.

Oh Lord. It was all so obvious. Or at least, all except for …

He put the bowl down, the slop still untasted. He made his way over to Sir Roger and tried to keep his voice casual. 'Is Humphrey still in the tent with Sir Hugh?'

'Yes, why?'

'No particular reason. I just need to go and find Martin.'

Edwin hurried through the camp. There was only one possible answer, and it would explain every incident – except one. Edwin was sure in his heart that he was right, but if he was, then how to explain that single anomaly? He didn't want to speak out until he could prove everything absolutely; but if he waited too long to resolve everything to his satisfaction, then he might have another death on his hands. He needed to talk to Martin, and he needed to do it now.

He slowed as he approached the earl's camp, aware that he still wouldn't be let anywhere near the pavilion. Instead he made his way to the cooking area, where to his relief he saw the tall figure and managed to attract his attention.

Martin saw his urgency and came towards him. Edwin pulled him away behind a tent so they couldn't be seen.

'There haven't been any further attacks on the earl since the battle, have there?'

'No. Why?' Martin thought for a moment. 'Could it be because the man who was trying to kill him was himself killed in the battle?'

This seemed to give him some satisfaction, but Edwin had to disappoint him. 'I've got a different idea.' He pointed to a patch of ground in a sheltered corner behind the tent. 'Sit there and tell me again about the night the lord earl's pavilion caught fire.'

Martin looked puzzled, but he did as he was bid. 'You know what happened. I went to bed and —'

Edwin shook his head. 'No, I mean tell me *exactly* what happened. I want to hear every single little detail, everything you saw or heard or felt. Concentrate, now. Think yourself back. Start from the moment I left.'

He watched in silence for a moment as Martin sat back and then closed his eyes. 'They were eating. Philip took some of Matthew's, which made Adam angry.'

Edwin listened with care as Martin continued, sinking himself further into the events of the evening. They had gone back into the central space. Salisbury had sent his squires away. Adam had given the page some bread – Martin smiled as he recalled it. 'Just like him to do that.' He had checked the jug of wine was full. He had gone … 'No, wait.' His eyes still closed, he rubbed at the back of his hand. 'I spilled some wax on my hand. Nothing serious. And I'm sure I didn't upset the new candle. Besides, if I had then one of them would have noticed – they were there for a long while after that.'

Edwin stared into the middle distance as the tale went on, trying to lose the here and now and to see and hear things as Martin had done on that night. And then, his reward.

'Say that again.'

Martin opened his eyes and repeated the piece of information he'd just given. Then he gave a whistle. 'You mean …'

Edwin nodded, feeling the excitement rise. 'Yes.' And, oh Lord, there was more. 'And it also means I'm right about something else.'

He repeated his own words: 'Say that again …' Yes. It was the final thread in the pattern.

He began to rise, but Martin put out a hand to stop him. 'Oh no. Not this time. You're not going anywhere until you tell me exactly what you've got planned.'

'Don't worry. This time, I won't be able to do it without you.'

Chapter Fourteen

Edwin crouched behind the untidy stack of baggage in Sir Hugh's tent. Humphrey had been summoned back to the earl's side; he had left unwillingly, with a promise to be back as soon as he could, but he knew that orders from his lord were to be obeyed without question. The knight himself was lying on his cot, grey-faced, his breathing laboured, blood and pus seeping through his bandages once more. He was dying, and anyone who saw him would know that. But not everyone had seen him in person; those who hadn't might well have been fooled by Sir Roger's loud announcement around the camp that he had been mistaken earlier, that Sir Hugh's great strength and determination meant he now looked likely to recover.

Edwin was gambling on the fact that the right person had heard, and he stared at the darkening outline of the tent flap as the sun went down. Was he correct? He had to be – there was no other logical explanation. He tried to relax his muscles one by one so that he wouldn't get cramp in his confined space, for he didn't know how long he was going to be there.

He didn't know how much time had passed when he saw the tent flap twitch. He held his breath as he saw the shadow slip in.

He was right.

There had been no further attacks since the battle. But this was not because the perpetrator had been killed; it was because *everyone knew that Sir Hugh was dying.*

C.B. Hanley

Edwin's instinct was to jump up straight away, but he had to wait. Until he had witnessed the actual attempt, it could all be denied, and although he was sure in his own mind, there was no substitute for proof.

The figure stood looking down at Sir Hugh for a long moment, and then with deliberation it picked up a blanket, rolled it into a ball and stepped forward.

Edwin waited until the cloth was actually being pressed against the motionless knight's face, and then he stood. 'Stop!'

John jumped almost out of his skin. He dropped the blanket as he turned in one smooth movement and drew his knife.

He saw Edwin, and, although he didn't exactly relax, his stance seemed to soften a little. 'It's you.'

Edwin was acutely aware of the knife, but now at least John was facing away from Sir Hugh, who was still breathing. He said nothing.

John realised he should make some effort to explain himself. 'I was just –'

'I know what you were doing. I know you were trying to kill him, and I know you've been trying to kill him since you joined the host.'

The hand holding the knife wavered. 'How can you possibly know that? How can you think that?'

'Move further away from him and I'll tell you.'

The only light came from the sinking sun and the camp fires outside, slanting in through the tent flap behind John so Edwin couldn't see his face properly. But he caught a shake of the head. 'No. Tell me now, here where we stand.'

Edwin shrugged. 'All right.' Hoping the gesture didn't look too obvious, he put his hands behind his back. 'I was fooled to start with by the fire in the lord earl's pavilion, which happened before Sir Hugh arrived and before you did. That was why I thought someone was trying to kill him. But that was an accident – my lord kicked a chair over in anger and didn't notice he'd sent wax and flame flying on to the canvas. No, the real attacks didn't start until you got here, and they were all aimed at Sir Hugh, not the earl.'

He seemed to have John's attention. How long could he keep him away from the injured knight?

'That night around the fire, you made a fuss about losing your knife, but of course you still had it yourself, and while you were off in the dark pretending to look for it, you threw it at Sir Hugh. When that didn't work you tried to poison the earl's evening meal, knowing that Sir Hugh was eating with him. I suspected Alf for a while, thinking he might have sent Dickon to put something in the pot. Or even Humphrey. But if either of them had done it they would have known which herbs and plants would cause a swift death. You didn't, which is why you failed. And you had no regard for who else might suffer, including innocent boys.'

John snorted. 'There's no innocent noble alive. They're all just as bad as one another.'

'Really? Even little Hugh, who you saw being attacked by bigger squires and thought it unfair? Even Adam, who stood up for him and took a beating when you wouldn't interfere?'

John said nothing. Edwin was trying to remain calm, but he could feel his anger rising. 'And then that day in the woods, it was you who picked up a stray arrow and killed Alan with it. The rest of the arrow-storm fell on that part of the column because the nobles are easy to see in their bright surcoats. But yours was aimed, and Sir Hugh was hundreds of yards from you – nobody could possibly have got that close to him except you. And it was only because Alan threw himself in front of the cart that you failed.'

The more he got worked up, the more John seemed to be calming down. His demeanour was relaxed, even confident. 'You're talking rubbish. After-effects of the shock of the battle, I expect. Why don't you go and lie down?'

Edwin continued. 'And at the docks – it was you who did some-thing to the plank.'

'Ah, now you know you're lying – we all helped them together, and you were there too. We came back to the camp together.'

'But you went back, didn't you? That's what Stephen meant when we spoke to him again about the lime. "We wouldn't have done it half so fast if you hadn't come back".'

'He must have meant all of us —'

'And he called you John. How did he know what your name was? Nobody mentioned it while we were all there the first time. He could only have known it if you'd gone back and spoken to him again. What did you do, offer to buy him that drink? Send him and his friends off to a tavern while you damaged the plank with the tools you carry in your bag?'

John looked less sure of himself now. 'But —'

Edwin shook his head. 'It's all true. It's the only explanation that makes sense.'

Now he started to bluster. 'Ha! Is that all you've got? You reckon they'll hang me on your say-so? They wouldn't take your word to save me that time, why should they take it to condemn me now?'

He had steered the conversation in exactly the direction Edwin wanted. He tried to keep his voice casual. 'But these great men will hang us on a whim if it suits them, won't they? You said that to me yourself.'

He'd scored a hit, and John knew it, but he made one last attempt. 'Well, if this is what you think, then why? Why would I want to kill Sir Hugh, and why in God's name would I choose to do it now and not any of the other years I've been in his service?'

Edwin kept his hands behind his back, his fingers curled around the hilt of the hidden dagger. He was approaching the moment of danger, and he might need it soon. 'Because it was only on the day that you joined this host that you found out what Sir Hugh had done.'

John froze.

'When we met up with you, Sir Hugh was telling you all about discipline. He was telling you that if you stepped out of line and tried to plunder anything, you'd be punished. He reminded you that in France three years ago he'd hanged a man for stealing from a church.'

'But …' John was struggling now. Edwin still couldn't see him properly but he could sense his agitation, feel the heat, smell the sweat. 'So what? We all knew that already.'

Edwin's right hand clasped the hilt of the dagger. 'But it wasn't until that moment that you found out that the man he hanged was your son.'

He was prepared for an attack, but he wasn't prepared for the wail of pain and misery that escaped John's lips. It shook him, but if he was going to get the confession he needed, he had to be remorseless. 'Three sons, all dead, you said. And because you mentioned your wives dying in childbed I just assumed they'd all died as babies. But one didn't, did he?'

'My eldest. Richard.' The voice was a whisper.

'He grew up. You taught him to shoot. You kept the bow he used as a boy and you still carry it everywhere. You loved him, and when he died you mourned him. You looked out for other little boys, made them toys, taught them to shoot – because you missed your own son.'

Edwin stopped for breath, and then let the silence form and stretch out.

It was John who caved in, unable to stand the void. 'We got separated into different units. He went off with his, and all I heard later was that he'd been killed. I was broken, but at least I thought he'd died in battle.'

'Until Nigel finally said it out loud, that day,' said Edwin. 'I saw you talking to him, and I heard you. "Say that again," you said. And I thought you were arguing, you were daring him to say something to your face that he'd said under his breath, so you could fight about it. But the tone of your voice was all wrong. You actually couldn't believe what you'd heard, so were asking him to repeat it, probably hoping you'd heard wrong.'

John was looking into the distance. 'All those years … and nobody told me the truth.'

'They wanted to spare you.'

'Spare me? Oh aye, spare me the news that that murdering bastard had hanged a boy of seventeen.' He took a step back towards Sir Hugh.

'No. I meant spare you the news that your son was a thief and a defiler of churches. That he was disloyal to his lord and deliberately disobeyed his orders. That he brought shame on himself, and on you.'

John gaped for a moment, as if unable to believe that such cruel words could be coming out of Edwin's mouth. His voice broke. 'No! It's not true! He was a good lad, and Sir Hugh killed him. And if my son wasn't allowed to die in battle then neither was he. I was going to … but now I don't care if there's marks as long as he's dead.'

He stepped to the cot and raised the knife, at which point Edwin said, loudly and clearly, 'Now!'

It was over in moments. Martin, wearing his mail, ducked through the tent entrance and made for John. A panicked slash of the knife barely glanced off the links of his hauberk before he had the man pinioned. Sir Roger stood up from where he had lain concealed on the ground on the far side of Sir Hugh's bed; he removed the blade from John's now unresisting hand and tucked it in his own belt. He reached out to touch Edwin's shoulder. 'Well done. We'll take him away to the lord earl – you stay here until I send word.'

Edwin nodded and watched Martin drag John out, his arms like iron bands round him, the captive's feet hardly touching the floor. His knees felt shaky all of a sudden and he collapsed to the floor beside the bed. With a trembling hand he reached out to brush the hair away from Sir Hugh's perspiring forehead: the dying knight had remained unconscious through it all.

Martin had seen the captive bound and put under guard. Indeed, he'd checked the knots himself just to make sure, and set no fewer than four men to stand guard all night, two on and two off in watches. If the prisoner escaped then there would be hell to pay all round. John's struggling and swearing, as Martin had half-carried and half-dragged him through the camp, had subsided to what looked like a limp acceptance of his fate, but Martin gave the guards permission to gag him if he started again.

As he walked back to the earl's pavilion to explain everything to him, the enormity of what the man had done – had tried to do – struck him anew. To betray his lord, to attempt to kill him … it was almost inconceivable. It was against every law of God and man, an inversion of everything that was natural.

His own revulsion was mirrored in the lord earl's face when he told him all about it. Of course, he didn't do it as well or as smoothly as Edwin would have done; Edwin would have explained every little happenstance and made it all sound perfectly logical. Instead Martin blurted out the main facts and said that both he and Sir Roger had heard the man confess.

As he went on and the full scale of the situation became clear, the earl began to exhibit not just disgust but rage. Martin could see it coming in the thin lips, the tightly controlled gestures. And it dawned on him that the earl was not just angry with the man John – who was so far below him as to render his motives irrelevant and meaningless – but with Sir Hugh himself. In essence, the cold fury in his lord's voice was because Sir Hugh had been so slack in the choice of men to accompany him on the campaign that the earl himself had been put in danger.

Of course, thought Martin, this wasn't because he was afraid for his life, or at least not entirely. It was because of the balance of power in the kingdom, the number of other lives depending on him, and what would happen to them all if he died suddenly. There would be chaos.

The earl concluded. 'We'll hang him first thing in the morning and he can count himself lucky.'

'Lucky, my lord?'

Those slate-grey eyes bored into Martin's. 'There are worse punishments available for those guilty of treason.'

Martin felt momentarily queasy. He was still not quite over the sight of the injuries he'd inflicted on the men on the ship, but at least that had been in the heat of battle. The idea of watching while a screaming man was tortured and punished made his stomach turn. He would need to harden himself to such things, of course. But then again, the punishment had to fit the crime. If someone, for example, had hurt Joanna, what would he be prepared to do? He'd wield the iron himself.

He'd almost missed the earl's next sentence, and he had to repeat it to make sure he'd understood correctly.

'Sorry my lord, but you want Sir Hugh to be brought to the execution?'

'Yes. His man, his responsibility. He will see justice done in person.'

Moving the knight would kill him, surely – although he was going to die anyway so maybe it would be a mercy to hasten his end. 'If you'll excuse me, my lord, I'll go and arrange that now.'

'Go. No, wait.'

'My lord?'

'If, as you say, Weaver had a hand in this, tell him to be there too. He can witness justice – and it will do him good to see what happens to men who betray their lords.'

Once outside the pavilion, Martin hesitated. How best to go about it?

The smell of cooking gave him his answer.

It was late but Humphrey and his men were eating their meal after serving and clearing away everyone else's. He welcomed Martin and listened to his story with an increasingly grim expression. Together they made their way to Sir Hugh's part of the camp, where the circle of men was even smaller and more subdued, huddled round their fire.

Martin looked at them with suspicion. Had any of the rest of them been in on it? Was there still danger?

There was somebody moving inside the tent. Martin drew his sword and prepared himself, but the figure who emerged was Edwin. He was startled at the sight of the weapon, holding up his hands, and Martin sheathed it again.

Edwin spoke to Humphrey, keeping his voice low. 'He's still alive. He's even come close to waking up a couple of times; I'm almost sure he recognised me for a few moments.' He held the tent flap open and Humphrey went in.

Martin stood erect outside the tent, hand on sword, daring any to come near and challenge him; the protection and privacy he could offer Sir Hugh and Humphrey was the last thing he could do for them. Under his breath he filled Edwin in on the sentence of death and the arrangements for the execution. He told him that the earl wanted him there, but refrained from adding the second half of the sentence.

He could hear murmurs from inside the tent. He tried not to listen, but with Edwin so silent and the other men starting to sleep, it was difficult not to.

'Father. Father, can you hear me?'

A groan that might have been one of recognition.

'I ask your forgiveness, Father. I know I've always been a disappointment to you. I'm not a knight, not brave like you.'

The ghost of Sir Hugh's voice. 'All right, boy.'

'And – I also ask your blessing. What I do isn't what you do, but the lord earl looks favourably on my work.'

'Serve the earl … in your own way, I suppose. Bless you.'

Humphrey made a sound that could only be a sob. 'Thank you, Father, thank you.'

Martin heard him get up, but the hoarse whisper sounded again. He could just make it out. 'No. Stay with me, boy.'

Silence fell inside the tent, and Martin stared at the starry sky. Sir Hugh would be all right with Humphrey sitting right by him, and Sir Roger's tent was only yards away. He could go back to his lord. And he could learn to serve him in his own way.

———•◦•———

Hangings always took place at dawn, apparently, although Edwin didn't know whether that was to cut short the terror of the condemned or the anxiety of the executioners; he could hardly put one foot in front of the other as they made for the edge of the woods. A suitable tree had been found the night before, one of its branches tested for strength.

Alongside him, one of the men carrying Sir Hugh's litter slipped, and Edwin shot out a hand to steady it as he regained his balance. Sir Hugh groaned and opened his eyes, but they were closed again before they reached their destination. His bearers laid the litter down on a bare patch of earth at the edge of the tree-line, where he would be able to view the proceedings if he regained sufficient consciousness. Edwin had been shocked at the command to bring the dying man along, considering it unnecessary cruelty, and he'd been even more horrified by the sharp words the earl had addressed to his knight, expressing his disappointment. Edwin sincerely hoped that Sir Hugh had not heard, or had at least not been conscious enough to understand, for it would have broken him more than the French weapons ever did. Half a century of loyal service – more than a lifetime for many people – to the earl and his father, all come to this.

The earl and Sir Roger were both riding, and they took position some yards back from the chosen site in order not to scare their mounts. Edwin wished he could be shown as much consideration, but of course he was worth much less in his lord's eyes than the horse, wasn't he? Sir Roger dismounted and made his way over to press Sir Hugh's hand before he took station next to Edwin. He shot a look that Edwin interpreted as an inquiry about his welfare, and he managed the barest nod in reply.

Sir Hugh's archers and sergeants marched into the clearing. Most of them lined up, staring straight ahead, while a small group formed a knot under the spreading branches of the tree – an oak, Edwin noted, hoping that by concentrating on the leaves he could shut out the rest of it. They threw a rope over the selected bough and then huddled around a figure in their midst.

Eventually they moved back and left John standing alone. For a moment he looked like he hadn't a care in the world, despite the noose around his neck and the hands bound behind his back; he glanced around him at the green glade and inhaled deep breaths of the dawn air, fresher here than in the packed camp. But then his gaze met Edwin's, and Edwin almost took a step back at the malevolence contained within. This was not the John he thought he knew. Misdirected, in more ways than one.

'So, here we are then. You've saved me twice – are you going to do it again?' The voice was harsh, mocking.

Edwin risked a glance around at the earl, but he had been momentarily distracted by Sir Hugh, who had groaned and started to stir, so he was paying no attention to the scene before him.

'No. You were going to kill Sir Hugh and you have to pay the price.' Edwin hoped he'd sounded firm, but he clamped his mouth shut straight away in case the chattering of his teeth should betray him.

John managed a snort, the rope not yet tight around his neck. 'Justice, is it? And where was the justice for my boy when he had him killed?'

Sir Roger interposed before Edwin could open his mouth again. 'That was also justice, as you well know. He disobeyed orders; he robbed a church; he was punished.'

'He was just a boy!'

'Boys die in war all the time.' An unusual savageness entered the knight's tone. 'As we both well know.'

John bit back his retort and bowed his head. 'Again, I'm sorry about your lad. For what it's worth, now.'

Sir Roger said nothing, so John turned back to Edwin. 'Bet you wish you'd dropped me in the sea now, don't you?'

'The sea would have spat you out, dammit!'

The hoarse bellow had come from Sir Hugh, who with his last breaths was furiously trying to raise himself into a sitting position, his wounds all breaking open again. He spat blood. 'Traitor! The sea wouldn't want you – you'll burn in hell!'

John regarded the dying man coolly. 'Then I'll die knowing that we'll go to hell together.'

Sir Hugh made an incoherent noise as he clutched at his stomach and spluttered through the blood foaming in his mouth. He managed a strangled roar. 'I'll live longer than you, by God! Even if I have to pull the rope myself!' But the effort of speaking was too much for him, and he fell back on to the litter with blood spreading alarmingly across his bandages and dribbling through his beard.

'I'll do it.'

Edwin hadn't even noticed that Humphrey was there. At a nod from the earl he stepped forward and took the free end of the rope from Sir Hugh's sergeants, who moved aside. But he wouldn't be able to haul John up on his own, surely?

'And I.' Edwin was hardly aware that the words had come from his own mouth, but he found himself moving into the open space. 'I condemned him; I should be prepared to carry out the sentence myself.'

The earl said nothing either way, so Edwin took hold of the rope, preparing himself. The hemp was rough against his palms; he could feel every fibre of it.

A third pair of hands appeared above his own. 'And I, my lord, for Sir Hugh is my friend.' Sir Roger had spoken loudly for all to hear, but only Edwin and John caught the second part, whispered close. 'And so was Peter. Thank you for being kind to him.'

John, beyond speech now that the moment had come, nodded. Sir Roger paused and readjusted the rope around his neck, moving the knot from the back to a position just under John's left ear. 'On my word, pull suddenly and as hard as you can.'

Edwin's eyes met John's for one last fraction of a moment, just as Sir Roger shouted 'Now!'

It was over quickly. The force exerted by three men was enough to jerk John off his feet and high into the air quite suddenly, where he kicked and spasmed for only a few moments before hanging heavy and still.

Along with the others, Edwin held tight to the rope, bearing the weight and unsure whether he wanted to run away or vomit. What were they to do? Should they tie it somewhere? He looked at the composed figure on the nervous mount.

After a short pause, the earl gestured. 'Tie it off and leave him an hour just to make sure. Then you can take him down and bury him.'

The ghost of a murmur of gratitude came from the other archers, and Edwin was glad – for John and for any future passers-by – that the body wouldn't be left to rot, as often happened with hangings.

There were other men around him now, others taking the rope and making it fast, so he was able to stagger away. He tried to pick the hemp fibres out of his hands; how long would he feel them there? Sir Roger wouldn't meet his eye, and Humphrey looked as bad as Edwin felt. They made their way over to the litter.

'Father?' Humphrey knelt down and took the callused hand. 'It's done, Father. For you.'

But Edwin could see that it was no use, for Sir Hugh was dead.

It was afternoon, and Edwin stared at his feet as he sat. Some of the men were half-heartedly preparing a fire, so they could get a pot over it to boil something ahead of the evening meal. Sir Roger was polishing his sword, lost in his own thoughts. On the ground in front of Edwin was a bow.

It wasn't John's mighty warbow, for they'd buried that with him. Nobody would waste such a fine weapon under normal circumstances, but none of the rest of the group could draw it fully, and besides, nobody wanted to touch it for fear of bad luck. So it had gone into the grave with him, into the final mass burial pit that was being kept open until they left, for more of the wounded were expected to die before tomorrow.

The bow in front of Edwin was small and slim. John had made it lovingly for his son, had taught him to shoot with it, and his son was dead. It had been on his back when Nigel told him the sorry news, and Nigel was dead. It had stood by while John taught Peter to shoot, and Peter was dead. John had carried it and cherished it until his own life had been choked out of him by a rope, an oak tree and three men that very morning.

It was cursed. As men stepped around the camp to gather wood, to stoke up the fire or to chop food, they gave it a wide berth.

At last Edwin could bear it no more. He stood and picked up the bow. It was light and balanced; a thing of beauty. 'If any man wants to stop me,' he announced a little more loudly than he'd intended, 'let him do it now.' There was silence, so he stepped forward and threw it in the fire.

He felt a little foolish after such a grand gesture, but nobody argued and there was nothing further to say. He sat down again and pulled out his letters. They were stained with the sweat he'd shed during the battle, but still more or less legible. *Most worshipful husband, beloved wife* ...

His concentration was broken by a sigh from Sir Roger, who had put down his sword.

'Edwin. You have served the lord earl and Sir Hugh well, again. And look at you.'

Edwin shrugged.

'And we still have the problem of Sir Geoffrey and your mother to reconcile. Tell me, what did he actually say?'

Edwin held the letters out without speaking, but Sir Roger handed the top one back with the nearest he could come to a smile. 'I don't need to know what's between husband and wife.'

He read Sir Geoffrey's letter with care, then folded it and sat tapping it on his knee while he stared into space. Then he stood and held it out. 'I need to talk to someone. More than one, in fact. Let me see what I can do.'

Edwin watched him go and took up his letter from Alys again.

Martin fiddled with the goblets, placing and replacing them. Adam had folded the same cloth three times, he would swear. Humphrey was likewise dawdling over his tasks, and over in the corner Brother William was sharpening his pen as slowly as he could, fumbling as he tried to keep it steady and whittle with just the one hand. Fortunately, the earl was telling little Hugh something so he wasn't paying the rest of them much attention.

Martin could feel the sweat on his palms. There was no telling what the lord earl's reaction was going to be. He liked to keep people off balance with unexpected ideas and suggestions, it was true, but Martin was fairly certain he wouldn't appreciate it when the tables were turned. Maybe they shouldn't try. Maybe – *Stop that! Are you a coward? You'd give up your life for a friend but you won't risk humiliation? What sort of knight are you going to make?* The goblet slipped out of his hand and he put it down firmly and turned away. *Only a few more moments. He'll be here soon.*

In fact, here he was: Sir Roger was entering the tent. Last chance to back out. No. There would be no turning back. He caught the knight's eye and nodded.

Sir Roger took several paces towards the earl and then fell to his knees. The other four, after a swift look at each other, did the same: Martin and Adam to Sir Roger's right, a little behind him; Brother William, awkwardly with his bound arm, and Humphrey to the left.

The earl, as might be expected, was taken aback and did not look pleased about it. He gazed at them all, steadily, his mouth set into a straight line. Martin felt his knees starting to shake. He looked at the floor.

'Well?' The earl was addressing Sir Roger. 'I assume there is a purpose to this and you are not just paying your respects?'

Sir Roger inclined his head. 'By your leave, my lord, we ask a boon of you.'

Martin risked a look at the earl. There was no telling which way this was going to go, but just now all he did was raise his eyebrows. 'Five boons? Do you not think that is too many for one evening?'

Sir Roger's voice was still steady. 'It would be, my lord, but all of us are in fact making the same request.'

The voice gained something of an edge. 'Well? Speak, then – I can come to no decision until I know what you're asking.'

Sir Roger puffed out a breath and Martin realised that even he was nervous. 'My lord, we – all of us – humbly petition you to take Edwin Weaver back into your service.'

The wait was agonising. When he spoke, though, the earl's voice was still steady. 'Hugh. Go now to your lord father, tell him from me that I hope to see him tomorrow morning before we go our separate ways. Take your own leave of him at the same time. Return in an hour.'

A barely audible 'Yes, my lord,' and the boy was gone. The axe was going to fall now.

The irritation was building, but the earl was still restrained – just. 'Look at me, all of you. I can't talk to you while you're staring at the floor.'

Martin raised his face and saw the earl's gaze sweeping slowly down the line. 'Martin, Adam. Yes. I understand your loyalty to a friend. Can't blame you, I suppose. Brother William – he's helpful to you, I know. But you others?' He skewered Humphrey with a glare. 'He couldn't keep your father alive, could he? Why would you want him back?'

Humphrey managed to get past the hurtful reminder without reacting, although he did flush. 'My lord, neither Edwin nor anyone could stop my father from fighting through the thickest press of the battle, and nor would I have wanted them to. It was his life. But what Edwin did was precious: he stopped him from being shamefully murdered in his bed. Thanks to him, my father saw justice done and died proudly of the wounds he sustained in battle.' The pain showed through as he risked a final defiance. 'In your service, my lord.'

The earl made no immediate reply, turning instead to Sir Roger. 'And you?'

'My lord, Edwin is a good man, an honest man. He owes everything he has to you, and that makes him devoted to your service —'

'Ha! Honest, you say? What of this deception with his mother?'

Sir Roger ploughed on. 'My lord, I truly believe that Edwin had no idea of this marriage plan – that the news was as much a surprise to him as to you.' He faced only a stony silence, so he made his last throw of the dice. 'My lord, you are known as a just man. You would never, I am sure, blame a man for something he did not do. If you are unhappy with the situation, please, I beg of you, take it up with Sir Geoffrey and forgive Edwin. Take him back.'

Martin realised he was holding his breath. Dear Lord, this was risky in all sorts of ways. To start with, they were all perfectly aware that the earl would be happy to blame a man for something he hadn't done if it suited his purposes, but he saw himself as upright and wouldn't appreciate being given any hint otherwise. Secondly, in deflecting the blame away from Edwin they were dropping Sir Geoffrey squarely into the earl's sights. But it was the lesser evil: his shoulders were broader than Edwin's, and the situation had been of his own making, after all.

There was still no outburst. Instead Martin found the earl pointing at him. 'Fetch him here. Now.'

———

Edwin knelt by the grave. He'd said a prayer for the souls who had left their bodies beneath this earth, far from their homes, and he pleaded for their swift passage through purgatory. Especially Peter and D– *Edith*, as he could say to himself in the silence of his own mind. They'd been shriven on the morning of the battle along with everyone else, thank the Lord; most of the priests had remained ashore. And surely God would ease the path of children?

Now he was praying for himself. What was he going to do? He was no longer part of the earl's household, but he couldn't stay here, at the other end of the kingdom. He was no longer part of Sir Hugh's household, either, for Sir Hugh was gone; Edwin had been there when the shroud was wrapped around his cold, grey face, and had watched as the nails were hammered into the coffin. No mass grave for a knight; he would go back to his manor to sleep in the familiar earth of home. *Home.* The dead man had one; Edwin didn't. Could he possibly tag along and follow the Conisbrough men north? The earl might not notice, as he was going to Lewes himself, and once he got back he could speak with Alys, with Mother, and – dear Lord – with Sir Geoffrey to see what could be done. Would he even be able to keep his house, the home he'd promised would be his wife's to share? Would he —

A tap on his shoulder roused him and he looked up to see Martin.

'Stand up and smarten yourself up. My lord wishes to see you.'

'What? What for?'

Martin paused. 'To be honest, I'm not sure whether we've made it better or worse. If worse, I'm sorry. But we all pleaded for you.'

'For me? Who? Sorry, what are you saying?'

Martin hauled Edwin to his feet and ineffectually brushed at his tunic. 'I'll tell you on the way. But come on – it won't help if we keep him waiting.'

By the time Edwin entered the pavilion he was both overcome with gratitude that five – five! – men had put themselves at risk for his sake, and terrified of what the earl was going to say to him. He was there sooner than he expected or wanted to be, so there was nothing for it. Trying to keep his eyes away from those standing at the edge of the space, lest he burst into embarrassing tears of thanks, he fell to his knees before the earl. He had no weapon in his hand, at least – though a lord didn't need a sword to cause a man's death, as Edwin well knew.

The earl leaned forward. 'Speak truth to me now, Weaver.'

'Yes, my lord. Of course, my lord.' He'd never spoken anything else – but whether he was going to be believed one way or the other was yet to be seen.

'It is the belief of Sir Roger here that you did not know of this proposed marriage between Sir Geoffrey and your mother. Is that true?'

'I had no idea, my lord, I swear it.'

The earl drummed his fingers on the arm of his chair. 'You must have known something. Come now – the truth!'

Ignoring the atmosphere in the room, Edwin sat back on his knees and thought. What had he known? Or what should he have guessed at? He risked looking the earl in the eye. 'I knew that Sir Geoffrey and my father were friends, my lord. I knew that Sir Geoffrey promised my father when he was dying that he would let no harm come to my mother. But I thought ... well, that's the sort of thing Sir Geoffrey would say, wouldn't he? Protecting people is what he does.' He knew he was rambling, but he couldn't stop now that the thoughts were streaming out. 'As to the rest, I ...'

It hit him like a hammer. 'It's been right there in front of my face, hasn't it? And I never saw it. I've been completely blind.'

The earl now had an air of puzzlement, as well he might, for Edwin supposed that not many men in danger of their lives or livelihoods tended to rattle on to themselves while on their knees before him. 'Sorry, my lord.'

The tapping on the arm of the chair continued. Edwin stayed where he was. The earl had very fine boots, and the rush matting of the floor was interwoven in a pattern that was almost mesmerising.

The noise ceased. Edwin held his breath. This was it. His future.

'Very well.'

Very well what? What did that mean?

'I accept that you did not know of this foolishness. I also recognise that a man who gains the respect and loyalty of his companions is worth having around. You may take up your position again.'

Air was expelled from numerous mouths all at once, and the atmosphere in the room seemed to grip less tightly around Edwin's head. He should thank the earl, he should get up and take what was being offered. But if others took risks for him, why should he not do so for another? The words came out before he could stop them. 'And what of the marriage, my lord?'

He'd done it now. And he'd been so nearly home. Martin was wincing and even Sir Roger was shaking his head.

The earl was staring at him in disbelief. 'You don't seriously …'

Edwin shrugged. He'd been cast out once already. Could it be worse a second time?

'The rest of you – out!' There was no gainsaying; the others slipped from the pavilion one by one, Sir Roger still shaking his head and Martin giving him one long, last significant look. His friends had saved him, and he'd thrown himself back in the mire.

It was too late to do anything about it now, anyway. Should he duck? Should he run? He remained with his knees fixed to the floor.

The earl was giving him a long, considering look, and Edwin boldly matched his gaze – he couldn't make things worse than they already were.

'You have some nerve, Weaver.'

Edwin said nothing.

The earl let out an exasperated noise and reached out his hand, snapping his fingers for wine. Realising there was no squire or page in attendance, he got up himself and poured it before re-seating himself, taking a gulp and glaring at Edwin again.

Edwin let the silence develop, and eventually the earl sighed. 'Right. Here is what we are going to do. You will head back north with the men of Conisbrough. You will take Sir Hugh's body with you. I can't spare Humphrey, he's too useful – God knows I've never had a better organised household campaign – but you can return his father's body to his manor and give the news to his elder son. Tell him Sir Hugh died in my service and there will be no issues with his inheritance. Got that?'

Edwin nodded. It was a shame the earl hadn't said something along those lines to Sir Hugh before he died, so that he might not have gone to his grave thinking he'd brought shame on his lord. But it was too late now.

'You will then go to Conisbrough. You can tell that old dog Geoffrey … ach. Tell him that he does not have my blessing but he may marry if he chooses, and I will recognise any heir to his manor. His wife will not sit at my table while I am in residence but she may otherwise share his bed and board at the castle. Clear?'

Edwin nodded again. It was better than he could have hoped for, and please God he could make some sense of it once he could speak to them both in person. And he would be going back to Alys and a roof that was safe over her head.

The earl now relaxed back into his chair. 'I will go to Lewes with the rest of the household, but I will be back at Conisbrough for Christmas, by which time I expect my hall to be finished – you and Geoffrey can hurry the masons along between you, I'm sure. And there's no point you then coming back south and north again – you'd just spend all your time on the road. Remain in Conisbrough, see to it that the new bailiff settles in and has all he needs. Now there is to be peace in the land I can no doubt manage without your … skills for a few months.'

Edwin was reeling. None of this could have worked out better if he'd planned it, and he gave fervent thanks to God.

'Go on, now, get out of my sight before I change my mind. And send the others back in.'

Edwin rose and stammered his thanks as he stumbled towards the door, knees a little stiff.

Once outside he allowed the smile that had been hiding to emerge and spread all the way across his face, and he had to restrain himself from skipping, which would have looked inappropriate to say the least. But in his head and in his heart he was dancing.

There was peace, and he was going home.

historical note

The naval engagement known as the Battle of Sandwich took place on St Bartholomew's Day, 24 August, in the year 1217. It was just over two years since King John had agreed and then reneged on the document known to us as Magna Carta, and about eighteen months since Louis had first arrived, at the behest of many English barons, to replace him on the throne. In the meantime John had died, at which point many rebels switched their allegiance from Louis to John's 9-year-old son Henry. A combined force of French and baronial troops had been defeated at Lincoln in May 1217 (as depicted in one of Edwin's earlier adventures, *The Bloody City*), but Louis himself had been at Dover with half his army, so all was not lost. He returned to London to consolidate and plan, and awaited reinforcements from France that were being mustered by his wife, Blanche of Castile, who happened to be King John's niece.

The fleet set off from Calais. If it had reached London and joined up with Louis's existing forces, he would probably have been in possession of sufficient resource to carry the day; England would have been ruled by King Louis I rather than King Henry III. Therefore, it was imperative that the ships be stopped before that happened, which meant preventing them from landing and blocking their route up the Thames to London.

Sandwich is today several miles from the coast, but in 1217 it was a sea port, and William Marshal, the regent, called all the nobles who were loyal to the young king to assemble there to form an army that would take to the sea. His main problem in this endeavour was that 'loyalty' was something of a nebulous concept; many of England's nobles – including the Earls Warenne, Salisbury and Arundel – had already switched sides more than once. The great men of the realm were fighting as much for their own positions as they were for their king, and if they felt that they would be better served by having Louis on the throne, or by removing their peers from the picture, they would take steps to ensure the correct outcome.

Earl Warenne's personal role in the battle was less glamorous than the one he plays in this book. A contemporary French chronicle called the *History of the Dukes of Normandy and the Kings of England* tells us that he 'fitted out a ship with knights and men-at-arms where his banners were', but that he did not embark himself. A famous illustration of the battle by the thirteenth-century historian Matthew Paris includes the figure of Warenne standing with the regent and others on the shore while the engagement takes place out at sea. His ship did take an active part, though, as described here: it was commanded by Richard Fitzjohn, who was both King John's illegitimate son and Warenne's nephew (I'll leave you to work that one out for yourselves …). The description of the earl taking on three knights as he boarded the enemy ship is based on a specific account of the event from the contemporary *History of William Marshal*, the protagonist actually being one Reginald Pain, a knight of Guernsey.

The English fleet, as depicted here, initially headed out to sea and passed to the south of the French; however, by dint of excellent seamanship, they came about and then approached the French at speed with the wind and the sun behind them. Warenne's ship was the first to reach the French command vessel, known as the 'great ship of Bayonne' – which was so loaded down with men, horses, baggage, treasure and the pieces of a trebuchet that it was barely out of the water – followed by the huge cog belonging to the regent. It is not clear who commanded this vessel in Marshal's absence, so I have felt free to give the role to the Earl of Salisbury, who was the young king's uncle. All of the principal sources for the battle agree that lime was flung at the French before the ships engaged, blinding and choking those on board; Matthew Paris's illustration shows archers shooting balls of it. The great ship was rammed, and then grappling hooks were thrown as they were lashed together; the English boarded and carried the day in a crowded and brutal encounter.

After the battle was over, the French common soldiers and sailors were massacred. A group of bloodthirsty men from the English fleet did attempt to kill the knights as well, but they were saved by the English lords for ransom; thirty-six French knights were captured from the command ship, including their leader Robert de Courtenay, a kinsman of Prince Louis. As the ranking nobleman he (and his ransom) were claimed by the avaricious William Marshal, who had already awarded himself most of the lands belonging to the late Count of Perche who had been killed at Lincoln. Hubert de Burgh, having overshot the turn, sailed serenely back into the carnage just as it was all over, capturing two ships for his own gain.

Eustace the Monk, 'the wicked pirate', was dragged out from where he was hiding in the depths of the ship's hold; he did make a huge ransom offer but must have known his life would be forfeit. The *History of William Marshal* says that he was offered the choice of being beheaded on the trebuchet or beheaded on the rail; nobody knows what his answer was, but the sentence was carried out by one Stephen of Winchelsea, and the severed head was later paraded on a spear around the towns of the south coast that he had terrorised for years.

As is usual with mediaeval battles, estimates of casualties vary wildly between sources. The *History of William Marshal*, keen to embellish the victory, claims 4,000 dead 'not counting those who jumped into the sea and were drowned', while the French

History of the Dukes of Normandy plays it down and says that only Eustace's flagship and some smaller vessels were captured at all, with all nine of the other large ships making it back to Calais. What is clear is that much money and treasure, intended for Louis to pay his troops, was captured: members of the victorious fleet shared it out 'in bowlfuls' and there was still enough left over to endow a hospital dedicated to St Bartholomew in Sandwich.

Some of *Give Up the Dead*'s characters are based on real historical people, including William and John Marshal, Eustace the Monk and the Earls Warenne, Salisbury and Arundel. Arundel did have seven daughters and two sons, the younger called Hugh; he was aged around seven in 1217, although there is no evidence either way as to whether he was a page in Warenne's household. However, it was the custom for noble boys to be sent away to train with their father's lords or allies, and Hugh was in later life closely linked with the Warenne family, so I thought this arrangement plausible.

The rest of my cast is fictional: Edwin, Martin, Adam, Brother William, Humphrey, Sir Hugh, Sir Roger, and all the other squires and men. However, the make-up of the earl's retinue and – with the possible exception of Edwin – the parts that each of these characters play in it are based on what we know of noble households at the time. An earl had knights who owed him service; they in turn had men of their own who might be mounted sergeants, foot sergeants or archers, depending on their wealth and resources. Any army on campaign would number non-combatants such as grooms and cooks among its population; an earl would have a clerk and a marshal to deal with his correspondence and his travel arrangements respectively.

The attack on the camp in the absence of the royalist army is entirely fictional. However, such things did happen, and Louis did have men on the ground in the south-east, so it would not have been a bad tactic under the circumstances. If they had managed to kill or capture the king or the regent – who, as we know, remained on shore – then the defeat at sea would have been negated. Many of the victims in any thirteenth-century war, whether in battle, siege or plundering attack, were children or other non-combatants. Much is made of the concept of 'chivalry', but at the time this was simply a code that sought to govern the behaviour of knights towards other knights; anyone else, and particularly anyone not rich enough to pay a ransom, was afforded no such protection.

Conditions in an army camp were generally unhealthy, as might be expected when a large number of people and animals were camped in close proximity with little proper sanitation. Outbreaks of food poisoning were common, as were diseases such as dysentery; indeed, on some campaigns the casualties from sickness outnumbered those from combat. Such large groups found it difficult to carry with them all the provisions they would need, so foraging in and/or plundering of the local countryside was an accepted tactic – albeit a seemingly counterproductive one when the war was being fought in your own country.

Any army would include among its number experienced soldiers who had fought in previous campaigns and who, in some cases, had survived serious injury. The nature of hand-to-hand combat meant that broken and severed limbs were common; survival rates were low due to the dangers of blood loss and infection, but occasionally somebody got lucky. Alf is one of these; the fact that he was treated by an Arab doctor probably increased his chances of recovery, whatever he might say himself.

There was no such thing as a pension, so a man disabled by active service would simply have to make his way in the world as best he could. He would not, however, be an outcast: his former comrades would probably treat him no differently, and after the initial shock of his appearance, new acquaintances would get used to him. Very few people in the thirteenth century reached middle age without some kind of lasting scar or health problem, and attitudes to disability were more liberal than we might think. Alas, not every condition was treatable; those who suffered from other ailments, such as the appendicitis which strikes Humphrey's man Rob, were doomed.

———

Archery in 1217 was not quite as well developed as it would become in the following couple of centuries, but it was an established military practice. The law making Sunday archery compulsory was not passed until 1252, but local competitions (friendly or otherwise) took place on an *ad hoc* basis and there were certainly skilled bowmen around who formed a significant part of any army.

Bows were not as long as they would be later – perhaps a maximum of 5ft – but they could still propel an arrow at great speed from a draw weight of 80-100lbs. The technique was to start with the bow held in front of the chest and then to push and pull at the same time, which helped to even out the strain; repeating this over and over again was a feat of skill and endurance that required extensive training. Arrows were loosed in volleys (with the commands being 'nock, draw, loose', *not* 'ready, aim, fire'); they were generally made of ash, which tends to grow very straight, with fletchings of goose feathers. The iron or steel arrowheads could vary in shape from narrow, pointed, mail-piercing bodkins to triangular broadheads, effective against both horses and men and extremely difficult to remove once embedded.

The outcome of the Battle of Sandwich was the Treaty of Lambeth, finalised three weeks later, by which Louis agreed to relinquish his claim to the throne in return for a huge payment of 10,000 marks (£6,667) of silver. He sailed back across the Channel at the end of September 1217; he would never set foot in England again, but when he later assumed the throne of France as Louis VIII he fought successfully against the English in his own realm as he sought to expel them from French soil.

The treaty was meant to impose peace, but of course that was easier said than done in a land where the nobles had been deeply entrenched on opposing sides for years, and where many of them held competing claims to the same titles and lands. Disputes, conflict and outright violence would continue throughout England for some years, as Edwin will soon discover.

Further Reading

Carpenter, D.A., *The Minority of Henry III* (London: Methuen, 1990)

Hanley, Catherine, *Louis: The French Prince Who Invaded England* (London: Yale University Press, 2016)

Lynn, John A. (ed.), *Feeding Mars: Logistics in Western Warfare from the Middle Ages to the Present* (Boulder: Westview Press, 1994)

McGlynn, Sean, *Blood Cries Afar: The Forgotten Invasion of England, 1216* (Stroud: The History Press, 2011)

McGlynn, Sean, 'England's Medieval Trafalgar', *BBC History Magazine*, July 2012

Stanton, Charles D., *Medieval Maritime Warfare* (Barnsley: Pen and Sword, 2015)

Acknowledgements

As ever, my thanks are due to many people and it is a pleasure to be able to acknowledge them here.

Matilda Richards, until recently my editor at The Mystery Press, has believed in and supported this series from the start; I will miss her and her acute observations, but I hope that her new venture brings both success and happiness.

Joy Hawkins, an academic medievalist specialising in the history of medicine, and Alison Convey, a GP, between them set me straight on all sorts of matters to do with amputation, food poisoning and appendicitis, for which I am extremely grateful. Sorry about the emails full of gruesome questions.

Sean McGlynn, as ever, was happy to discuss all things thirteenth-century in return for tea and cake; his work on Eustace the Monk and the Battle of Sandwich has been of particular help this time round.

Three splendid volunteers read through full drafts of the work before I finalised it: many thanks to Susan Brock, Maddy McGlynn and Stephanie Tickle, whose comments on everything from equine behaviour to semi-colons were gratefully appreciated, even where they diverged to a considerable degree …

I am fortunate to have many friends on Twitter who were generous either with specific help on points contained in the book, with general medieval goodness, or with all-round support and encouragement. They include (but are in no way limited to) James Aitcheson, Sophie Ambler, Andrew Buck, Jim Jones, Phyl Jones, Marion Livingstone, Levi Roach, Richard Sheehan and

Paul Webster; many thanks to all of them and to the rest of the Twittersphere.

And finally, a grateful shout-out to the small but perfectly formed Wiveliscombe library; despite the threats being cast at it from all sides, it remains doggedly open to serve its rural community. The staff, 'friends of' and volunteers are all heroes.

About the Author

C.B. HANLEY has a PhD in mediaeval studies from the University of Sheffield and is the author of *War and Combat 1150–1270: The Evidence from Old French Literature* and *Louis: The French Prince Who Invaded England*, as well as her Mediaeval Mystery series: *The Sins of the Father*, *The Bloody City*, *Whited Sepulchres* and *Brother's Blood*. She currently writes a number of scholarly articles on the period, as well as teaching on writing for academic publication, and also works as a copy-editor and proofreader.

Also in this series

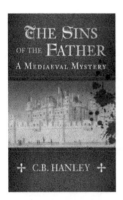

1217: England has been invaded. Much of the country is in the iron grip of Louis of France and his collaborators, and civil war rages as the forces of the boy king try to fight off the French. Most of this means nothing to Edwin Weaver, son of the bailiff at Conisbrough Castle in Yorkshire, until he is suddenly thrust into the noble world of politics and treachery: he is ordered by his lord the earl to solve a murder which might have repercussions not just for him but for the future of the realm.

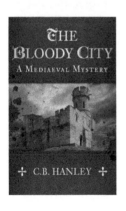

1217: Lincoln is not a safe place to be. A French army has captured the city and the terrified citizens huddle in the rubble of their homes as the castle, the last remaining loyal stronghold in the region, is besieged. Edwin Weaver finds himself riding into grave danger after his lord volunteers him for a perilous mission: he must infiltrate the city and identify the traitors who are helping the enemy. Edwin is pushed to the limit as he has to decide what he is prepared to do to protect others. He might be willing to lay down his own life, but would he, could he, kill?

1217: Edwin Weaver has returned to Conisbrough from his blood-soaked adventure in Lincoln, but he has no chance to rest: preparations are underway for a noble wedding at the castle. When the household marshal is murdered and a violent band of outlaws begins terrorising the area, the earl asks Edwin to resolve the situation; but Edwin is convinced that there's more to the situation than meets the eye and, with growing horror, he realises that the real target might be someone much closer to the earl.

1217: The war for the throne of England is far from over, but as commoner-turned-earl's-man Edwin Weaver waits to see where his lord's loyalties lie, a message arrives from Roche Abbey: one of the monks has been murdered. The abbot needs help to find the killer and Edwin soon finds himself within the unfamiliar and claustrophobic confines of the abbey, where faces are hidden and a killer stalks unnoticed.